Yagos: The Marriage Contract

Kattarin L. Kirk

DEDICATION

Dedicating the first fruits of my labor

to my Lord and Savior, Jesus Christ.

"As you harvest your crops, bring

the very best of the first harvest to

the house of the Lord your God."

Exodus 23:19a

CONTENTS

Chapter 1

Stepping out of the shower she hummed along to *Jingle Bells* as the music blasted out of her phone. Reaching for her towel she rubbed her bleary eyes and stifled a yawn. It had been a long trip from Colorado to Yagos and she hadn't been able to sleep on the plane as her little sister had. One of Celine's many talents was to fall asleep no matter where she was, a skill that Karrine had always admired but never mastered.

Reaching for her clothes she groaned when she realized she had forgotten to bring them downstairs with her. Debating for a moment she weighed her options. She had woken up to a note taped to her door saying her aunt and uncle had taken Celine out to see the sights but didn't want to wake her up. The note said there was food in the fridge for her but not to expect them back before lunch. She could text her sister, see if they would be home soon enough to bring her a change of clothes but that could be a while and she was starving. It wasn't that far to the guest room. She could make it in less than a minute.

Making sure the towel was wrapped securely around her, Karrine grabbed her phone as she headed out of the bathroom and started for the stairs. Just as her foot hit the first step a movement caught her eye and she screamed. The man looked startled but whether it was because of her scream or her clothing, or lack thereof, she wasn't sure.

"Who are you?" She yelled the first thing that came to mind.

"Who are you?" He asked, sounding about as confused as she felt.

"What are you doing here?" Suddenly realizing she didn't even know how to call emergency services in a foreign country, "Are you breaking in?"

"What are you doing wandering around in a towel?"

"I asked first!" She realized how childish that sounded the moment the words left her mouth. "What are you doing here?"

"Karrine?!" Aunt Fern's voice echoed down the hallways. "What's wrong?" Coming around the corner she gave a scandalized gasp at the scene she had just stumbled on. "Karrine! What are you wearing?"

"You?" The stranger glanced at Fern then back to her, "You are Karrine?" His gaze swept over her from head to toe and back up again, sending an involuntary shiver she didn't want to interpret running down her spine, as a slow smile spread across his too handsome face.

Pulling the towel a little tighter around herself she gave him her best icy glare, irritated when he just grinned back at her. "Who are *you*?!"

"Oh dear," Aunt Fern put both hands to her cheeks as she stared at Karrine, looking like she was about to faint or cry. Alarmed Karrine watched her, unsure of which option she would end up picking. Or why exactly she was so distraught in the first place.

"Well . . ." the man in front of her drew out the word, causing Karrine to shift her focus back to him. "It appears that I'm your fiancé."

*

Steffan Dalton stared up the stairs where his fiancée and her aunt had disappeared. They had been gone for a while and he was not sure what he was supposed to do while he waited. Over the years he had visited this house for various social events. He was comfortable enough to know his way around but not enough to make himself at home.

Briefly, he considered leaving, but he had waited his whole life to meet the woman he was going to marry, so he couldn't leave now. Then again she did not exactly seem prepared to give him a warm reception, maybe leaving was his best plan. Instead, he started pacing the floor, still considering his options when the phone in his hand started to ring a familiar tune. Glancing at the screen he debated for only a moment before answering the call. "Hello, Cam."

"Please tell me you are not ignoring your fiancée to answer my call?"

"No," he glanced again at the stairs before deciding to cut his losses and go towards the living room after all. "She's not in here at the moment."

Something in his tone must have tipped his friend off because Steffan heard him chuckle on the other end of the line. "I didn't think you'd been there long enough to manage to mess anything up yet. What did you do?"

Irritated, even though he knew none of this was Cam's fault, he clenched his hands into fists. "Why do you assume it is my fault?"

"Because I've known you since we were kids and it's almost always your fault."

"True," he agreed, striving to keep his tone mild, knowing his irritation was at the situation and not his best friend. "But normally because I was trying to execute one of your stupid plans."

Again Cam just chuckled, "Feel better?"

Not wanting to admit it he moved the phone so he could get his laughter under control while he tried to think of a suitably sarcastic reply. Instead, all he could think of was the text message that had caused him to take an early lunch and come over in the first place.

Karrine arrived last night. Why don't you come over for lunch and meet her?

He hadn't thought twice. Responding to Grover Sandor's text message that he was on his way he had headed over to their house. He had knocked when he arrived but when no one answered he let himself in, assuming they were just on the other side of the house and did not hear him. The fact that the door had not been locked seemed to further justify this conclusion. He had been heading towards the living room when the girl in the towel appeared.

"Steffan? You still there?"

4

Readjusting the phone, he considered sitting down while he talked to his friend but decided he had too much restless energy. "Yeah, sorry I'm here."

"I take it meeting the fiancée wasn't as simple as you were hoping?" Cam asked, switching from teasing to sympathetic.

"It was supposed to be," Steffan muttered. "I mean we have always known that this day would come but when she saw me. . . I don't know Cam, something was off. It was like she didn't even know I existed."

*

"Karrine!" Even a few minutes in, Fern Sandor still looked shocked beyond belief that her niece, still dressed in only a towel, was ranting about random men showing up from nowhere and making ludicrous claims as they broke into people's houses. "Darling, that is no way to talk about your fiancé!"

"My what?!" Karrine knew she sounded shrill but she couldn't help it.

"Oh!" Fern took the folded clothes that were lying on the bed and pushed them into Karrine's arms, pointing her towards the dressing screen so she could change. Who still had dressing screens in their house anyway?

"Why did you call him that? Why did he say that?" She demanded, trying to calm herself down as she pulled on the jeans, belatedly remembering how grateful she was that Celine hadn't been there when the lunatic broke in.

"Darling, don't say things that way. I know it was an awkward first meeting, but it's not like you did not know . . ." A long pause stretched between the two of them as Karrine waited for her to explain. "You did know didn't you dear? About Steffan?"

"Steffan?" She echoed, pulling the shirt over her head and stepping out from behind the screen. "Who the heck is Steffan?"

Under any other circumstances she would have felt bad for Aunt Fern, the poor woman looked about ready to cry but considering she had just announced that Karrine had a mysterious fiancé she'd never heard of, sympathy wasn't her reigning emotion at that moment.

"You don't know?" Fern pressed one hand to her forehead, covering her eyes and shook her head. "Your mother. She never told you, did she?"

"Tell me what?!" Karrine demanded, feeling her temper rise again.

"Oh my," Aunt Fern frowned and rubbed her temple, suddenly looking liked she had aged ten years in the last ten minutes. Sitting down on the bed she wrung her hands, a phrase Karrine had never understood until this moment.

"Aunt Fern, what is going on?" Karrine asked again, starting to feel like she was in some sort of strange parallel reality where no one could hear what she was saying, or more likely, were not listening.

"All right, I am going to call your uncle, then we need to sit down and talk this all out from the very beginning. Don't worry dear; we will get everything sorted out soon enough."

She couldn't help but wonder whose version of 'soon enough' they were going by. What kind of things could they have to 'sort out' between her and the attractive burglar?

*

Steffan was just winding down his conversation with Cam when he heard a door open and close. Hearing a girl's laugh he frowned for a second, a deep voice rumbled, too low for him to hear but enough for him to realize that Grover was home. Who was with him was anyone's guess. Before he could try to figure it out, he heard footsteps and then his fiancée and her aunt reappeared.

"Hey, I will call you back."

"She's there isn't she?"

Knowing Cam would just call back if he hung up on him without an explanation, he settled for the best non-answer he could give. "Um-hmm."

"Is she pretty?"

The woman standing in front of him wearing jeans and a t-shirt with hair just starting to curl was just as intriguing as the wide-eyed, furious, scared women wrapped in a towel he had first walked in on. Turning his back to the women so they would not see his grin he tried to keep the emotion out of his voice, "Very." He hung up to the sound of Cam's laughter. Careful to change his appreciative grin to a polite smile he turned back around as he slipped his phone back into his pocket. "I apologize for that."

7

"It's not a problem Steffan," Fern Sandor assured him. Karrine perched on the couch, glaring at him with a silence that spoke volumes. Wringing her hands, the older woman did her best to smile at him, "Apparently there has been a . . . misunderstanding. As soon as Grover gets here I am sure we can get this all figured out."

"Will we still be . . . engaged?" Karrine seemed to stutter over the last word and Fern shifted uncomfortably.

"Yes," Fern nodded at her, "You will."

"Then I don't understand how we can get this sorted out." She retorted, moving her glare between him and her aunt as if she wasn't quite sure where to direct her ire. "How can I have a fiancé if I never knew I was engaged?"

"You never knew?" Steffan repeated her words and felt his own eyes widen at the revelation.

"Know what?"

A miniature version of the woman sitting in front of him waltzed in, Grover Sandor on her heels. She looked like a teenager, maybe fourteen or fifteen with wide brown eyes and blonde hair piled on top of her head but that was where the similarities seemed to end because while Karrine looked like the weight of the world was resting on her thin shoulders this girl seemed as carefree as they came.

"Nothing for you to worry about Cina," Karrine assured her with a smile that would not have fooled the most gullible person.

"Actually, this does affect you, Celine," Grover told the girl with a kind smile. "It affects both of you girls. Why don't you sit down?"

Despite the fact that he had known he was engaged to Karrine Sandor for years, he couldn't help but suddenly feel like an outsider looking in as the patriarch of this small family arranged themselves around the living room. He was just about to excuse himself when Grover motioned towards him. "First, let me introduce everyone. Girls, this is Steffan Dalton. Our families have been friends for years. Steffan, this is Karrine and Celine Sandor..." there was a dramatic pause as Grover took a breath, "Karrine is your fiancée."

"You're *what*?" Celine jumped to her feet and turned on her sister, an odd mixture of horror and delight playing out across her features. "You're engaged? Why didn't you tell me?"

"Because I didn't know Celine!" Karrine's words must have been sharper than she intended because her face immediately fell; she reached up to tug on her sister's hand, pulling her down onto the couch next to her. The teenager resisted at first but a murmured word between sisters had her leaning into Karrine's hug. Apparently, she was more than willing to forgive a sharp word, considering the circumstances.

"Girls, Steffan," Grover nodded at them each in turn. "First, Steffan I have to apologize. When I invited you over, I intended to say, 'for dinner'. I didn't see your reply until Fern called me. That's why we weren't here to greet you." Grover waited for his nod before turning to the girls. "And girls, we have to apologize to each of you. Karrine, Fern gave me a brief account of what happened, including telling me you were not aware of what was going on. I am sorry, we thought your mother had explained all of this to you but . . ."

"Maybe she didn't have time," Celine suggested, pain distorting the delicate features of both young women. Karrine kept her arms around the teenager and focused on her uncle, doing an admirable job of ignoring him the whole time.

"What was she supposed to explain to me?"

Steffan watched helplessly as Grover and Fern exchanged a look before the older man took a deep breath. "Girls, because you were raised in the States you don't know much about Yagos' customs. The fact is that arranged marriages, especially among the wealthier families, have been a part of our culture since our country was first founded."

Shock and irritation showed on Karrine's face while Celine's registered the wonder of a teenager's overactive romantic imagination. Steffan hid his smile at the reactions of both sisters but wisely stayed quiet as their uncle continued his explanation.

"When you were born Karrine your father arranged a marriage for you . . . to Steffan."

Now irritation morphed into full-blown fury as she glared at him. "I've been engaged since I was born, and no one told me?"

"We thought your mother had," Fern tried to explain.

"Don't you dare blame this on her!" Karrine shouted, releasing her sister as she jumped to her feet.

"We're not," Grover assured her, standing up also and patting her shoulder in some attempt at sympathy. "But your mother was an American and it was never a secret that she did not approve of your father arranging your marriage. For years she tried to get you out of it, except your father had already had the marriage contract drawn up and the only clause it had to break it was if there were some irreconcilable difference between the two of you," he indicated first Steffan then Karrine.

"Does, not knowing he existed count?" She demanded, crossing her arms over her chest defensively as she sat back down next to her sister.

"I'm afraid the clause said that if there were irreconcilable difference both sets of parents would have to agree to break the contract. With the circumstances now . . ."

"Now I'm an orphan so there's no chance of that happening," Karrine sighed, all her emotions playing across her face as she slumped back into the couch. Still not looking at him she shook her head, "So what, I just have to marry some stranger? How is that fair?"

Unable to dredge up any resentment at her words he just stayed quiet, watching his fiancée struggle to accept her new reality and wondering how long she would pout for. It lasted less than a minute before she straightened again and glared at the room in general.

"What if I don't? What if I refuse?"

"Then you will lose your entire inheritance from your father," Fern explained, "Including your place in the family business."

Karrine rolled her eyes in a gesture that made her look surprisingly endearing instead of the aloof expression he was sure she was going for. "So what? I still have my inheritance from my mother, I don't need Dad's money or his business."

"Maybe not," Uncle Grover sighed. "But we just learned of

another clause in the will. If you do not marry Steffan within one month of your twenty-first birthday then both of you girls will be provided for but guardianship of Celine will transfer to your Uncle Kenneth, your father's, and my older brother."

Even Steffan felt his face blanch as he watched the horror and terror cross the faces of both Sandor girls. Unable to keep silent any longer he straightened, "That is simply not right."

"How could Dad do this to us?" Karrine whispered. Wrapping her arms around a suddenly trembling Celine, and completely ignoring him. "We've never even met Uncle Kenneth."

"I'm sure no one ever expected to have to use that clause," Aunt Fern explained. "But with your mother's accident . . ."

"I am so sorry." He was not exactly sure what made him say the words but for the first time Karrine looked over at him with an expression other than a glare. She stared at him for a long moment as if to judge the sincerity of his words before she nodded.

"Thank you."

Reeling with the new information about his fiancée and her family he looked over at Grover. "You said we have to be married one month after Karrine's twenty-first birthday. How long do we have?"

Once more Grover and Fern exchanged a look, but it was Karrine who answered. Hopelessness tinged her voice, "Two weeks, we have to be married in just two weeks."

Chapter 2

Karrine hit the call button and waited for an answer as she stared blankly at the simple yet beautiful cream-colored walls of the sitting room. On the other side of the mahogany door, Celine was sleeping blissfully, probably dreaming of romantic arranged marriages and mysterious family members from other countries. She smiled at the thought. Celine, ever the optimist, had spent her last minutes of wakefulness trying to convince her older sister that this marriage could be a good thing.

"This is like the perfect romance story Krin," the teenager explained as she lay in bed, next to her sister, ignoring the movie they had put on.

"This isn't a book Celine," she reminded her as gently as she could. "It's real life. My life and yours."

"Will you do it?" The girl asked, "Will you marry him?"

"Of course I will," she smiled and hugged the teenager, stroking her hair like their mother used to back before grief and work had overtaken her life. After that she had been too busy to take care of her daughters most of the time, forcing Karrine to take her spot in Celine's life. "I'm not going to let anyone take you away Celine, I promise."

"I don't want you to give up your life for me Krin," the girl told her seriously but she could see the fear in her younger sister's eyes of what would happen to her if Karrine refused to go through with the marriage.

"You're my life kid," she repeated the words their mom had said so many times before. *"Now get some sleep, you look exhausted."*

Comforted by her sister's reassurance she had fallen right to sleep, leaving Karrine to turn off the movie before she slipped out to make the phone call.

"Hey, you!" Contessa "Tessa" Franklin didn't even wait for her to finish her greeting before she launched right into the conversation. "How's Yagos? And who names a country Yagos anyway? I mean, I know we've always known about it because of your Dad but it's still a weird name for a country. It sounds like something someone made up for a book. So, what's it like there? Have you found any good mountains to climb yet? How's the other side of the family? How's Celine? It's so quiet around here without you two. Are you going to be home soon? I miss you! What time is it there anyway?"

Karrine just listened in amusement as her cousin jabbered on. She had learned years ago not to try to interrupt Tessa when she was on a roll but to just let her go on and on until she finally took a breath, then they could have a normal conversation. For now, she just let Tessa's familiar voice soothe her as she tried to gather her thoughts. By the time Tessa finally paused to catch her breath she knew what she wanted to say.

"I'm getting married."

There was a long pause before Tessa started talking again, "Is this some kind of joke? Because it's not funny Karrine."

She laughed but there was no humor in it and there was no way to hold back the tears that sprang to her eyes. "Trust me I know. There's nothing funny about this Tessa, and I really wish there was."

Another pause as Tessa tried to process what Karrine was saying. "Tell me everything."

So she did, it took less time than she would have imagined to explain how her life had managed to fall apart in just one afternoon. By the time she was done she felt amazingly better, knowing she was doing the right thing. Tessa didn't even bother to ask what her decision was. She already knew.

"I'm getting on a plane Krin, I'll be there in two days."

A part of her wanted to object, tell her it wasn't necessary, that she, the same woman who had scaled Mt. Everest for her eighteenth birthday, was strong enough to handle this on her own. Instead, she just hung up and curled into her pillow, letting the tears fall, knowing her best friend would be there soon enough to help her figure this mess out.

*

"Poor girl," Cam sat back as Steffan finished explaining the whole situation to him. "What are you going to do?"

"What can I do?" Pushing to his feet Steffan paced the Persian rug that Cam owned only because his mother had insisted on having his apartment professionally decorated when he had moved out.

"You could not marry her."

Steffan shook his head without stopping his pacing, "I can't do that. If we call off the wedding then she loses guardianship of her sister. We have no choice."

Cam nodded slowly, "What about the contract? If you have two weeks there may be time to get it checked out, perhaps see if there's a loophole?"

"Her mother's side of the family are international corporate lawyers Cam," Steffan said, turning to face him finally. "And her mother hated the plan if there was a loophole they would have found it."

"Still might be worth looking at it," Cam pushed him a little further. "For her sake."

"Or we end up getting married and she sees my looking into the contract as a sign that I was trying to get out of it. That this wedding is not what I want." Steffan flopped back onto a chair that was probably equal to the cost of college tuition.

Cam frowned that thoughtful, inquisitive look that ensured he never had to spend an evening alone. "Is this wedding what you want Steffan?"

If anyone else had asked the question he would have ignored them or laughed them off but this was his best friend, the closest thing he had to a brother. So, he took a deep breath and tried to consider the question, "I'm not sure." He shoved both hands into his thick brown hair pressing his palms into his temples. "I mean ever since I was a child I've known I had this fiancée out there." He rubbed his temple then started pacing again, unable to sit still.

"But she has never known about me. Her whole world was just turned upside down so for her sake I wish she didn't have to go through with this but for me . . . I'm not sure what I would do if the wedding was called off."

"What else?"

Steffan didn't stop pacing but shot him a sideways look, "What do you mean?"

Cam leaned forward, digging his elbows into his knees. "I mean there is something you are not saying, what is it?"

For a moment he sat there, considering how to put his emotions into words but then he stood again, pacing the expensive rug as Karrine's scared but angry face flashed in his mind again. "Nothing."

"Right," Cam laughed but got to his feet. "You know I'll find out, sooner or later. But if you want to keep your secrets for now then go right ahead. Either way, it is almost nine and I have a date, so unless you want to tell me what it is you don't want to admit, I have got to get going. You crashing here?"

"Nah," Steffan rubbed his head but grabbed his jacket. "Who's the girl?"

"A waitress I met the other day," Cam grinned. "If tonight goes well maybe she will be willing to attend that tedious business dinner I have on the calendar in a few weeks."

He just shook his head, not really surprised by what he was hearing. Cam had spent his adult life doing a very elaborate job of not getting entangled in relationships. He only dated casually, never taking the girl on more than one or two actual dates and then having them as convenient companions for business dinners or functions. More than once Steffan had seen his friend play matchmaker, setting up one of his dates with some friend or associate he had come across. Somehow he always managed to slip out of the relationship before anyone got their feelings hurt.

"Hey Steffan," Cam called out before Steffan made it to the door. "When do I get to meet her?"

"The wedding is in two weeks," he called back. "I'm sure you will get an invitation . . . as long as it doesn't get lost in the mail."

His friend's laughter followed him out the door as he got in the car and started towards home, idly wondering what his fiancée was doing at that moment.

*

"So, what's she like?"

He hadn't even turned on the lights when Kennedy's voice reached him a second before she turned on a lamp. Just like something out of a movie she was curled up in a chair in the corner, just waiting for him, his supposed guard dog lying at her feet as she used one stockinged foot to rub his belly. Tossing his jacket over a chair he grinned and headed into his kitchen, deciding to have a little fun at his sister's expense. "I am sorry who are we talking about?"

"Oh, don't even pretend to be clueless Steffan Dalton! You know I'm talking about Karrine!"

"Karrine?" He drew out her name. Pulling a confused look he turned to look at her, handing her a soda but choosing water for himself as he fed the enormous English Mastiff, Solo, his dinner, and debated what he was going to cook for himself. "That name seems familiar somehow. Who is she again?"

Kennedy hit his shoulder, doing her best not to laugh. "Oh, I don't know . . . maybe your fiancée! You know, the one we have been waiting to meet since forever! Come on! What is she like? Is she pretty? Is she nice?"

Laughing he finally decided on fish and started pulling out ingredients. "Have you had dinner?"

"I had a salad." One look at the way she eyed the fish and he added some more to the pan, knowing she would wait until the last moment before asking for some. "So . . ." when he just smiled, she jumped up to sit on the counter. "Come on big brother! You're killing me here!"

Laughing he finally turned to face her, "All right, all right, yes I met her and she's . . ." he frowned, trying to think of the best way to describe Karrine Sandor. "Well she is beautiful, but she also seems very stubborn."

"Is she excited about the wedding?" Kennedy demanded, moving into a chair so he had room to work.

Not willing to lie to his sister he shook his head, "Not exactly. She didn't know about it."

"Excuse me, she what?"

For the second time that day, he explained the story, this time leaving out the part of how he first discovered Karrine, scared, angry, and wrapped in a towel demanding to know who he was. By the time he finished Kennedy was indignant.

"That's horrible. What are you going to do?"

Despite himself, he smiled. That was his little sister, she expected him to be able to fix anything and until now he could not think of a time he had ever failed her. "That's just it Kennedy, I am not sure if there is anything I can do. If we fail to get married then she loses custody of her sister, if we go through with the wedding, she may hate me forever."

"No, she won't," Kennedy shook her head confidently. "There is no way that will happen."

"Oh?" Pulling the pan off the stove he handed her a plate, "Why is that?"

"Because of who you are," she took the plate and happily popped a bite in her mouth, nodding her approval. "No one ever hates you for long Steffan, no one can."

Grinning at her confidence he put the pan in the sink and started on his own food, sending the dog to the living room where he would not be able to beg. Then he asked his sister enough questions to start her talking about herself instead of asking more questions about Karrine.

*

"Are you awake?"

Not wanting to open her eyes Karrine groaned at her sister's question. "That depends? Am I still engaged to a guy I didn't know existed before yesterday?"

"'Fraid so, and judging from your reaction I'm guessing you still don't think it's that romantic?"

Opening her eyes she smiled at her sister, "Sorry Cina, I guess I'm just not quite as optimistic as you are."

"Eh," Celine shrugged in her usual, carefree way. "I'm used to it."

"You get it from Dad you know." Smiling a little at how much the teenager reminded her of their late father she sat up a little, positioning the pillows so she could lean back against the headboard more comfortably. "He was always optimistic, no matter what was going on. Dad used to say that as long as we had each it would always be okay."

"Are you mad at him? For arranging your marriage and not telling you?"

She smiled and rubbed her eyes wondering how honest she should be. "I was. Yesterday when I first found out I was furious, but last night I was dreaming about Dad and I realized something." She didn't wait for Celine to ask but continued to explain, "I was eight years old when Dad died, what would have been the point of telling me I was engaged? And even if he did, I don't know if I would have remembered. Chances are he never mentioned it because he didn't want to upset Mom, but even if he had what would have been the point in telling a child her future was planned out? It just would have made them argue if Mom really was so opposed."

"So you're really not mad?" Celine asked again, looking like she wanted to believe that but not sure she should.

"About an arranged marriage?" She bit back a groan at the very words, "Oh I'm mad and confused but it doesn't matter. What matters is making sure you're taken care of, so I guess that means

I'm getting married."

"What about the contract?" Celine asked. "Is it possible there's some sort of loophole in it?"

Shaking her head she tried not to yawn, "I wish there was. But if Mom was really so set against this then I can't imagine there'd be a loophole she didn't find. Still . . ." she shrugged, "I'll ask Aunt Meredith and Uncle Donovan to look into it. It's worth a shot, right?"

Celine leaned forward and hugged her impulsively, "You know you're the best sister ever, right? I wish you didn't have to do this for me Krin."

Pushing her back a little she looked the fourteen-year-old in the eye, "Listen to me Celine, I would do anything for you, anything. And if marrying a random stranger is the worst I have to do to make sure that you're taken care of, then I think we're really doing pretty good, got it?"

Celine had tears in her eyes but she hugged her again, "What if he's not a good guy Karrine? I mean he's cute and all, but what if he turns out to be a serial killer or something?"

Laughing even as a tendril of fear snaked around her heart, she wrapped her arms around her kid sister, "Hey, Uncle Grover and Aunt Fern seem to like him. How bad can he be? And you know what Uncle Andy would say, God took care of us in Colorado, he's not going to stop just because we're in Yagos."

"I guess God's in control Krin but you always say there's still evil in this world," Celine leaned back to look at her, worry dimming her brown eyes and frown lines marring her normally happy expression. "How do you know we can trust him?"

Knowing she had to be honest she didn't even try to hold back her sigh. "I don't know if we can Cina, but you heard Uncle Grover, he said our families have been friends for years. I can't imagine Dad coming up with a marriage contract to someone from a bad family. And there's no way Mom would have let it stand if she had concerns about my safety."

"I don't know Krin . . ."

"We'll look into it, okay?" Karrine hugged her one more time. "But first we have to get dressed." Her face heated at the thought of her first meeting with her fiancé but she turned away before her sister could see it and ask questions. The last thing she wanted to explain was why she'd been wandering around in a towel listening to Christmas music in August.

Chapter 3

Steffan was already at work when his phone rang. He didn't recognize the number but answered anyway paying more attention to the paperwork he was trying to deal with. Tired and distracted his voice was sharper than he'd intended, "Dalton."

"Um . . ." the hesitant female voice made him frown but he just waited, his patience wearing thinner by the second. "Is this Steffan Dalton?"

"Yes," he sat up a little straighter, thinking the voice sounded familiar but unable to place it. "May I help you?"

Terse laughter came across the line, "I guess we'll find out. This is Karrine Sandor, your f--" she broke off as if she couldn't bring herself to finish the word, "Well you know who I am."

"Yes," he couldn't help but smile, "Yes, I do. How are you Karrine?"

"I wish I knew," she muttered then rushed on, apparently not wanting to give him time to respond. "Listen, I hope this isn't a bad time but can you meet me somewhere? I have a lot of questions and if we're supposed to get married in two weeks then we have a lot of planning to do."

He looked at the paperwork accumulating on his desk, debating. After he had finished school last year, his father had turned the company, Sailor IT, over to him. Just like its name suggested his IT company focused on tracking ships and their cargo, along with dealing with their technology needs. They catered to a very select crowd, Karrine's late father's company, Sandor Shipping, being first among them.

Sailor IT had been his idea when he was only sixteen but without the money, education, or resources to start it, he had gone to his entrepreneur father, Charles "Charlie" Dalton, to help him. As soon as Steffan graduated from college Charlie had turned the company over to him. As much as he loved running his own business the work could be tedious. Taking a break to meet with his beautiful fiancée seemed like it would be well worth the hours he would have to put in later to make up for it.

"I would love to, should I come back to your aunt and uncle's?"

"No." The answer was a little too quick and he frowned, wondering why she didn't want him at the house, but not confident enough in the rocky ground they were standing on to risk asking her about it. As it turned out he didn't have to. "I'm sorry it's just that I would like a chance to talk to you without worrying my little sister."

Surprised and more than a little sympathetic to the cause of trying to figure out how to take care of a younger sister he nodded. "Absolutely, where would you like to meet?"

"Got any mountains in this country?"

Taken aback by the question he frowned, "No, none to speak of. Why?"

Her sigh came over the line, "Forget it. Um . . . I don't know anything about this country so why don't you tell me. Just name the place."

"How about I come and pick you up? We can decide after that."

She hesitated long enough he was sure she was going to turn him down, but just as he was about to suggest a little café within walking distance from her aunt and uncle's she surprised him. "Okay, when will you be here?"

Surprised by her willingness, and not wanting to give her a chance to back out he looked at the folders open in front of him, trying to decide how much he could afford to leave until later and what absolutely needed to be finished up today. Finally deciding he could come back to the office after he met with her, he pushed back from his desk and grabbed his jacket. "I can be there in twenty minutes."

"Fine," the word was suddenly sharp, business-like, instead of hesitant and he found himself wondering if her mood could change as quickly as her tone. "I'll be ready," then she hung up before he could reply. With an amused smile on his handsome face he stared at the phone and headed to his secretary's desk.

"Hey Mrs. Coren, I need to go out for a while."

The older woman looked up at him with a stern expression. She'd worked for his father for years, serving at various companies as Charlie Dalton bought and sold them but when

Sailor IT had started she'd insisted on coming to work for him, stating that someone would have to be around to keep him in line. And that was a job she took very seriously. "Oh? And when exactly do you plan on being back? You have an appointment at four."

Glancing at his watch he mentally debated, "See if you can reschedule it for tomorrow morning. If not, then I will make it work."

"And what reason should I give for rescheduling," she demanded before he could walk out the door. Not bothering to hide his smile he shook his head indulgently, they both knew she wouldn't bother giving a reason for the reschedule it was just her way of keeping tabs on him. The woman had been a constant in his life for as long as he could remember and he was more than happy to let her get away with it.

"Tell them I am meeting with my fiancée to deal with some last-minute wedding details."

The surprise on her face was worth every moment of difficulty she had ever given him and he used her rare moment of speechlessness to escape out of the building.

*

Fifteen minutes after hanging up with her fiancé, Karrine left a note for her sister and aunt. She was glad Aunt Fern had been able to convince Celine to go sightseeing after their day had been cut short yesterday, allowing her to leave without having to explain herself. Locking the door behind her she walked outside, second-guessing her simple outfit of dark blue jeans, royal blue silk blouse, and high-heeled black knee-length boots for about the hundredth time since hanging up the phone. She threw on a black coat to ward off the chill, something that still confused her since it was winter in August.

Right on time, a sleek BMW pulled into the drive and stopped in front of the stairs. Impressed by his punctuality she closed the door behind her as he jumped out of the car. Walking slowly she took the time to study her fiancé, taking in how tall he was, and how the slacks and polo did nothing to hide his fit physique. His light brown hair and chocolatey eyes watched her back as he opened the passenger side door for her.

When she reached his side, he leaned forward like he was going to kiss her cheek but she ducked around him, sliding onto the plush leather seat and making a show of reaching for her seatbelt. When he didn't close the door she finally looked up. Staring at her, he waited for her to meet his gaze, he smiled and said, "You look beautiful Karrine."

The compliment from her handsome fiancé set her heart racing as if she had just made it to the top of Everest, again. She couldn't even manage a smile before he shut the door and rounded the hood, sliding in behind the wheel with all the confidence in the world.

"Where are we going?"

"There's a beautiful stretch of coastline about thirty minutes from here." He grinned over at her, "There are no mountains, but you can't beat the view. Beautiful blue water, white sand, and an incredible restaurant that can make just about anything you can dream up. Interested?"

She thought about telling him no, suggesting they go for a walk instead but there didn't seem to be any way for her to get out of this engagement fiasco, so she might as well start playing nice now. "Sounds fine."

"O-kay," he drew out the word enough to tell her he was hoping to get a little more of a response, but she wasn't sure she had the emotional energy to even try. Instead, she asked the question that had been on her mind since he had first introduced himself as her fiancé last night. Or rather since Uncle Grover had introduced him as such when she was a bit calmer.

"How long have you known about the engagement, about me?"

Sympathy crossed his face and one hand came off the wheel like he wanted to reach out to her, a part of her recoiled, not wanting comfort from a virtual stranger. However, when he put his hand back on the wheel another part of her, a part she didn't want to examine too closely, mentally regretted the lack of contact. "I have known basically my whole life." Apparently concerned she'd take that the wrong way he rushed to add, "About the engagement that is, I know next to nothing about you."

She smiled, a little relieved to find out they were on equal footing. "Well, that makes two of us."

"Steffan."

Karrine frowned, not sure why he was telling her his name, "Excuse me."

A mischievous smile crossed his face, "I was not entirely sure if you knew my name since you haven't used it since we met yesterday. I just thought I would remind you."

Her lips twitched a little as she fought a smile but she didn't let it spread, "I used your name when I called you."

Judging from the look he shot her he had noticed the way she let the sentence hang in the air, purposefully not using his name this time. He just grinned, letting the matter go. "All right Karrine, the first thing you should know about me is that I'm a born-again Christian, the second is I don't even pretend to understand American football."

This time she wasn't able to keep the smile off her face and she chuckled, relaxing a little bit into her seat. "Well that is one thing we have in common," she hesitated just a beat, "Being a believer that is. However, if you're not willing to at least tolerate me following the Denver Broncos then this engagement is already doomed."

Tipping his head back a bit he laughed out loud, "If that is the worse problem we encounter then I'd say we are off to a good start."

A mix of amusement and mock disbelief had her shaking her head, "I'm not sure you understand how important football really is."

Still chuckling he stopped at a streetlight and waited for some pedestrians to cross the street, "All right, football aside, what else should I know about you, Miss Karrine Sandor?"

"My sister is the most important person in my life," she angled slightly towards him to emphasize her point. "I would do anything for Celine, including marriage to a stranger."

For a moment he looked at her as if trying to decide whether or not to answer. A car honking behind him forced him to turn his attention back to the road. "Karrine, I will be honest with you, I had no idea about the guardianship clause in the contract. Also, I always assumed you knew about our engagement, the same as I did." The light turned green and he accelerated. "When I first heard you didn't know about the engagement I would not have blamed you for walking away from this whole thing but now with the guardianship clause . . ."

"Now you realize why I don't have a choice," or at least she hoped he did.

"Something like that," he admitted. "But Karrine if we do decide to go through with this then I should make myself clear, I don't believe in divorce. If we get married, then it will be for life."

The thought of divorce had never crossed her mind but she had to give him credit for being upfront. If she'd had more time to think about it, she probably would have considered it at some point. Even though she had always been taught marriage was for life, the idea of filing for divorce before the ink was even dry on the marriage license so she could maintain guardianship of her sister was more than a little tempting. Yet, Steffan was making himself clear, divorce was not and never would be an option.

"I've met your Uncle Kenneth," Steffan once again broke the silence as he slowed for a sharp corner that offered them a beautiful view of the beach. "If you don't want to go through with this marriage then I will understand, and I'm sure Celine would be well taken care of."

Anger was her first reaction but years of training on how to handle herself in polite society kept her from immediately exploding. One look at the sincerity on his face and she felt the fury drain out of her. He was trying to help, give her the best options in an impossible situation, she couldn't blame him for that, no matter how much she might like too.

"Our mother died just a few weeks ago." She heard his sharp intake of breath and took some perverse pleasure in being able to surprise him, even with such a horrible fact.

"I am so sorry, I heard your mother had passed away, but I didn't realize it had happened so recently." He frowned but didn't look at her as he slowed for another turn, "It would have been right around your birthday."

"The week before," she turned to stare out the window again, not wanting him to see the tears in her eyes. If he showed her the least bit of sympathy, she was sure the dam would break, and it would take hours before she would be able to get the tears under control again. "Our Dad died before Celine even turned one. Then losing our mom . . . We came to Yagos for a visit and to get away only to discover we may not be allowed to go home. I can't make Celine go live with a man neither of us have ever met before. I won't do that to my sister, she deserves better."

Steffan smiled at her but it wasn't the same smile that had taken over his whole face like when he had laughed earlier at her football jokes. "I hope your sister knows how lucky she is to have you in her life."

Digging her fingernails into her palms to help keep the tears at bay she just shrugged, "Me too." Desperately needing a distraction she turned back to the window, too exhausted to even attempt a smile and finding it easier to just keep her face averted instead. "So you're a Christian and you don't like football. What else do I need to know about you?"

"Well . . ." he drew out the word as if trying to come up with the most important information for her to know. "Let me think, I'm twenty-three, my favorite color is green and I have a dog named Solo, you aren't allergic are you?"

Unable to help herself, she laughed, having a hard time shifting from a conversation as serious as an arranged marriage and guardianship of a fourteen-year-old to innate facts like his age and favorite color. "No, I'm not allergic, and neither is Celine. In fact, she's always wanted a dog but Mom wouldn't let her. She insisted that she wasn't home enough to take care of it and she wasn't sure Celine would be responsible enough."

"Well, I'm sure Solo will be thrilled to have someone besides just me to lavish him with attention. What about you Karrine, any pets?"

"A goldfish when I was eight," she turned just enough to see his reaction, almost laughing when he just looked at her in shock.

"A goldfish? Seriously? That's it?"

"I'm afraid so."

"That is almost depressing," he informed her seriously, making her laugh. If it hadn't been for the ridiculousness of the fact that she was being forced into an arranged marriage, one she neither wanted nor needed, she could almost find herself enjoying this little question and answer session with her new fiancé.

*

"Why did you ask me about mountains?"

They had just sat down in the restaurant and were waiting for the waitress to come to take their order when Steffan surprised her with the question. For a moment Karrine just looked at him, as if she wasn't sure what he was talking about, or, more likely, debating if she should answer. Instead, she absently wrapped her hands around the cup of coffee in front of her, mixing in cream as if it required all of her concentration.

"Have you ever been to Colorado?"

She still refused to use his name but he ignored that. "No, I have never been anywhere in the States."

Karrine glanced up at him, brown eyes curious, "Why not? Weren't you curious? If you knew about me didn't you know where I was from?"

Steffan sat back, wondering where she was going with this, "Yes, I knew about you but you have to remember I thought you knew about me too. I just never saw a reason to seek you out."

"You weren't curious?"

"Of course I was," he frowned, wondering how to explain an entire culture of arranged marriages and various other customs to a woman who hadn't even known such things still existed until yesterday. "But I was living my own life and I just assumed you were doing the same thing. All I knew was the wedding would take place sometime after your twenty-first birthday until then there was no real reason to seek you out."

"Not even to settle your curiosity?"

She wasn't going to let this go and he studied her for a moment, trying to decide what the underlying cause was for her questions, almost certain there was something he was missing. "Like I said I was just living my life, finishing school, and then working to build my business. My goal was to make sure I was turning a profit before we eventually married." He hesitated, wondering if he should tell her the rest of the story or not. There had been a few times he had almost given in to the urge to seek her out but hadn't. After only a moment of indecision, he continued. "When I heard your mother had passed away I considered coming out to Colorado, to try to support you, but your aunt and uncle didn't think it would a good idea."

Confusion and grief covered her face, making her look even more vulnerable but she continued to stare at her coffee, not willing to meet his eye. "Why not?"

Steffan rolled his shoulders back, glad he had shed his suit jacket in the car but wishing he could ease the tension between the two of them just as easily. "I think they were concerned it would make you feel ambushed. From what I understand your mother never supported the idea of an arranged marriage and there was some concern that if you felt the same way my presence at her funeral would not be welcome."

A shadow passed over her face but before he could question her about it the waitress appeared. The teenager, a niece of the owners, greeted him warmly, sending a curious look at Karrine but still pasting on a friendly smile. "So what can I get you? Do you want to order something off the menu Steffan? Or let Auntie surprise you? Unless you've come up with some new recipe to challenge her with?"

Laughing at that, Steffan directed the questions to Karrine, "What sounds good?"

"How about pasta?"

Something was off about the way she said it, there was a shadow in her eyes that hadn't been there before but Ria was waiting for his order and he didn't have time to worry about it right then. "Whatever Jessica wants to make will be fine Ria, and tell her thanks."

"You've got it," the girl smiled and checked to make sure that Karrine did not have any allergies before heading back to the kitchen, leaving them alone again.

"Do you come here a lot?" Karrine asked before he could try to start the conversation again.

Unable to help feeling like he was walking into some sort of trap he nodded, "Off and on. There's some great surfing in this area and Jessica always makes sure we have a good meal when we finish."

"So do you bring all your dates here?"

His shoulders tensed a little at the passive-aggressive note that had crept into her voice but he ignored it. "Nah, just the ones I am engaged too."

Karrine alternated between being irritated with herself for sabotaging her lunch with Steffan and blaming him for the whole arranged marriage fiasco in the first place. Rationally she knew he'd had about as much control over the marriage contract as she did but her emotions were too chaotic for rationality to matter much right then.

As worked up as she was the only thing she knew that would calm her down, was if she could go rock-climbing. Since Yagos was a large island between New Zealand and Australia, the chances of finding mountains to climb without jumping on a plane first didn't seem very likely.

The thought of flying far away and leaving this whole mess behind was more appealing than just about anything else yet there was no way she could do that. She had been raised to face her problems head-on, not run away from responsibility but she would be willing to ignore all of that, if not for Celine.

Leaving meant giving up guardianship of her sister and she couldn't do that to the girl. Brandaliyn "Brandi" Sandor had been a good mother once, but when her husband died she had moved back to Colorado to be closer to the support of her family because she had been so distraught. As much as she loved her daughters, she dedicated the majority of her time to her work. Karrine had been as much of a mother as she was a big sister to the girl. She was not about to send her away just to make her own life a little, or even a lot, easier.

For a moment she looked at her phone, debating whether to call Tessa, but her cousin was probably on a plane already on her way to Yagos. Even if she was at an airport on a layover there was nothing she could do to help right then, not really, it was better to just wait.

Karrine laughed at the thought, but even to her own ears, there was an edge of hysteria to the sound, warning her that trying to stay patient and wait for her cousin to arrive would just end up driving her crazy. Who knew what state she would be in by the time Tessa finally did get there. She needed to find something to do, somewhere to climb, and she needed to do it soon.

*

"Karrine?" Aunt Fern's voice drifted through the door just before she knocked. "Karrine, honey are you home?"

"I'm here Aunt Fern," she smiled at the older woman who had tried so hard to befriend her. Even before Karrine had found out about the engagement Aunt Fern had tried to be there for her. The woman cared, Karrine could not fault her for that, but a caring aunt she had never known wasn't what she really needed at present. She needed a mountain to climb, preferably one that had a cave she and Celine could hide out in for the rest of their lives.

"Celine's outside," Aunt Fern explained. "She got a phone call as we were coming home, someone from Colorado I believe."

"Probably Karra, her best friend," Karrine explained, working hard to be polite. "Did you two have fun?"

"Oh yes," Aunt Fern's eyes brightened at the question. "We saw some of the sights around Jifte, the capital city, then we went shopping in Teller. I'm exhausted but Celine's still going strong. I finally convinced her to come home and have a little bit of lunch before we go out again. She wants to go horseback riding and I have some friends who said they would be happy to take her down the beach. Would you like to come?"

"No, but thank you," she smiled at the older woman. "For helping Celine to have such a wonderful time I mean. I appreciate it."

Aunt Fern smiled back but it was tinged with sadness, "Karrine, I'm not sure how much you remember about your life here in Yagos before your father died, but I used to spend a lot of time with you. Grover and I could never have children but we always delighted in being able to spoil you and your sister. Despite the circumstances, it is a joy for us to have you back."

Surprised by the sudden revelation she impulsively hugged the older woman, an embrace, Fern gladly returned. "Thank you, Aunt Fern."

"Of course dear," pulling back Fern blinked away a suspicious amount of moisture in her eyes. "Well, would you like some lunch dear?"

"Um, no, I already ate," she smiled but changed the subject rather than explain further. "Aunt Fern do you know if there are any sort of cliffs in Yagos? Preferably close by? Or even a rock-climbing gym?"

The woman thought for just a moment and then smiled, "Actually there is. A park, less than an hour from here with some beautiful cliffs. I've heard lots of rock-climbers go out there to climb. It's not hard to find, but I can get someone to drive you if you like."

"No," she smiled, relieved even if there were no mountains, there were at least some cliffs to climb. "A GPS and a car will work just fine."

Chapter 4

Karrine grunted with satisfaction as she found a handhold and pulled herself up on the ledge. She wasn't at the top of the cliffs but she was high enough to have a great view and she took a few minutes to enjoy it as she guzzled her water. A glance at her watch warned her that she would need to head back sooner rather than later if she was going to make it in time for dinner. Her stomach growled right on cue, making her realize just how long ago her lunch with Steffan had been.

Slowly but confidently she began the climb back down, unhooking her line and recoiling the climbing rope around her waist, keeping her body close to the rock as she went. Reaching the bottom, she returned the wave of some other climbers who looked like they were just finishing up too. In no mood to make small talk she avoided making eye contact and headed out to the parking lot, she had just slipped into the front seat when her phone started to ring.

"Hello."

"So I fly all the way across the world only to arrive at the house where you're supposed to be staying and you don't even have the decency to be here when I arrive? What's up with that?"

Recognizing the voice immediately she started the car, "I didn't think you would be here until this evening at the earliest. How'd you get here so quick?"

"I flew. Where are you?"

"I needed to climb," knowing Tessa would understand that answer in a way few others would she left it at that. "I'm in the car; I'll be there in forty-five minutes to an hour. And if your flight was anything like mine then I suggest you take time to get some sleep, you're probably exhausted."

"Good plan," Tessa agreed, for once not lecturing her about climbing alone. Her voice lowered, "Are you okay?"

Not wanting to lie to her cousin she took a deep breath as she thought how to answer, her mind quickly flitting through everything that had taken place since she had arrived in Yagos. "Honestly? I have no idea. But I'm better than I was, I got a good climb in so at least I'm not about to jump out of my skin."

"Well it's a start, I'll see you when you get here, drive careful."

"I will, and Tessa? Thanks for coming."

"I always will Krin, all you have to do is call."

*

"Hello Solo, where is our boy? Hmm?"

Steffan smiled as his Mum's voice drifted to him from the other room. Nor was he surprised that the dignified Genève Dalton was the first person Solo had sought out. Following the dog's path, he found his Mum curled up in her favorite chair, reading glasses on and laptop half shut, setting aside whatever charitable cause she was working on, so she could give the enormous English Mastiff her undivided attention.

Leaning against the doorframe he took a moment to just absorb the scene in front of him. His mother, still in her pantsuit, with her heels, kicked off and lying on the floor haphazardly beside her. The one hundred eighty-pound dog doing his best to stretch his way into her lap without actually lifting his paws off the ground so he could avoid getting into trouble for climbing on people. It took Genève only a moment before she noticed him standing there, taking her glasses off she offered him a sympathetic but perceptive smile.

"Your sister said you met Karrine yesterday."

"Yeah," rubbing the bridge of his nose he went to sit in the chair across from her, appreciating how she set the laptop aside so she could give him her full attention. "Did she also tell you that Karrine had never known about our engagement?"

His Mum nodded, "She did; I'm so sorry Steffan."

Snorting he leaned back in his chair, "For me? Why? It's Karrine you should be feeling sorry for. Her Mum just passed away a few weeks ago and now she finds out she has been engaged since she was a baby. Not just that but if she does refuse to go through with the wedding she loses guardianship of her teenage sister. Which by the way, I have been meaning to ask you, whose idea was that?"

"Hamilton's," his father, Charlie Dalton, explained as he walked into the room, kissing his wife and clasping Steffan's shoulder briefly before patting Solo's head and making himself comfortable on the couch. "He added it as an addendum when they found out that Brandaliyn was pregnant again. He told me as a courtesy but since it didn't directly affect you I had no real reason to object. I questioned the wisdom of it but he insisted if something were to happen to him and Brandi he didn't want Karrine to have to raise a child on her own, this was the best way he could think of to protect her, to protect both of them."

"Then why send her to a single older man neither of them knows?" Steffan demanded, not willing to let Hamilton Sandor off the hook that easily.

"He wasn't single at the time," his father explained, looking sympathetic but there was a hint of steel in his eyes that warned him Charlie would not let his son unfairly blame his old friend for trying to take care of his daughters the best way he knew how. "Kenneth's wife passed away years later when Karrine was a teenager. When the contract was written, Grover and Fern were not in a situation at the time where they could take care of the girls if something had happened."

"Added to that, was the fact Hamilton expected the girls to be raised in Yagos," Genève stated. "Had he not passed away they would have known their uncle . . . and Karrine would have known about your engagement, but God had a different plan, however that does not mean He has given up control."

"I know that," Steffan rested his arms on his knees and sighed, letting the anger drain out of him. Sensing his master's tension Solo came over to sit beside him, whining and setting his massive head on his knee, as if to ask if he was okay. Absently petting the dog he focused on his parents again. "I do know He is in control, but watching Karrine go through this . . . knowing there is not a way to fix it for her, it isn't exactly the easiest thing I have ever done."

"You care about her."

He nodded at his mother's statement, "It's hard not to. I have known about her my whole life, I have spent years wondering what she was like when I might meet her. Since I was a teenager I have spent a good deal of time praying for her. Actually meeting her just reinforces whatever feelings I have developed, not lessens them."

"And that is why I said I was sorry," his Mum explained, a soft smile on her face.

Frowning at her he leaned back again, still absently petting Solo, "I'm not sure I understand."

"You are her fiancé Steffan, soon you will be her husband, you will be the one who will have to help her through all of this," his Dad told him. "And none of it is going to be easy."

"Yeah," Steffan rubbed his head again. "I am starting to figure out nothing about Karrine Sandor is easy."

"Maybe not," Genève gave a dainty shrug but did nothing to try to hide the smile playing on her pink stained lips, "But I doubt it will ever be boring."

*

"Have I told you how glad I am you're here?" Karrine kept her arms wrapped around Tessa, making her words muffled but still understandable.

"Once or twice," Tessa laughed but she didn't pull away from the embrace and Karrine knew her cousin was doing the best she could to lend her strength. When she'd gotten home from rock-climbing she had immediately been greeted by her cousin, who'd arrived a short time before with her own parents, Karrine's Aunt Meredith and Uncle Donovan. The family had still been exchanging hugs when Celine had gotten back. The teenager had been almost bursting with excitement wanting to tell her sister and the rest of the family all the things she had seen and done that day. Not the least of which was the horseback ride she had taken on the beach. Then by the time Celine had finished filling them in on all the details, it was time for dinner. Now was the first chance the two cousins had managed to find time to talk.

After a long while, they pulled apart and Karrine sat down on her bed while Tessa chose to pull the overstuffed chair close to her side. They shut the door that separated Karrine's room from her sister's so they wouldn't waken the exhausted teenager.

"I want to hear everything," Tessa began, making Karrine smile. "But first there is something you should know."

Seeing the tension in Tessa's face she gave a humorless laugh, "Whatever it is Tessa I doubt it can be worse than what I have heard the last couple of days." When her cousin didn't smile she felt herself tense, "Tessa? What's going on?"

"Mom and Dad knew about your engagement."

All the anger, the frustration, and betrayal she had felt toward her parents since she first found out about the arranged marriage, the emotions she'd worked so hard to release in her climb today came rushing back, this time it was directed at her aunt and uncle. Yet it was different though, and the biggest difference was, they were still alive. Leaning back against the headboard she closed her eyes against the tears that threatened.

"Did you know?" She stared at her best friend, praying with everything in her that the answer was no. "Did you know anything about this? Did you ever hear any of them mention something like this?"

"Of course not!"

There was enough outrage in her cousin's voice to make her feel guilty for even asking and she reached out a hand, touching Tessa's shoulder lightly. "I'm sorry Tessa, but I needed to ask."

Never one to hold a grudge Tessa sighed and reached up to squeeze Karrine's hand, "I know, but I swear Karrine I would never keep something like that from you." Tessa smiled, "I couldn't even if I tried. We've been best friends since we were kids Krin. Do you really think I would have been able to keep a secret this big from you?"

"No," she sighed, this time she couldn't hold back the tears. "But then again, I never would have believed my parents could have arranged something like this, or that your parents would have kept it from me, and yet somehow they did."

"Oh Krin," crawling over beside her Tessa pulled her into a tight embrace. She let her cry out all the crazy emotions from the last few weeks, grief over losing her mother, fear at the thought of raising her little sister on her own, and now all the emotions this engagement had stirred up since she had arrived in Yagos. The tears fell and she started to wonder if they would ever end. A bone-weary exhaustion stole over her and the combination of the cathartic tears and the comfort of having her best friend with her once again lulled her into a deep sleep.

*

Karrine woke early, blinking against the sunlight that was coming in through the windows she must have forgotten to close the night before. For just a moment she laid still, slowly letting the events of the day before, come back to her. Starting with her lunch with Steffan then rock-climbing in the park. She remembered Celine's excitement about her day of sightseeing in Yagos, and then her talk with Tessa. The memories ended in the revelation that her aunt and uncle, the couple who had helped raise her and Celine, had known about her engagement all along, and never told her. Turning her head she saw Tessa, still sound asleep on the other side of the bed, her back to the window so the sun wouldn't bother her.

Moving as quietly as she could, she draped a blanket over her cousin, smiling at the way Tessa curled into it without ever waking up. Pulling the curtains closed so the sunlight wouldn't disturb Tessa she opened the door to check on Celine. As she had expected the teenager, probably still exhausted from her adventures the day before, was sound asleep, she didn't so much as stir when her sister looked in on her.

Taking her time getting ready for the day she headed downstairs in search of some much-needed caffeine. As soon as she stepped into the kitchen she saw Aunt Meredith already there, sipping a cup of coffee that she knew would have cream but no sugar stirred into it.

All the feelings of betrayal from the night before came flooding back but her aunt just smiled sweetly at her. "I thought you and Tessa would stay up so late talking you would be sleeping until noon, just like when you were teenagers."

Pouring her own coffee she mixed in cream, adding a little bit of sugar before sliding into a chair opposite of her aunt at the kitchen table. "We did talk." A shadow passed over Aunt Meredith's face but she didn't apologize, instead, she just took another sip of her coffee and waited for Karrine to say her piece. "Why didn't you tell me? Why didn't *she* tell me?"

"Oh Krin," Aunt Meredith set her coffee down and rubbed her forehead as if she had a headache come on suddenly. "She wanted to, so did I but . . ."

"But what Aunt Mer?" Karrine demanded, slamming her own cup down and ignoring the way the liquid sloshed all over the table. "How complicated could it have been? She had twenty-one years to tell me I was engaged!" She didn't even notice the tears streaming down her face until her aunt reached over to wipe them away as she had when she was a child. Angry and not ready to let it go she pushed her hand away. "Don't."

Slowly Aunt Meredith pulled her hand back, hurt showing in her eyes but Karrine steeled her heart against it. "Sweetheart, I know you're not going to understand this but your mother did what she thought was best. She never wanted this arranged marriage for you and she spent years trying to find a loophole in the contract so she could get you out of it, but it is ironclad. The only catch was if there was some moral objection from the family and if both sets of parents agreed to call it off. Only Steffan never crossed any lines, he was a good kid, a strong Christian and he is building himself a very successful business. He will be a good provider for you Karrine, there was really nothing your mother could find to object too."

The world spun a little faster as she tried to process everything she was hearing. "A good kid? A good provider? What did you do have someone follow him?" Her eyes widened as the implications of that set in, "Was someone following me? All this time was someone giving Steffan or his family reports on me? Was it you?"

"Of course not." Aunt Meredith reached over to grasp her hand but she snatched her hand back, too angry to be comforted. "Karrine we would never do that to you. We would never have let someone follow you."

"You had someone follow Steffan, why should I believe you didn't do the same to me!"

"We did not have anyone follow Steffan," her aunt gave a long-suffering sigh and took a long swallow of her coffee. "Your father's family acted as a go-between for all of us. They kept an eye on both you and Steffan, just to make sure there was nothing in either of your lives that the families would object to."

"Unbelievable," rubbing her eyes she tried to process everything she was hearing but before she could hope to wrap her mind around it another thought came to mind and the world shifted again. "You knew about the guardianship clause? And that I had to be married within a month of my twenty-first birthday? Didn't you? At Mom's funeral, when Aunt Fern and Uncle Grover asked if I was still coming to Yagos you knew all of this and you still didn't say anything?"

"Karrine," Aunt Meredith spoke in a quiet voice as if trying to calm her down, but she was too upset.

"No. No!" She was almost hysterical now but she didn't care, only the fear of waking up her sister kept her from screaming at the top of her lungs. "You let me come here completely unprepared. You didn't warn me. You didn't tell me I was supposed to be getting married in just two weeks. How could you do that to me? How could you do that to Celine?"

"Oh, Krin I didn't want to." Aunt Meredith was crying now too but she was beyond the point of caring. "I didn't know the wedding had to be one month after your birthday and I didn't know about the guardianship clause, if I had I would have told you, I swear I would have, but it wasn't until after you called Tessa that I went back and looked at the contract."

Even as angry as she was, her aunt's words made sense, and desperately she wanted to believe her, but she wasn't willing to forgive her. "You still should have told me about the engagement."

"I know that now," Aunt Meredith agreed. "But I had promised your mother I wouldn't. She wanted to let your first visit back to Yagos go unspoiled. I was going to tell you as soon as you got home but now . . ."

Done listening Karrine shoved back her chair, leaving her coffee on the table and grabbing a banana from the fruit bowl instead. Running back up to her room she quietly slipped inside. Grabbing her purse she changed into clothes more conducive to rock-climbing. When she went back down her aunt was right where she had left her.

"When Celine wakes up tell her I went out, I'll be back later."

"Where are you going?" Aunt Meredith demanded, tears still falling down her face.

"Climbing." Without any more of an explanation, she found the keys to the car that Aunt Fern had let her borrow the day before and headed out the front door, leaving her family, her engagement, and all the secrets and betrayal behind.

*

Steffan had woken early when Solo decided he wanted to play at five in the morning. Having made it back in time for his meeting the day before he didn't have much at the office waiting for him. Deciding to call it a casual day he walked to work in khakis and a polo instead of his normal suit, bring Solo along for the day. While the dog slumbered at his feet he got caught up on all of his work he'd put off to have lunch with Karrine the day before and even managed to get ahead on a few things. By the time he had finished the weekly staff meeting at ten, he was ready to be done with work for the day.

Heading out of the office he let Mrs. Coren know he was leaving and would be gone for the day unless something came up, in which case he did have his phone on him. For a moment he just stood outside the office building, debating his options. He could go home, give Solo his second meal of the day and scrounge up some lunch for himself. Or, grab his car and head over to see his parents and kill some time with his family. Cam was another option; his best friend was probably working but more than likely he would be willing to spend his lunch break on a rematch handball game. Somehow none of those ideas held much appeal.

Instead, he headed to his apartment only long enough to change his clothes, feed Solo, and grab his car. It was time to see what his fiancée was up to.

The drive to the Sandor house was short but he noticed the new car in the driveway as soon as he pulled up. Snapping on Solo's leash he instructed the dog to heel as he went to knock on the door. A young woman answered, dark blonde hair fell in ringlets to her shoulders and big blue eyes regarded him with a mixture of curiosity and suspicion.

"Can I help you?"

There it was, the perfectly polite voice with just a hint of an accent and attitude that reminded him of Karrine. "Is Karrine home?"

"That depends," the woman crossed her arms and rocked back on her heels, shuttering her expression so she gave nothing away. "Who are you?"

More amused than intimidated he shifted Solo's leash to the other hand, quietly instructing the dog to sit and stay. "I am Steffan Dalton, her fiancé, who are you?"

Something flashed in her eyes but unlike Karrine, this woman knew how to hide her emotions and it was gone as quickly as it appeared. "Contessa Franklin, but everyone calls me Tessa," she held out a hand, "I'm Karrine's cousin and her best friend."

Shaking her hand he smiled at the confident grip and steady gaze. "Nice to meet you, Tessa. Is your cousin here?"

She regarded him for just a moment, sweeping her gaze over him and the huge dog at his side before stepping back to allow him entrance. "Actually she's not but if you would like, you're welcome to come in and wait." Realizing she wasn't asking, he stepped inside as Tessa closed the door behind him, "While we wait it will give us a chance to talk."

Tessa led him into the living room, taking a seat on the couch and offering Solo her hand to smell while he took a chair opposite her. The Mastiff sniffed her hand for a moment before licking it, making fast friends with the confident and curious young woman.

"So Steffan, tell me about yourself."

Leaning back in his chair he held her stare, "What do you want to know."

"My parents tell me you have your own company, what do you do?"

That's how he found himself explaining Sailor IT to the intriguing young woman. Tessa asked insightful questions and she followed his explanations with surprising ease. He was telling her how he had first come up with the idea when the door opened again and his fiancée walked in. At least he thought it was his fiancée but the young woman staring at him in confusion didn't look anything like the expressive, defiant, strong-willed woman he had found himself daydreaming about.

Dressed in some form of spandex pants, a tight-tank top accentuating her form and well-used shoes, she entered with a duffel bag slung over her shoulder. There was no jacket in sight despite the six degrees Celsius weather, he could only hope there was one in her bag and that she hadn't forgotten it. Her hair was pulled back into a tight ponytail, keeping it off her face. She looked completely confused to find him there. Her gaze kept flicking between him, Tessa, the dog, and back to him again.

"What are you doing here?" She finally asked.

Remembering his manners a little too late, he stood, "I came to see you but Tessa said you were out so she's been keeping me company while I wait."

Tessa hadn't bothered to stand but stayed where she was, her legs folded up under her as she watched the exchange, "How was the climb Krin?"

Karrine switched her attention from staring at him to smiling at Tessa but it didn't quite reach her eyes. "It was . . . necessary."

"No Mount Everest huh?"

Karrine smirked but shook her head, "No, not even close." Looking at him again a shadow passed over her face and she frowned, "I should go change, excuse me."

Reclaiming his seat Steffan absently patted Solo's head as he stared at the floor, trying to decipher his own reaction. Karrine hadn't been dressed immodestly by anyone's standards, he had seen plenty of women at the gym or the handball courts in much more revealing clothing but he had never had trouble remembering how to talk around them.

Solo whined, reminding him he was not alone in the room and he looked up suddenly, seeing that Tessa was staring at him with a knowing smile on her face. Not wanting to speculate what was causing that smile he cleared his throat.

"I apologize, what were we talking about again?"

"The fact that you like my cousin."

Forcing a chuckle he purposefully leaned back in his chair again, doing his best to look relaxed. "Well, she is my fiancée so I suppose being able to get along will be beneficial in our marriage."

"That's not what I meant and you know it," Tessa smirked at him. When he stayed quiet she opened her mouth to say something else but Karrine walked back in before she could. He sucked in a quick breath, checking her face quickly to determine if she had overheard the conversation but she seemed to be blissfully unaware as she settled down on the couch next to her cousin.

"So, what did you need to see me about?"

*

Karrine had not been trying to be rude but as soon as she spoke Tessa kicked her leg and she knew she had crossed a line. Before she had a chance to apologize though Steffan smiled at her.

"I thought you might like to meet Solo here, I told you a little bit about him yesterday."

"I remember," her eyes falling on the huge animal at his feet and she couldn't help but grin. "Celine is going to love this guy. May I pet him?"

"Of course. Solo," Steffan got the dog's attention and pointed across the room. Immediately the animal hauled himself up and lumbered across the room, tail wagging as he came to lay his head in her lap. Giggling like a child she rubbed his ears, delighting in the attention of the dog.

"Is Celine up yet?" She asked Tessa, "She'll love this."

"She went for a walk with Dad but they should be back anytime, I'll go check."

Still petting the dog she just nodded when Tessa excused herself, leaving her and Steffan alone in the room. Chancing a glance up at him she looked away quickly when she realized he was watching her. She felt the heat rush to her cheeks and knew she was probably blushing so she dipped her head, letting her hair fall over her face in hopes that would keep him from noticing. Keeping her attention on the dog she searched for something to say.

"So, you really just came over to have me meet your dog?" When he didn't reply she looked up and realized he was frowning at her. "What is it? What's wrong?"

Leaning forward Steffan rested his arms on his knees, "Karrine, you realize that in order to fulfill the stipulations in the contract and for you to keep custody of your sister we have to get married . . . in a little less than two weeks."

Tensing at the mention of the engagement she nodded, "I remember."

"That means we will be living together," he spoke slowly as if she were a child trying to understand a difficult subject. "You, Celine, myself, and Solo. I thought it would be best if you and your sister could at least meet the dog before that. And maybe get to know me a little bit better."

Her hand paused on the dog's head and she slowly withdrew it as his words started to sink in. Something in her face must have concerned him because suddenly he was sitting next to her, reaching for her hand.

"Karrine? Are you all right?"

"We're getting married," she turned to look at him in shock. "We're getting married in a couple of weeks. We're going to liv-" her voice broke on the word and a hand flew to her mouth as humiliating tears filled her eyes again, "live together and we don't even know where!"

"Okay," he reached out to take her hand, remaining calm in the face of her panic. "Karrine, first you need to take a deep breath. We will figure this all out, I promise."

Closing her eyes she worked hard to fight the tears that were threatening to fall, "How are we going to figure this out? None of it even makes sense."

"Krin?" Celine walked into the room but upon seeing her sister's tears she rushed right to her side, ignoring Solo and shooting death glares at Steffan. "Krin what is it? What happened?"

"Celine," Uncle Donovan came to the threshold and called the teenager back. "Come here sweetheart; let's give Karrine and Steffan a few minutes to talk, hmm?"

Taking a deep breath she forced a smile at her uncle but shook her head. "It's okay Uncle Don, you're all welcome to stay. Celine should get to know her future brother-in-law after all," she felt her smile falter at her own words but thankfully it was enough to distract her sister. Celine looked curiously at Steffan while Uncle Donovan and Tessa both came back into the room. Squeezing

Celine's shoulder she helped the teenager off the floor as Steffan moved back to his own chair so the girl could take his spot. "Celine, I know you met Steffan the other day," she waited for the teenager's nod to confirm. "And this," she smiled at the English Mastiff that was currently standing there panting, waiting for someone to give him attention, "is his dog, Solo."

*

Steffan watched as Karrine went from nearly frantic to calm in mere seconds. Things were starting to fall into place and he was beginning to learn a little bit more about his fiancée. Starting with the fact that Celine was more than her little sister, she really was Karrine's whole life. He would have to remember that if he wanted to make their marriage work.

"Steffan," Karrine's uncle came over to shake his hand, sizing him up then giving a nod that he hoped signaled his approval. "Donovan Franklin, it's nice to meet you."

"Likewise," he smiled at the man then grinned when Celine giggled as Solo tried to lick her face. "I think you found a new best friend there Celine." The teenager laughed and pushed the dog back a little, prompting him to scold the animal, "Solo, behave yourself." The Mastiff whined but sat down, letting Celine continue to pet him but no longer trying to climb in her lap.

"At least when we move to Yagos we'll finally have a dog Krin," the teenager laughed at her sister, not noticing the way Karrine suddenly blanched. Digging out his car keys he smiled at Celine.

"Solo has a tennis ball out in the car, there are some treats out there too. If you want, you can take him out to the back yard and play fetch with him for a while. You think he loves you now, but if

58

you do that he will be your best friend for life."

"Sounds like fun," Tessa jumped to her feet and grabbed the keys. "Come on Cina, I bet I can throw the ball further than you."

The teenager hesitated but a nod from her sister had her smiling, "Yeah right, you throw like a girl, Tessa."

"I am a girl."

"Bet I can throw it further than both of you," Donovan teased the girls as he got to his feet and called the dog to his side. As soon as the group had filed out of the room Steffan turned to Karrine.

"You didn't think through the fact that you would be moving to Yagos, did you?"

"No," taking a deep breath she exhaled slowly and turned to face him. "I hadn't, but I assume you have. So . . . where will we live?"

He considered her for a moment, debating how to answer, he had always believed that honesty was best. "I have my own business; I think I told you that, so I assumed we would live here in Yagos but if you have any objections I could try to figure out a way to move my headquarters or how to do my work from home."

"No," she took a shaky breath but shook her head, "At least for now the only work I have is whatever is required of me at my Dad's company. Staying in Yagos makes sense, Celine and I could both probably use a fresh start."

Curious about the hint of regret he saw lurking in her eyes he smiled and made himself nod. "As for where we would live I assumed you and your sister would just move into my place rather than try to find a house between now and then."

"How big is it?"

And this was where they ran into an issue, "It's small Karrine, it only has two bedrooms but I could put two beds in one room if that would make you feel more comfortable."

Relief shone in her eyes and she nodded, "That would be good, Celine, and I wouldn't mind sharing until we figured something else out."

He had to hide his surprise since he had meant adding another bed to his room and not her sister's but the relief in her eyes kept him from voicing those thoughts out loud. "If you want to tell me what you would like, I can start looking for a place right away but we still have to talk about the wedding."

"Right," she sighed but pulled out her phone, tapping a few keys before looking at him again. "August 10th." At his confused look she shrugged, "That's the Saturday after next, two days from our one-month deadline. Does that work for you?"

It occurred to him this was not the way they should be having this conversation. They should both be excited, happy, even if they weren't in love, they shouldn't be acting like it was more of a business deal than a wedding. Of course, that was the whole problem. To Karrine, this was nothing more than a contract, one she wanted nothing to do with but would sign so she could take care of her sister. Even if he felt differently it wouldn't change a thing.

Chapter 5

"You want to do what?" Karrine stared at her aunts with a mixture of shock and confusion but neither woman looked like they were going to back down.

"Karrine you are getting married in eleven days and although we can hire a wedding planner to do a lot of things we still need to find your dress and find dresses for your bridesmaids." Aunt Fern put her hands on her hips and stared her down. If she hadn't been so stressed she would have started laughing at the sight of the small woman glaring at her with such defiance. Instead, she threw up her hands.

"Fine," she forced herself to smile at her sister who was already bouncing up and down with excitement. "Let's go shopping." Celine giggled and launched herself at Karrine, almost knocking her down with her hug. Across the room, she met Tessa's eye and her cousin gave her an encouraging smile as she wondered whether or not she would have the energy to keep smiling as they picked out a dress for the most important day of her life.

"There are some other decisions you have to make too dear," Aunt Meredith told her. They had not spoken again since yesterday but when she had told her family last night that she and

Steffan had set a wedding date, Aunt Mer had immediately begun helping her with the details, making calls to her family in Colorado and making lists of decisions that had to be made.

Not exactly in a position to refuse help she frowned but Tessa stepped in, "Can they be made while we drive Mom? We really should get going; we have a lot to do today."

"Come, the driver is already waiting," Aunt Fern ushered them all outside but Karrine balked at the sight of the limo in the driveway.

"Aunt Fern, you've got to be kidding, you want me to go wedding dress shopping in a limousine?"

"I just thought it would be more comfortable," the woman defended herself but the smile she was fighting suggested she wanted to show off her niece at least a little bit.

"Please Krin," Celine begged her sister. "Can't we take the limo?"

Unable to resist her sister she sighed but waved a hand towards the car, "Oh why not? Come on let's go shopping."

It only took a few minutes to get settled in and as soon as they were safely sequestered inside, the driver had them on their way to the first store. Aunt Meredith turned to look at her. "All right Krin, the first thing you need to decide is who you want your bridesmaids to be."

"Actually that's second, first is whether or not you want Steffan's mother and sister to be involved in picking out your dress," Aunt Fern told her. "If you do, I need to call them right away."

Rubbing her head she sighed, trying to process everything she was hearing without letting the emotions overtake her, she nodded. "Yes, Aunt Fern, Steffan's family deserves to be involved, go ahead and invite them. As far as bridesmaids go, Tessa and Celine, would you like to be in my wedding?"

*

Karrine decided she liked Genève Dalton the moment she met her. Sophisticated and elegant from the top of her perfectly coiffed hair to the tops of her exquisite three-inch heels. The woman should have been extremely intimidating but instead, she had breezed inside and offered Karrine a tender smile. "I know you do not know me but first let me say how sorry I am about losing your mother and for how chaotic everything has been since you have arrived in Yagos. I can't imagine how hard this must all be for you. I do want you to know I've been praying for you for years Karrine, and I am certainly not going to stop now. If you ever need anything, all you have to do is call." Then she had slipped her a business card with her cell phone number written on the back before giving her a small hug, "Now, let's find you a wedding dress."

Kennedy was a strange combination of her mother's grace and kindness, her brother's confidence, and an attitude that had to be all her own. She had come in behind her mother, taken one look at Karrine and Celine and grinned, "So you're my new sisters. I always wanted sisters, I mean Steffan's great but there are some things you just can't talk to a brother about, know what I mean?"

Unable to hide her smile she laughed but nodded her agreement at Kennedy's observation, "As a matter of fact I do. I never had a brother, but I had some cousins who did a pretty good job of filling in for me and there are definitely some things I never would have wanted to talk to them about."

"Tell me about it," Kennedy grinned then gave them each a hug, hugging Tessa and both aunts for good measure, and informing them they were family now too, or at least they would be in less than two weeks.

Feeling a bit like she had just been caught in a hurricane masked as an eighteen-year-old girl Karrine grinned at her soon-to-be-sister-in-law, "Kennedy, I know we don't know each other very well but would you like to be in my wedding? I would love to have you as a bridesmaid."

So, the bridal party was set. She had asked Celine to be her maid-of-honor but the teenager had insisted Tessa should have that honor. So with her cousin serving in that position with Celine and Kennedy as her bridesmaids, and her Uncle Donovan would walk her down the aisle to give her away. Once those plans were in place they moved on to other important decisions. In between trying on dresses, picking out colors, fielding questions her aunts, and future mother-in-law asked about things like what font she wanted for the invitations and what cake they should serve, she barely had time to breathe much less think.

Three hours into their shopping day, they finally managed to select deep purple and peach for the wedding colors. They decide the bridesmaids should wear tea-length dresses in the same purple with spaghetti straps which crisscrossed down the back for the two girls, and a strapless dress with a sweetheart neckline for Tessa. Peach colored roses with purple ribbons were chosen for the girls to carry and silver shoes would complete their outfits.

Now if they could just find her wedding dress.

After several more hours of looking they called it a day, "We can look more tomorrow," Aunt Fern suggested. "Don't worry dear, we will find you something."

"Actually dear, we may already have something." Aunt Meredith slipped an arm around her shoulders, removing her hands with a look of hurt when Karrine tensed at the contact. "I spoke to your Grandmother when you were trying on your last dress and she sent me this." Holding out her phone she let Karrine take a look.

A beautiful pearl white dress with puffed sleeves and exquisite beadwork on the bodice trailed down to a full skirt and a long train. "It's beautiful Aunt Mer, I mean I don't like the sleeves but it's gorgeous. Where did it come from?"

"It was your Mom's." The older woman smiled and blinked back tears. "I figured you wouldn't like the sleeves but we can make some modifications to it."

"Oh, Aunt Mer," she blinked back her own tears as she looked between the dress and her aunt. "My biggest regret about this wedding is that Mom and Dad won't be here with me but having her dress, it would almost be like having her here."

"That's what we thought too," Aunt Meredith agreed. "Say the word and your Grandmother will get on a plane and bring the dress here. That should give us just enough time to get the adjustments made. What do you say?"

"Aunt Mer, that beadwork, they can't adjust that in a week."

"No, but they shouldn't have to, you and your Mom are about the same size, other than taking off those sleeves there shouldn't be too much they'd have to do."

Impulsively she hugged her aunt, holding her tight and letting herself be held, taking the comfort that was offered and drawing from her strength. "Thank you, Aunt Mer."

"You're welcome sweetheart," her aunt whispered back, her voice thick with tears. "I love you."

Knowing the words were more than just affection but also held an apology she pushed her confused emotions aside and squeezed her aunt a little tighter, "I love you too."

*

Steffan had gotten a call asking him to meet Karrine's family for dinner to go over wedding plans. He knew his mum and sister had been out all day with his fiancée looking at dresses and going over plans for their wedding. He had gotten more than one phone call at the office asking him to make some decision or another, most of which he neither understood nor cared about but he did the best he could, already looking forward to getting past August 10th so they could put all this wedding nonsense behind them.

Pulling up outside the Sandor house he prayed for patience. He wasn't sure what to expect from the dinner but after a long day, all he wanted was to go home, feed Solo and then call Cam for a good game of handball. Instead, he was sitting in his car, trying to find the energy to go inside and enter the wedding planning chaos.

The front door opened and Karrine stepped out. Seeing him in his car she hesitated for a moment before giving a tentative wave. Unable to resist the vulnerability he could see on her face even from such a distance away. He climbed out of the car and headed towards her.

"Your mom and sister are inside," she said by way of greeting.

"Yeah? Did you guys have a good day shopping or whatever it is you were doing?"

Her lips tilted up in the barest hint of a smile and she nodded, "Yeah, actually we did, I even found my wedding dress."

He wondered if he was supposed to be excited at that or at least interested but since he was neither he just nodded, "That is good."

This time Karrine fully grinned, "Don't worry; I don't expect you to be excited about any of this. It's not like either of us asked for it."

"At least I knew it would happen someday," he pointed out as he leaned against the side of the house, enjoying these few minutes to talk to her before they went inside.

"True," she shrugged, "But you didn't ask to get a fourteen-year-old girl in the mix either."

"No," he shook his head, noting the way her eyes narrowed in anger at his easy agreement even though she was the one who had made the point. "But I like Celine; she seems like a nice kid." He paused a moment, trying to sort out what he wanted to say, "Karrine . . ."

The door opened and Tessa stuck her head out, "Hey you two, everyone's wondering where you went." Glancing between them she frowned, "And I'm interrupting something, sorry."

Karrine smiled when her cousin disappeared back inside but she gave a little shrug, "I guess we should go back in. Like I said, your Mom and sister are already inside. Is your Dad joining us too?"

"I think so but I'm honestly not sure, I was at work and Mum called to say I should come here for dinner to go over some wedding plans. That's about all I know."

"Yeah, that has pretty much been my whole day," she reached for the door but he beat her to it, holding it for her as she walked inside. "Make this decision or that one and then someone else telling me where we were going next. I hardly knew which end was up."

"Well let's hope tonight goes better than that."

*

"Steffan, you need to decide on your groomsmen," his mum explained as they went over wedding plans before dinner. "Since Tessa, Celine, and Kennedy are the bridesmaids you will need to pick three."

"You're a bridesmaid?" he looked at his sister in surprise. "How did that happen?"

"Karrine asked me and in exchange, I promised to tell her stories about you," his sister smart-mouthed back.

"Like you know any," he chuckled but smiled at Karrine, trying to tell her thank you with his eyes but not sure whether or not she understood.

"Groomsmen, Steffan," Mum reminded him with an indulgent

smile. "Focus."

"Right," thinking for just a second he shrugged. "Cam will be my best man, no question. But as for other groomsmen . . . Karrine do you have anyone you'd want to be in the wedding?"

"Me?" She frowned at him, but he just shrugged.

"You asked my sister to be a bridesmaid, the least I can do is return the favor."

For a moment she just looked at him but whether she was trying to think of someone she wanted in the wedding or if she was trying to figure out if it was a genuine offer he couldn't tell. Finally, she glanced at Tessa, "Ben and Luke?"

"That's what I was thinking too," her cousin agreed with a smile. "They'd love it."

Steffan waited patiently, hoping they would explain eventually. It only took a minute before Karrine looked over at him. "My cousins, Ben and Luke, they're the closest thing, Cina, Tessa, or I have ever had to brothers."

"Ben and Luke?" He repeated the names in amusement. "Your family comes up with names like Karrine, Contessa, and Celine but your cousins' names are Ben and Luke?"

Meredith coughed to cover a laugh while the others just grinned in amusement. It was Karrine who answered, "Aunt Jules is . . . kind of the wild child in the family. She is the youngest in her generation and she has always made a point of doing things differently than the rest of the family. She also happens to be a huge Star Wars fan."

It only took him a moment to make the connection, "Luke Skywalker?"

"You got it," Tessa laughed.

He searched his brain; he didn't know much about Star Wars but Ben didn't sound familiar. When he asked the family smiled.

"Ben is Andy's middle name," Meredith filled in for him. "Her first choices were Yoda and Anakin, but Andy convinced her not to name them after bad guys or characters that weren't human, much to our relief. Getting her to agree to Ben for her oldest was a bit of a fight but apparently it's the name of someone or another in the movies. Once she remembered she gave in." She looked to Karrine for help

"Obi-Wan," Karrine filled in for her. "I think he's introduced as Ben Kenobi in one of the movies. Anyways, since Uncle Andy got to pick the first name she got to pick the second. Thankfully she decided to go for something that still sounded normal but was easily recognizable as being a Star Wars name too."

"So she settled on Luke," he summarized, earning him a nod and a smile from his fiancée.

"She really wanted Luke to have a twin sister so she could name her Leia," Celine added with a grin. "Instead Mom decided to surprise her when I was born and she made it my middle name."

"Celine Leia," Kennedy repeated with a grin. "That's awesome."

The girl just shrugged but there was a trace of sadness on her face, "I was born on Aunt Jules birthday, Mom felt like it was appropriate."

Reaching over he squeezed her shoulder in a kind of half-hug like he would if it were Kennedy, "It's a good name." He looked back to Karrine, "Ben and Luke sound like they will make good groomsmen, no matter how they got their names."

*

Over the next week, things were hectic. Karrine felt like she was always being dragged one direction or the next, making decisions about a wedding she still wished she could get out of. Then she would look at Celine and she remembered why she was going through with it at all.

Her Grandma flew in with her Mom's wedding dress in tow. A friend of Aunt Fern's agreed to do the simple alterations it would require. Genève Dalton knew someone who would make the wedding cake and someone else, she couldn't remember who had found a church large enough to accommodate all of the guests. Not that there were going to be many people coming in on such short notice but apparently the church where Steffan and his family attended was too small. Karrine had let her friends know about the wedding, sending out emails and text messages with a brief explanation, but most of them were climbers like her who would rather spend their money flying to their next adventure rather than fly in for her wedding. So, outside of her family, there would be no guests on her side of the aisle.

She kept telling herself it didn't matter, the whole reason she was going through with the wedding was for her sister. And it was true but that didn't mean it hurt less. In fact, the pain just kept coming in waves, because her Dad should have been there to walk her down the aisle, her Mom should be there to help her with her veil, her friends should be here celebrating with her, and the man at the other end of the aisle should have been the love of her life, instead of the means to an end. So on days when her emotions got too strong, and things were too overwhelming she would go climbing. She escaped to the park and left everything out on the rocks.

It was strange that August in Yagos felt like April in Colorado, but the advantage was that most people in the country were spending their winter skiing instead of rock-climbing so most of the time she was out there on her own.

Three days before her wedding she had just finished a climb and was headed back to her car when she realized someone was already there. Leaning against the vehicle with one foot propped up. Karrine slowed down, squinting against the sun as she tried to see who was waiting for her. Reaching in her bag she fingered the Ruger 9mm handgun she always kept with her at her family's insistence. Uncle Andy had taught her to climb but he had also taught her how to protect herself, insisting that a young woman should never go out in the wilderness by herself without protection. Until now, she'd never had to use it.

"You can leave it in the bag Krin, I promise not to bite."

The familiar voice had her dropping the bag where she stood and running into his waiting arms. Tears came to her eyes as he wrapped her in an embrace, holding her close and waiting for her to cry herself out as she had done so many times in the past.

For a minute she was that eight-year-old little girl all over again, grieving over her father, adjusting to a new country and watching her mother slowly bury herself in work, while the rest of the family, practically strangers to her, stepped in to take care of her and her infant sister. It was after Uncle Donovan had found her climbing thirty feet into a tree that they had decided something had to be done. Uncle Andy owned his own rock-climbing gym and it seemed like the logical place. She had taken to it immediately and he had taken her under his wing. He taught her to climb, first at the gym, then on mountains, teaching her to leave her emotions on the rocks focusing only on where the next foothold or hand grip would be.

"I'm glad you found some rocks," he finally whispered when her tears dried up.

Unable to help herself she laughed, "Yeah. Me too."

"Good. Then we can save the lecture about why you should never climb alone and not tell someone where you're going for later."

Knowing she had broken one of his cardinal rules she tried to defend herself, "I really just needed some time alone."

"Time alone when your foot slips is what gets climbers killed," Uncle Andy lectured but he flicked her ponytail in a gesture that told her he wasn't going to push it. "Grab your bag kid, I promised your aunt Jules I'd bring you home so she could see you right away."

"How did you get here?" She asked, realizing she didn't see any other familiar cars in the parking lot.

"Ben dropped me off before he and Tessa went to pick up some food. Apparently, they found a place that has Italian take-out. The real question is why didn't you call us? One phone call Krin and your aunt and I would have been here days ago. All you had to do was ask. The only reason we waited until now was so

Jules could finish her court case first. I could have come earlier though and I would've if you'd asked. You know we are always here if you need us. When we didn't hear from you we assumed you were handling things, but judging from that crying episode just now we were wrong."

"I know." She jogged back to grab her bag, fishing for the keys and tossing them to her uncle, too emotionally spent to want to drive back to the house.

He waited until she slid into the passenger seat and strapped her seatbelt before he started to pull out. "So if you know, why didn't you call? If ever there were a time you needed someone to talk to, I'd say it was when you found out you were engaged and had to get married in two weeks."

Closing her eyes so she wouldn't have to see his reaction she leaned her head back against her seat. "Uncle Andy, did you know? Did you know about the marriage contract?"

"No." He hit the brakes harder than normal, put the car in reverse and pulled back into a parking spot. When she didn't look at him he reached out to grasp her chin and turn it towards him. "Karrine, I would never have let you come to Yagos on your own if I had known what you were walking into. But I know why you had to ask because after I did find out about the contract, I also learned your grandparents, and your other aunts and uncles did know. Jules and I didn't though, I promise."

He had never lied to her, not once in all of her life. There were times he had refused to answer her questions and other times he'd told her the truth knowing how much it would hurt her but he had never lied, and she didn't think he would start now. Letting out her breath she nodded slowly.

"Good, thank you, Uncle Andy. I don't know if I could have handled it if you had known."

"I didn't," he told her again, shifting the car into drive again. "But I do now so I'm listening. Tell me what has happened so far."

Chapter 6

It seemed like every day more people arrived from Karrine's family. He spent more time meeting them than he did talking to his fiancé. The advantage was he genuinely liked them, and he was learning more about Karrine every day. Everyone in Karrine's family had been kind but from the moment he had arrived at the house that day, Jules Shaw had him under a microscope and no one seemed very inclined to help him get out from under it.

"Steffan, tell me about your business, how did it begin?"

"Mom, go easy on him," fifteen-year-old Luke was engaged in a chess match with his grandfather and didn't even look up as he spoke.

"He's about to marry your cousin, Luke," Jules replied with a slight smile that seemed more threatening than welcoming. "This is me going easy on him." The rest of the family smiled but continued their conversations, apparently unwilling to come to his defense.

"All right, it started when I was a teenager and used to go to the office with my Dad . . ." He was almost through the explanation when Karrine walked into the house, laughing as she talked with a man who looked to be fifteen or twenty years her senior. The strong resemblance to the chess-playing Luke told him this was Uncle Andy. The smile on Karrine's face told him they were close, and her outfit said she had been rock-climbing again, something he was quickly learning she did whenever she got overwhelmed.

She stopped when she saw him and the happiness on her face slowly faded from genuine laughter to a polite smile. "Hi, I didn't realize you were here."

"Should I apologize?" He asked, only half teasing.

Her lips twitched but she didn't reply, "Uncle Andy this is Steffan Dalton, Steffan this is Andy Shaw, Aunt Jules' husband, and Ben and Luke's father." With the introductions out of the way she glanced around the room with a frown, "Where's Celine?"

"Outside playing fetch with Solo," he explained with a smile. "Your Grandma is with her."

"Oh," walking across the room she glanced down at the chess game Luke was playing with her Grandpa, putting one hand on her cousin's shoulder in a protective gesture. "Are you winning?"

"You know it," the kid grinned up at her and she laughed, giving him a side hug before moving to meet her Aunt Jules in the middle of the room.

"Hi sweetie," Aunt Jules stood and wrapped her arms around her, whispering something in her ear too quiet for him to hear. He saw her nod before she pulled back, carefully avoiding his gaze probably so he would not see her wipe away her tears.

"I have to go change clothes; I'll be right back down."

Jules sent him a look over her shoulder, said a quiet word to her husband, and followed Karrine out, apparently leaving Andy to take up the interrogation where she had left off. Sizing him up Andy continued to stand, meeting his gaze as Steffan did his own assessment.

He was a man of average height with the lean body of someone who kept in shape, the muscles in his arms made him wonder if perhaps he was a rock climber like Karrine. His light blonde hair was kept short unlike his son, Luke, who kept his just a little too long to be socially acceptable. Bright blue eyes narrowed in suspicion that warned him this was another family member who had not been aware of the marriage contract and certainly was not happy about it. Andy let the silence hang between them a moment longer than what was comfortable before he spoke.

"Steffan is it? Why don't we take a walk?"

It wasn't a request and he had never been fond of taking orders from strangers but he stood, following the other man out of the house and wondering if he needed to bring his dog along for protection. Instead, he waited only until they were off the porch before he started the conversation, figuring his odds were better if he were the first to speak.

"You and Karrine seem close. I haven't seen her that comfortable with anyone but Tessa since she arrived."

"We are," Andy sent him a sideways glance not elaborating. "She doesn't trust you."

Not sure if he should be offended or amused he settled for a nod, "I had noticed. But she doesn't know me yet either. I will earn her trust, hers, and Celine's, and then I will earn yours and the rest of the family's."

"Oh yeah?" Andy's facial expression stayed neutral, "How are you going to do that?"

"By taking care of them," Steffan stopped and faced off with him, "You have my word."

"Yeah?" Andy repeated the question and rocked back on his heels, "But whether your word means anything or not still remains to be seen."

*

"Sweetheart I'm worried about you. This engagement isn't exactly the conventional way of doing things."

Karrine laughed as she pulled out clean clothes. "Aunt Jules you are the most unconventional person I've ever met!"

"Well I can't argue with that," her aunt chuckled but it didn't wipe the frown off her face. "But sweetie this is a little different. Be honest, if it weren't for the guardianship clause with Celine, would you still go through with this wedding?"

"No," she frowned and sat down on the bed beside her aunt. "But it is in the contract Aunt Jules so what choice do I have?"

"I don't know," Jules frowned and tapped her fingers against her knee. "I do know God hates divorce, if you go through with this then there's no going back Karrine. Are you sure you understand that?"

She opened her mouth to answer then stopped, not wanting to just brush off her aunt. Without a word she went into the bathroom and climbed in the shower, letting the hot water wash over her as she tried to collect her thoughts. In the other room, Aunt Jules was quiet, not even attempting to make conversation but giving her the space she needed. If she knew her aunt then the older woman had her head bent as she prayed, for what exactly Karrine wasn't sure.

Forcing herself to think about her aunt's questions she tried to imagine the future. Her choices were clear, get married, find a way to make Steffan part of her, and Celine's lives so Celine could have a future. Her job would be what it had always been, to be the one to make sure her little sister got through school, got through college, and made a good life for herself. Or she could stay single, lose guardianship of her sister to an uncle she had never met, and to a fate, she could not predict or control. But Celine was fourteen, in four more years she would be out of the house and Karrine would still be stuck in a marriage she neither needed nor wanted.

Which said nothing about Steffan's future? He seemed willing to go through with the marriage for some twisted reason she couldn't even begin to understand. Maybe it was because he had always known about their engagement and he'd had more time to resign himself to it. Or maybe he was just a glutton for punishment. But she wasn't and she was not at all sure this marriage was a good idea.

Turning the water off she grabbed a towel and wrapped it tightly around her body, almost laughing at the thought of how she had first met Steffan and gotten into this mess in the first place. Instead, she forced herself to breathe deeply and headed back into her room to get dressed. As predicted Aunt Jules had her head bowed, lips moving in silent prayer but she looked up when Karrine came back in.

"Have you prayed about it?"

She resisted the urge to roll her eyes at the question. She was a Christian, she knew God created everything and Jesus had died for her sins but she doubted that God cared about her everyday life, and she didn't feel the need to pray about every little decision. Even as she thought it she wondered if she should pray, this wasn't exactly a little decision. Instead, she grabbed her clothes and started to get dressed.

"When Mom died I asked God to give me the strength, courage, and wisdom to raise my sister. I guess that gives me the only answer I need. Even if it means sacrificing my own future, I have to make sure Celine gets hers."

"All right," Aunt Jules nodded slowly then grinned, "But Karrine. Could you maybe do it without being quite so dramatic?"

Unable to help it she laughed at her own expense, sitting next to her aunt on the bed and nodding. "I suppose that was a little over the top, huh?"

Aunt Jules held up her thumb and forefinger a smidge apart, "Just a bit."

"But it doesn't change the facts Aunt Jules," Karrine shrugged as she started to brush out her hair. "I have to get married; I can't abandon Celine. I just can't."

"I know," Aunt Jules wrapped an arm around her shoulders, "I wish I could change this for you Karrine. I really do but . . . I have to believe this is God's plan, not just for you but also for Celine and Steffan, and His plan is always best. Even if we can't see how right now."

Resting her head on Aunt Jules' shoulder for a brief moment she sighed, "I really hope you're right."

*

Two Days Later

"I can't believe you're getting married tomorrow." Cam grinned over at him as Steffan stepped out to let the tailor check the fit of the tuxedo he would wear for his wedding the next day. "I mean I knew you would marry Karrine eventually, but I always expected to get the chance to meet the girl before your rehearsal dinner."

"Wait you haven't met Krin yet?" Karrine's cousin and one of his groomsmen, Ben, asked from across the room where he was trying on his own tux.

"I have not exactly had a lot of extra time," Steffan explained, getting what he hoped was an understanding nod in reply. "And you will meet her tonight. Just please Cam, will you do me a favor and try not to scare her away?"

"It will take more than Cam to scare Krin away," Ben replied with a lightness in his tone that wasn't reflected in his eyes. It was a warning and they both knew it.

Karrine would not walk away from her sister. For Karrine, this marriage was not about him or even about her. It was all about taking care of Celine and everyone in the family knew it. It made him wonder what kind of future they could have. Forcing down the doubts he took a deep breath in, replacing the doubts with a silent prayer for his future wife.

Silence fell over the group as the tailor worked away, checking their tuxes, making sure any final adjustments were made. After a while conversation started up again, easy bantering between Ben and Luke, Cam and Steffan, an inane conversation about their daily lives and reviewing the schedule for the next day to make sure they all understood. Just as they were finishing up the fitting Ben's phone rang.

With a glance at it, he looked up. "That's an alarm Tessa set for us. It means we only have thirty minutes before we need to be at the church for rehearsal. Trust me when I say you don't want to deal with Karrine if we're late."

"Then we had better leave."

Thirty minutes later on the dot, they were walking into the church that they had rented for the wedding. Karrine was there waiting for them, leaning against the wall and tapping her fingers against her leg.

"You're late."

"Not yet we're not," Ben grinned and flipped his phone around to show her the screen. "We still have one minute."

"Hmm," Karrine gave her cousin a glare but the smile on her face spoiled the effect and she shook her head. "Fine, you win. But we have reservations tonight so let's get started."

"Karrine," Steffan touched her arm and motioned for her to follow him into one of the Sunday school rooms, closing the door behind them. "One more time I just have to check. Are you sure about this?"

*

Everything in her wanted to shout, that of course, she wasn't sure. This wasn't how any of this was supposed to happen. The murmur of her family's voices came through the door like a knife to her heart. Meeting his gaze she tried not to notice how kind he was being, or how handsome he was.

"No, I'm not sure about this because none of this is how I imagined it to be. My Mom won't be here to help me get ready, my Dad won't walk me down the aisle and instead of my prince charming waiting for me there will be a stranger at the end of the aisle and a pastor I have never met. But I am going through with it. It's the only choice I have."

Without a backward glance, she walked out the door and almost ran into a stranger that would rival Steffan in the looks department. Whereas Steffan's hair was light brown this man's hair was so dark it was almost black and his hazel eyes seemed to twinkle with some hidden secret he didn't seem likely to share.

"Excuse me," she stepped back but before she could slip by him Steffan was at her side.

"Good, you are here."

"First, I told you I would be, and second, I followed you over. Did you think I would get lost?" The stranger didn't wait for a response but smiled down at her, "And from your description, I'm assuming this lovely lady is your fiancée?"

"Yes," Steffan rested his hand at the small of her back in a gesture that felt oddly protective. "Karrine, this Cameron Haddon but we call him Cam. Cam this is Karrine Sandor. He was with us at the tux fitting today but then apparently had a few things to deal with before he could meet us here."

"It's nice to meet you," Cam flicked Steffan a look that she couldn't interpret even as he reached out to shake her hand.

"You too," she started to say more but Tessa walked up just then, touching her shoulder with a smile of apology.

"Krin, Steffan, sorry to interrupt but we're ready to start. The coordinator wants to make sure that we all know the procession before we actually run through it."

"Yeah, okay," Karrine smiled at her cousin and indicated Cam, "Tessa, this is Cam Haddon, Cam, this is my cousin, Tessa Franklin."

"It is a pleasure to meet you, Tessa," Cam gave her a charming smile but Tessa only flicked a glance over him.

"You too. Krin, we should really get started."

Surprised by her cousin's brush off of the handsome stranger she had no choice but to let it go. "Okay. Let's go then."

*

"All right first both sets of grandparents will be escorted in. Then, as you have requested Karrine, your two aunts, Jules and Fern, will be escorted with their husbands following them. Genève as the mother of the groom will be escorted in after that. Charlie, you will come in behind your wife. Next Meredith, standing in as the mother of the bride will be escorted in. Finally, the bridal party processional will start, ending with Donovan escorting in the bride."

The minister continued, explaining how the flower girl and ring bearer would come in after the bridesmaids and groomsmen entered and checking to make sure they had the right order. First Kennedy would enter, escorted by Luke, then Celine with Ben, and finally Tessa escorted by Cam.

Steffan was trying to pay attention but most of what Pastor Jones was saying was going right over his head. Despite the circumstances, everyone was trying to put on a happy face and make the best of the situation, almost everyone that was. When the pastor instructed them to hold hands Karrine's grip was so tight he thought she might break a few fingers.

By the time they had moved on to the dinner, it had only gotten worse. He was almost certain her nails would leave permanent scars on her own palms by the end of the night. She managed to smile her way through the toasts, relaxing a little when their dinner was served and everyone's attention shifted away from the two of them.

They were just finishing their dessert when Tessa announced they would need to get going because they had reservations somewhere for Karrine's bachelorette party. His fiancée did not seem terribly thrilled with the idea, even when her cousin assured her she would have fun.

"We should get going too," Cam told him as the women collected their things. "We have our own party to get to."

Steffan shot his best friend a look but Cam ignored him. Turning his attention back to Karrine he put on a smile for her sake. "I'll walk you out."

Leaving the others to finish cleaning up the couple headed out into the cold night. She shivered but rejected the offer of his jacket. "I'm all right."

It was too dark to see her eyes but he could imagine the fear and turmoil reflected there. "I wish I could find a way to make this easier for you Karrine, I really do."

She was quiet for so long he was starting to think she wasn't going to answer but just as the door of the church opened again and some of her family started to come out she reached out to touch his hand, "I believe you, Steffan. Thank you for that."

"Have fun tonight," he leaned in to kiss her cheek, pretending not to notice how she flinched at the action. "I'll see you at the altar."

Chapter 7

Karrine couldn't remember the last time she had laughed so hard in one night. Tessa had chartered a plane to take them to a rock-climbing gym a few hours away in New Zealand. The owners had agreed to rent it out to them for several hours since it was after their normal business hours anyway so they had the place to themselves except for a few employees who stayed to keep an eye on things.

They had some competitions, racing each other up the rock wall and laughing uproariously as Karrine and Aunt Jules tried to give Aunt Fern, Kennedy, and Genève Dalton climbing lessons. Afterward, they had gone out on a scavenger hunt around the city before finally boarding the plane again to fly back home. Almost everyone crashed out on the flight back, barely waking up to file into the limo then later into the hotel room.

Despite the late-night, Karrine woke just before dawn. Celine and Tessa had shared the king size bed with her the night before but were both still sound asleep. Not wanting to disturb anyone she slipped out from under the covers, grabbing a hoodie to pull over her tank top. Walking out to the balcony she curled up in the lounge chair, watching the sunrise over the horizon.

"I thought I might find you out here."

She didn't turn at Tessa's voice but smiled at her cousin when she sat down in the chair next to her. "I didn't mean to wake you up."

"I figured that when you slipped out without saying anything." Tessa yawned and rubbed at her eyes. "You never could sleep in late when you had something on your mind. Remember when you first moved to Colorado and you lived with us? Your first day of school you were up at four in the morning! I thought Auntie Brandi was going to have a heart attack when she woke up and couldn't find you anywhere."

"I was sitting out in Aunt Meredith's rocking chair on the porch, curled up in a blanket, watching the sun come up. I couldn't understand why everyone was so upset."

"Aunt Brandi was on her way out to the car to drive around looking for you when she found you." Tessa reminded her.

Karrine smiled and shook her head at the memory. "Poor Mom, she'd just lost her husband, Celine was only a baby and then I pulled stunts like that."

"You were a kid Krin, a scared kid who had just lost her Dad and left everything behind to move to a foreign country with family you barely knew."

Karrine swallowed against the lump in her throat and turned to look at her cousin, "Flash forward fourteen years, and what's changed?"

"You're an adult now Krin," Tessa scooted her chair around so she could look at her. "You're not a scared kid anymore; you have a choice in the matter. Whether it's choosing to go through with the marriage or choosing to make it work. It's your choice, and you're not alone."

"It sure feels like I am right now."

"You know better Karrine Brandaliyn Sandor. Your family is here for you, I'm here for you and God is with you always. And . . . I have to say I don't know Steffan all that well but I'm pretty sure he'll be there for you too. If you let him."

*

Jesus looked at them intently and said, "Humanly speaking it is impossible. But with God everything is possible."

"You're up early," Cam walked out, patting Solo on the head and sitting on the porch next to his best friend. They had all slept over at Steffan's parents' house the night before but he had woken up early, walking outside to watch the sunrise and pray.

"Couldn't sleep, but I am getting married today, what is your excuse?"

"My best friend's getting married and my job is to keep everything running smoothly today," Cam grinned at him. "Since I woke up to a missing groom I'm not off to the best start."

Setting his Bible aside Steffan threw the tennis ball that Solo had been chewing on, sending the Mastiff running off after it. "Oh? It had nothing to do with a certain maid-of-honor who seems to have taken a disliking to you for some reason?"

Cam shifted a little, leaning back against his hands, "You noticed that huh?"

"Hard not to. What happened?"

"Who knows," Cam didn't turn to look at him but picked up the ball Solo brought back and threw it for him again. "Just be glad Karrine seems easier to get along with than her cousin."

"I am not so sure. At this point I think Tessa likes me more than my fiancée does," he admitted, squashing the urge to keep teasing his friend, sensing there was more to Cam's words than he wanted to admit.

"Karrine will come around. It might take some time, but she'll get there eventually."

"I want to believe you but . . ."

"Come now Steffan, where's your faith?" Cam didn't wait for an answer but motioned to the Bible as he threw the ball for the dog again. "What were you reading when I came out?"

"Matthew 19:26 *'Humanly speaking it is impossible. But with God everything is possible.'*"

"Including your wife coming to love you? Including becoming a father figure slash older brother for a teenage girl who just became an orphan a month ago? Or is there some exclusion clause that I've forgotten about?"

Steffan rubbed his forehead, "What if I can't be the person they need me to be Cam? If I cannot be the husband that Karrine needs or fill the roles that Celine needs? What if I fail them both?"

Cam scowled when Solo dropped the tennis ball covered in slobber onto his lap but he threw it anyway before he answered, "Why are you so sure that you will fail?"

"I barely know either of them! And it's not just Karrine's life and my own that I would be ruining it's also Celine's! She is just a kid Cam, and we both know how quickly a teenager's stupid mistakes can ruin the rest of their lives." The words hung in the air between them for a long moment. "I do not want to be responsible for causing either of them any more pain."

For a long moment, they sat in silence, taking turns throwing the ball until Solo collapsed at their feet, finally exhausted. Cam's expression remained dark and stormy, telling Steffan exactly who his friend was thinking of. He was just thinking about going inside and finding something to eat when Cam spoke again.

"Steffan, for years I've watched you pray for Karrine, for her family, for her faith, for your future together. You made the choice to love her long before you ever met her. Are you going to stop now? Love's a choice, Steffan. So that's what you need to do, choose to love your wife, love your sister-in-law, and keep praying that God will give you the strength and wisdom to be the husband, father, brother, and friend they need you to be. Somehow I doubt God's going to turn His back on any of you now."

He stayed quiet for a long moment, letting the wisdom soak in and finally finding the peace he had been so desperately seeking. "He hasn't turned his back on you either Cam."

"Yeah," Cam sighed with a heaviness which suggested he had not quite managed to find that same peace yet. "Sometimes I think I'm starting to remember that. In fact, I'm not sure if I ever really forgot, I may have just stopped believing it."

"Hey, there you two are," Ben stepped out of the house, unaware of the conversation he was interrupting. "Breakfast is almost ready, you two hungry?"

"Starving," Cam got to his feet, cutting off any chance of the previous conversation resuming. "Steffan, you coming?"

"Yeah," he smiled at his friend and Karrine's cousin. "I'll be right there." He waited for them to leave then bowed his head again, spending a few more minutes in prayer seeking wisdom and peace not just for himself and Karrine but also for Cam.

*

"Oh, Krin! Everything's so beautiful!"

"Celine, come back inside, you need to get your hair done," Karrine scolded her sister but she smiled to let the girl know she wasn't upset. As soon as the teenager was seated in the chair next to her with the hairdressers working away Karrine glanced at her, "How beautiful?"

Celine grinned and started chattering away, telling her about the lights and flowers that covered the huge sanctuary, the white runner that led up the aisle, and the arch Karrine and Steffan would stand under to recite their vows. Everyone chatted away about how beautiful it all seemed and Karrine smiled and agreed because it was beautiful. Only Tessa needed to know none of the decorations were anything like what she'd wanted.

Everyone chattered at once as they finished their hair and makeup, posed for pictures both in and out of the dressing room, timing it so Steffan and Karrine were never in the same area. Not letting the bride and groom see each other before the wedding wasn't a tradition in Yagos like it was in America but Celine had insisted on enforcing it. Indulging the teenager had been Steffan's idea, whether it was because he wanted her to like him or because he felt bad about everything Celine had been through and would go through in the upcoming months, Karrine wasn't sure but she was grateful for his attitude nonetheless.

"All right, it's time." Mrs. Haddon, Cam's mother, who was acting as the wedding coordinator came to the door and smiled at them. "Meredith and Genève as the mothers will stay in here for now, along with the bridesmaids but the rest of you come with me."

Karrine smiled at her Grandmother and her other aunts as they walked out then took a steadying breath. Turning to look in the mirror she studied herself for a long moment. Her mother's wedding dress was beautiful, they made a few alterations, cutting off the sleeves and changing the neckline along with a few nips and tucks here and there; the end result was it looked like it had been made for her.

"You look beautiful," Aunt Meredith slipped an arm around her waist, blinking back tears.

"Aunt Mer? Are you all right?"

"I was just thinking how much you look like your mother." Meredith dabbed at her eyes, careful not to ruin her makeup and speaking quietly so only Karrine could hear her. "Brandi always feared this day, the day when you would be forced to marry, but at the same time, she dreamed about it. About watching you walk down the aisle, listening to you commit to love, cherish, and stand by another human being until death do you part. In some ways, she had lost her faith but she still prayed daily that no matter how your marriage began you would be happy Karrine. She would have wanted to be here with you today, they both would have."

Closing her eyes she drew in a deep breath, trying to hold back her own tears. She still had yet to figure out how to forgive her family for the marriage contract, or for keeping it from her but she was doing her best to set it all aside, at least for today. It was supposed to be the happiest day of her life and even if it wasn't she still didn't want to ruin it for everyone else.

"I miss them, Aunt Mer."

"I know sweetie," her aunt wrapped her arms around her and held on tight. "So do I, but Krin your mom would be so proud of you. Taking care of your sister like this? You're doing the right thing, no matter how this wedding came to be it's the right thing to do."

"Genève, Meredith, we're ready for you."

Karrine kissed her aunt's cheek one more time, smiled at her soon-to-be-mother-in-law, and watched them walk out. A minute later Mrs. Haddon was back for the bridesmaids and Tessa smiled at her.

"You ready?"

"If I say yes would you believe me?"

Tessa smiled but shook her head, "No." Giving her a quick hug she pulled back, "But you can tell me anyway."

"Love you, Tessa."

"Love you too Cuz."

Bowing her head Karrine said a quiet prayer before Uncle Donovan knocked on the door. "You ready kiddo?"

Rather than answer, she hugged him, careful not to crush the boutonniere on his lapel. "Thanks for being here Uncle Donovan."

"Where else would I be?" He smiled at her but looked a little confused.

"I don't mean today, I mean I do, but," when he continued to look at her with that confused expression she took a breath and tried again. "Thank you for being here today but what I meant was thank you for always being there for me. Papa died when I was so young but you were always there for me, you were the one who came and talked to the boys that wanted to take me to dances, you took me to get ice cream when Mom and I would fight, you taught me to drive. You've always been there Uncle Don, you never tried to replace Papa. It was hard growing up without him, but you made it easier."

Uncle Donovan blinked and cleared his throat; she didn't mention the suspicious moisture in his eyes but returned the hug and smiled when he kissed her cheek. "I love you too Karrine."

*

Steffan smiled as he watched his little sister and Luke walk up the aisle, grinning when she winked at him. Next was Celine, escorted by Ben, who gave him a big smile as she took her place at the front of the church. Tessa and Cam followed, both smiling but neither of them looking very happy about having to walk together. He ignored them and smiled at his cousin's children who were acting as ring bearer and flower girl. Finally, the music changed and the doors opened as Karrine appeared at the back of the church, holding onto her uncle's arm, and he forgot how to breathe.

The walk up the aisle seemed to take forever but finally, she was standing in front of him and he smiled at her, trying to tell her silently how beautiful she looked. The pastor smiled at them both.

"Who gives this woman to this man?"

"Her family does," Donovan answered, kissing her cheek through the veil and placing her hand in Steffan's. She handed her bouquet to Tessa before facing him, taking hold of his other hand and gripping so tightly he didn't have to see the fear in her eyes to know how scared she was.

He knew it was not the right time but as the pastor asked everyone to bow their heads to pray he leaned forward and whispered in her ear. "I am here for you."

It wasn't what he had intended to say but he meant every word and through the thin fabric of the veil, he saw her eyes fill with tears as she nodded. He wasn't sure she believed him but that was all right. For now, what mattered was that he meant every word, in time she would see that too. As the rest of the church prayed along with the pastor he said his own prayer, silently making a commitment to prove to her he was there for her, even if it took the rest of their lives to convince her.

*

"I now pronounce you husband and wife; you may kiss your bride."

Karrine gasped and her eyes flew back to Steffan. They hadn't discussed this part of the ceremony but he smiled at her as he lifted her veil. "May I kiss you?"

Her breath froze in her lungs but she knew how it would look if she said no so instead she nodded. Smiling he leaned forward pressing a gentle but chaste kiss to her lips then kissed her cheek, inciting some "awes" from the crowd as he took her hand and led her back down the aisle.

The moment they made it past the two hundred and some guests she let herself take in a deep breath. Unbidden tears suddenly sprang to her eyes, she pulled her hand from Steffan's turning away quickly before he could see her tears. The rest of the wedding party would be there any second and she needed to get herself under control.

"Karrine?" Steffan turned her around slowly so she could face him. "Honey? What is it?"

"I-" she shook her head, unable to explain something she didn't understand herself. Taking her hand again he led her out of the room, off to a side room and closing the door behind them. "What is this place?" She frowned at the small room with the round table and assorted chairs.

"It's a classroom of sorts I think," he explained. "But more to the point it is somewhere we can talk for a minute. Are you okay?"

"I just . . . I . . ." she shrugged and tried to sort out what she was feeling. "I don't know. I guess I just realized we're married. I have guardianship of my sister, I'm married and my parents are gone. I have no idea how to handle any of this."

*

Steffan did the only thing he could; he drew his wife close and wrapped his arms around her. There was nothing passionate about the embrace, not even close, it was more the kind of hug he would give to a hurting friend but Karrine responded, wrapping her arms around his waist and hugging him back.

"I am here for you." He whispered in her ear. She gave a jerky nod against his shoulder and he heard her sob but no tears wet his shirt and he knew she would do anything not to let them fall. After a few moments, she pulled back.

"They're going to be looking for us," she finally said.

"They can wait," gently he wiped away the few tears that had leaked out onto her cheeks. "We can stay here until you're ready to face them again."

"Is never an option?"

He smiled, glad she was getting her sense of humor back, "Sorry but no, although I wish it was."

Karrine nodded and closed her eyes for a moment then took a deep breath, "Okay. Let's go."

He wasn't sure it was completely practical but he smiled, incredibly proud of her at that moment, for facing her fears and going back out to the reception when it was the last thing she wanted to do. Taking her hand again he led her out, leading the way back to the reception area and smiling at the concerned looks from both their families.

Not wanting to give his wife a chance to be nervous he swept her out on to the dance floor. The D.J. took the hint and started the music. He felt Karrine tense but he ignored it and just kept dancing, after a moment she relaxed against him and he drew her a little closer.

The reception flew by and Steffan watched as his wife slowly relaxed. She laughed with her family, danced half the night away, smiled her way through the speeches, and slowly relaxed enough that the stress of the last few weeks began to catch up with her. By eight o'clock she was sinking down in her chair, eyes drooping as she tried to carry on a conversation with her Uncle Kenneth, her Dad's older brother that she hadn't seen since she was a child.

Walking over he smiled at the man he'd met several different times. "Mr. Sandor, nice to see you again."

"Steffan Dalton," Kenneth shook his hand and gave him a warm smile. "It's always a pleasure. Thank you, I have not seen my nieces since Celine was just a baby, it has been wonderful to see them again."

"Why didn't we ever see you?" Karrine suddenly asked, frowning up at her uncle. "Why didn't you ever come to visit us in Colorado?"

Kenneth gave her a compassionate look, "You know Karrine even as a child you always asked the difficult questions." He sighed but finally just shook his head, "Not long before your family moved my wife was diagnosed with cancer."

"I'm so sorry," Karrine told him, compassion in her voice.

"Thank you, dear. She held on for several years before it ultimately took her. Then I spent several years trying to learn how to live my life without her. I wasn't in a good place. I stayed in touch periodically with your mother about things to do with business matters, but our relationship was already strained because of your marriage contract. At some point, I suppose it just became easier to stick to just corresponding about business and all but forgetting we were family. I am not making excuses mind you, if I could do things differently I would. However, the past is the past. I am hoping though, now that you and Celine are living in Yagos we'll get to see a lot more of each other. If that's okay with you of course."

Steffan looked at his new wife, waiting for her reaction but after a moment she just nodded. "I think I'd like that."

"Thank you, Karrine," standing Kenneth leaned close kissing his niece on the cheek. "Steffan, it may not be my place but I suggest you take your bride home before she falls asleep in her cake."

Chuckling he pulled back Karrine's chair and offered her a hand up. "I think that is probably a good idea. Are you ready to go?"

She looked nervous but she nodded anyway, "Yeah, let me just get Celine."

"Let her stay," he ignored the fear that widened her eyes and nodded when Kenneth Sandor quietly excused himself. "Tessa said Celine could stay with the rest of the family today and we'll meet up with them again tomorrow, she'll come back to the house with us then. Tonight, it will just be the two of us but it will give us some time to talk."

She was already shaking her head, "I don't think that's a good idea."

Reminding himself to be patient he reached out to take her hand. "Karrine, we are married now but I would never make you do anything you're uncomfortable with. However, we just effectively became the parents of a fourteen-year-old girl. I think that might be deserving of a conversation between the two of us without her listening in." Heat colored her cheeks and her brown eyes widened, her mouth opened and closed but no words came out. Taking pity on her he just shook his head. "So, now are you ready?"

Chapter 8

Karrine had intended to stay up and talk to her husband. Steffan had said that was what he wanted when they'd left the wedding reception the night before, but when she woke up in a strange room with early morning light streaming through the windows she was more than a little confused. Even more confused, when she realized she was wearing pajamas instead of her wedding dress and had no memory of changing.

The alarm clock beside her said it was nearly seven o'clock. She closed her eyes again but she wasn't tired, she knew herself well enough to know she wouldn't go back to sleep no matter how long she lay there. Tossing the covers back she climbed out of bed and shivered at the loss of warmth. She hadn't brought a suitcase with her so there was no point looking for her clothes, but she went to the closet anyway, hoping to at least find an extra blanket she could wrap around her shoulders. Instead, she found a whole assortment of clothes that had to belong to her new husband, which meant she must have been sleeping in his room.

A mixture of emotions swept through her, leaving her more confused than ever before and getting colder all the time. Grabbing a sweatshirt she pulled it on and headed out of the room, not sure if she was more afraid of finding answers or having to talk to her new husband to get them. She stepped out of the room and into a wide hallway with hardwood floors. Wandering down the hall she found her way into the kitchen where a pot of coffee was already sitting on the counter. Helping herself she found the milk in the fridge and went about fixing her coffee just the way she liked it.

"You are awake."

She jumped and whirled around, seeing Steffan leaning against the wall across from her, Solo sitting next to him. He was dressed casually, a leash hanging from one hand. "I . . . I didn't hear you."

"I took Solo out for a walk, we just got back but you looked like you were a little lost in thought. I did not mean to startle you."

"No," she shrugged but couldn't look him in the eyes. "I guess I didn't." Looking down at her pajamas she remembered she had no idea how she had gotten into them. "How'd I get out of my wedding dress?"

Steffan cleared his throat and she looked up, expecting to see a guilty expression but instead he was smirking. Feeling the heat rushing to her cheeks her eyes widened but he quickly shook his head. "It is not what you're thinking. You fell asleep in the limo on the way back here. I wasn't sure what to do so I carried you inside then called your cousin, Tessa. She came over and from what she said you actually woke up enough to talk to her and get changed. I am guessing you don't remember any of it?"

"No," she sighed, convincing herself she was relieved by the answer. "I . . . um . . . the room I was sleeping in, is it yours?"

"What?" He frowned at her then his face cleared. "The clothes in the closet, that's why you thought it was my room."

Shrugging she toyed with the end of the sleeve of the oversized hoodie. "Something like that."

"Surprisingly, it is my sweatshirt but most of the clothes in there don't belong to me. Half of them are Kennedy's from when she crashes at the house, the other half of the closet which I'm guessing is the half you saw are actually Cam's. He had to have some work done at his apartment last month and he stayed here. He left some stuff and just hasn't remembered to pick it up. I have a housekeeper that comes in twice a week, Kennedy must have borrowed that sweatshirt and then left it in the room. Remmi probably hung it up thinking it was Cam's."

"I'm sorry," sheepishly she looked up at him and gave a little shrug. "When I saw the clothes I just assumed . . . sorry."

"Please, don't be," Steffan gave her an understanding smile and moved out of the way, walking around her to get into a cupboard and pull some dog food out. Scooping some into a bowl he put it down for Solo. "If anything I'm the one who should be apologizing."

"You?" Karrine frowned at him, "Why?"

Steffan chuckled and reached around her to help himself to a cup of coffee, she wasn't sure why she paid attention to the fact he drank it black but somehow it seemed like something important she should know. "Karrine do you assume the worst about everyone or is it just me?" Before she could even try to come up with an answer he stopped her, "I'm sorry, that wasn't completely fair. You do not know me and you have been effectively forced to marry me anyway. Of course you assume the worst. Why would you not?"

For a second, she remembered being on a hiking trip with Uncle Andy in California when she was thirteen. He and Aunt Jules had taken her, Tessa, and Ben to Disneyland, and then Uncle Andy had taken them hiking the next day so Aunt Jules could sleep in. They hadn't been out long when an earthquake hit. Karrine had been ahead of everyone else on the trail and there was a sense of the ground falling out from under her. Somehow this conversation on the first day of their marriage felt a lot like the ground shifting out from underneath her.

"I'm not sure I understand."

"Yeah, I am not sure I'm making a lot of sense." Steffan sighed and ran both hands down his face. "When Tessa came by yesterday to help, we talked for a while."

For the briefest moment, she felt a flash of something that felt a lot like jealously but she pushed it away, knowing it didn't make any sense.

Steffan didn't seem to notice, "Karrine, I knew your mum only died a little over a month ago but until I talked to Tessa I really had not given that a lot of thought. Tessa told me you have never really had any time to grieve."

"That's not true," she objected even as a little voice inside her head warned that her cousin may have been right.

"I think it is," he gave her a sympathetic look. "From what Tessa said you were so busy taking care of your aunts, sister, grandparents, and everyone else you really didn't take any time to mourn. She said you barely even cried at the funeral. Then you came here and got married two weeks later. We barely know each other, and it is not like you had much choice. Even after meeting your Uncle Kenneth, I think you still would have married me to spare Celine the pain of another change. Karrine, I am much more shocked that you are coping enough to put one foot in front of the other than I am that you tend to assume the worst about me."

The last thing she wanted to do was cry but tears sprang to her eyes as she stared at her new husband. Pressing a hand to her mouth she turned away, not wanting him to see her cry. It didn't do any good though because Steffan came to stand behind her. Putting his hands on her shoulders he ever so gently turned her around, pulling her into his arms.

"I am so sorry Karrine, for all of this. I know it does not make it better but I want you to know I do understand, and I am not going to push you. We are in this together so whatever you need, I am here for you. All you have to do is tell me what you want me to do. Do you think we can handle that?"

Despite herself, she laughed through her tears, nodding against his shoulder, "Yeah, I think we can handle that."

*

"Tell me about Celine."

Steffan was making waffles and Karrine had managed to calm down enough to start feeling hungry. She was sitting at the kitchen table, with one leg drawn up under her. "What do you want to know?"

"Whatever you want to tell me," he turned enough to smile at her, but she didn't see it. Her attention was devoted to the dog that had finished eating and was now leaning against her legs while she petted him. In a moment he would be running out to get one of his toys for her to throw. Years later when they were old and gray this was one of those moments, he hoped he would remember. She glanced up with a confused look prompting him to explain his motivations for the conversation. "Celine is the most important person in your life, and she is now our responsibility. Learning more about her seems like a good place to start."

"She's a great kid," Karrine turned her attention back to the dog. "She's smart, social, fairly well adjusted considering she grew up without a dad, and her mom just died. She's had a hard time more recently, but she's been taking this whole thing about moving to Yagos and getting a new brother-in-law really well. I'm hoping it will actually end up being a good thing for her."

"How so?" He moved one of the waffles onto a plate along with a side of eggs and set it in front of her.

"Thank you this looks delicious." She smiled at him as she picked up her fork. "This last year Celine hit the teenage stage full force. Talking back, pushing the limits, normal kid stuff you know? But then mom died and Celine has been so depressed, I didn't know how to help her. That's the only reason I agreed to follow through with this trip, to get her out of town for a while."

Deciding it was best not to speculate on what would have happened if she had decided not to come to Yagos as planned he tried to stay on topic. "And has it been better since you got here?"

"Yeah, a lot actually." She sighed and leaned back in her chair, taking a bite of waffle as if to give herself a moment to consider her words. "Unfortunately, I don't expect it to last."

Surprised by that he got up to top off their coffee then sat back down, "Should we pray?"

"Oh yes," she smiled at him. "Sorry, I guess I got distracted."

"Not a problem," he reached out to take her hand, pretending not to notice her tense at the contact then said a quick but sincere prayer, thanking God for their food and asking for His blessing and guidance on both of them and their families, and wisdom in their new lives. When he was done there were tears in Karrine's eyes but he didn't say anything as she blinked them away. "So why do you not think Celine's good mood will last?"

"Because she's fourteen." Karrine took another bite of her waffle but still hadn't touched her eggs. "When it all starts to set in that we're actually living here for good, it's going to be difficult for her. In a few weeks when September comes and all of her friends are going back to school and she's not there with them . . . it won't be pretty."

Steffan narrowed his eyes, thinking that through, considering his words, and choosing them carefully before he spoke. "Actually, that is something we should talk about. School in Yagos doesn't break till just before Christmas. I know Celine already finished her ninth-grade school year in Colorado, but we need to talk to the school and figure out what grade she should be in. I imagine they will want her to go straight into the ninth-grade year here and finish it out with the rest of the class rather than wait several more months until the next year to have her start."

Karrine frowned but not in an angry way, taking a sip of her coffee and nodding slowly, "I hadn't thought of that, but I suppose it makes sense."

"We could wait a few weeks," he suggested, trying not to think how surreal this moment felt. They were talking about a young girl that they were suddenly both responsible for. Age of majority in Yagos was twenty-one which meant for the next seven years he and Karrine would be making decisions for Celine, and it all started today.

"I think that would be good," Karrine's thoughtful answer brought him back to the present and he realized she had finished her waffle but still hadn't touched her eggs.

"You don't like eggs?"

"Oh," she blushed and refused to meet his eyes. "I don't, I'm sorry. I probably should have told you but I didn't want to seem ungrateful."

Amused he took her plate and scraped it into Solo's food bowl, "Don't worry about it. Solo will love it, but you should eat some sort of protein for breakfast. What do you normally eat?"

"I normally throw together a protein shake but I don't have any of my mix with me today. Do you have any granola bars or something along those lines?" When he went to the pantry to find something for her, she went back to the subject at hand. "I don't know anything about the schools in this area. How do I choose one?"

He decided to ignore the fact she was still acting like she had to deal with things on her own. "The private school that Cam and I went to is one of the best in Yagos. Kennedy just finished there last year."

"Too bad, it would've been nice for Celine to have a friend, even if only for a few months."

"She's a great kid," he tried to give her a reassuring smile. "I'm sure she will make friends in no time."

Chapter 9

"Are you sure you really have to go?"

"I'm afraid so sweetie," Aunt Jules gave her a sympathetic smile that looked so much like her mother, for a moment it was like having a hand squeeze her heart so tightly it made her want to cry. Pushing away the pain she frowned at her aunt.

"But can't you stay just a few more days?"

Jules shook her head, "I'm sorry Krin, we had planned to but last night as I was praying about it I just . . . I felt like the Holy Spirit was urging us to go home. I can't explain why sweetie but we need to go, you need to stay and we both have to trust that God has a reason for all of this."

Not wanting to cry twice in one day Karrine just nodded and hugged her aunt again. "Okay, but promise me you'll come back and visit?"

"You know we will sweetie," Jules grinned, "Besides with you living in Yagos, Andy will probably decide we need an international site for the gym just so he has an excuse to come to visit you more often."

"I'll take it," she smiled and swallowed hard against the lump in her throat before turning to give her younger cousin Luke a hug good-bye. Celine, nearby, was trying hard to keep a brave face as she bid Jules, Andy, and their sons good-bye.

"You going to be okay?" Ben asked her quietly, taking her elbow and leading her over to the side of the room so they could talk.

"Of course, I will be," she smiled at the disbelieving look he gave her. "You don't believe me huh?"

"Not even a little. But you know who I do believe?" Ben pointed across the room to where Steffan was talking to Andy, listening intently and nodding at whatever the older man was telling him. "I believe Steffan when he vowed to love and cherish you and when he told me he'll take care of you and Celine. If I didn't I wouldn't be going back home for school."

Putting on a brave face she smiled, "I believe him too."

"No you don't," Ben grinned at her. "But you will, I'm going to be praying for you Krin, for all of you."

Not sure what to say she just gave him another hug, "Love you, Ben."

"Love you, too."

"Karrine," Uncle Andy walked over and smiled down at her, the same look, mixed with compassion and love, that he had been giving her since she was eight years old. "We'll be back to visit before you know it. I'm even thinking of opening up a new gym out this way."

Ben covered a chuckle, Karrine just grinned but gave her uncle a hug, "I miss you already Uncle Andy."

"Miss you too kid but you know we're always just a phone call away."

"A call and a transatlantic flight," she pointed out, trying not to focus on how lonely that made her feel.

"That's simply the details," he assured her.

Before long Andy, Jules, and their boys had left and Karrine and Steffan were sitting down in the living room with the family who was still in town, including Uncle Kenneth.

"So where are you three going to live?" Kenneth asked when there was a pause in the conversation.

"At my apartment for now," Steffan answered for them. "With my business and the girl's family business both here in Teller it makes sense to stay in the area."

"Wouldn't a house be better?" Kenneth asked.

Karrine exchanged a look with Steffan but they both shrugged, "I guess so but we haven't exactly had time to go house hunting. We got married less than two weeks after Celine and I got to Yagos."

"I'm sorry Karrine, I should have explained," Kenneth smiled at her. "It's just that our family owns several houses around Yagos. As the eldest of our generation, I oversee the family trust so the houses are one of the things I oversee. It so happens we actually have a house in Teller that the tenants just moved out of. It's yours if you want it."

"Really?" Karrine looked at Steffan, shocked by the offer. "You'd just give us a house?"

"It's a family home Karrine," Uncle Grover corrected. "It belongs to you and Celine as much as any of us."

"Speaking of houses in the family, what happened to Brandi and Hamilton's house?" Aunt Meredith spoke up. "The last time I talked to my sister about it she still owned it."

"If she didn't sell it then it should be listed in her assets," Uncle Donovan was already clicking keys on his laptop as he logged onto the network for the McKenzie & Franklin Law Offices, looking up the files from Brandi's estate. "Here it is, and since she left all of her assets to you girls it still belongs to you."

"So, we have two different houses we can live in?" Celine asked with eyes wide. "That's so cool!"

"Yeah," Karrine looked at Steffan and shrugged. "I guess it kind of is."

*

Steffan pulled up in front of the five-bedroom, three bath house and turned the car off. "First thoughts anyone?"

"It's beautiful," Celine was already halfway out of the car, heading up the walk to the old stone house. "It's like a miniature castle!"

"Karrine?" He frowned when his wife just stayed in her seat, staring at the house in front of them. "Are you all right?"

"It's just like I remember it, I don't think it's changed a bit in all these years. Even the garden looks the same."

"Your family has made sure it has been taken care of." He watched through the window as Celine ran up towards the house, kneeling to smell the flowers planted out front, before running over to inspect the wooden swing tied to a tree out front. He smiled at his sister-in-law's excitement, oblivious to the tears his wife blinked away.

"My Dad built that swing." Her words made him frown, realizing she didn't seem excited to be at the house but he stayed quiet, not wanting to interrupt her thoughts. After a moment she continued, "When they found out Mom was pregnant with me he built that swing, he told Mom every kid should have a swing."

Following her gaze, he saw Celine sit down on the swing and give herself a push. "They should, no matter what age they are."

Karrine's lips twitched at the picture her little sister made but it didn't stretch into a smile. "She was too young to remember any of this."

He thought about asking what she remembered, what memories of this house made her so upset but Celine was running back to the car and he rolled down his window, waiting for the teenager to reach them.

"Are you guys coming or what? Come on Krin, let's go inside!"

"Sure Cina," his wife smiled at her sister and climbed out of the car as the teenager ran off again, oblivious to Karrine's mood.

"Karrine," he climbed out behind her but she didn't turn around, just started towards the house with her sister, leaving him to follow them or not, as if it didn't really matter either way.

*

She felt like her heart was being torn in two. On the one side were all the wonderful memories being in her childhood home brought back; she could remember playing in the sunroom her mother had loved so much, hiding under her father's desk in his office, and getting caught by a maid as she tried to slide down the banister. She was so sure she would get into trouble for that stunt but the kind woman had just told her to start closer to the end so she wouldn't have so far to fall if something went wrong. In the dining room, she remembered sitting with her parents as they taught her about table manners and in the living room she remembered curling up in her mother's lap and holding still, a promise she could stay up later if she would settle down and just listen while her parents talked. Crossing into the kitchen she could almost smell the burned cake from when her mother, never much of a cook, had tried to make her a birthday cake from scratch for her sixth birthday, afterward they had instead gone to play outside while the cook whipped something up in time for the party.

But with every memory and every room came back the sense of betrayal that her father had signed a marriage contract for her while she was still a baby and her mother, although she disapproved, had done nothing to stop him. They had lied to her for twenty-one years, keeping the truth a secret till the day they died. They had told her she could do anything and be anyone and all along they had known that wasn't true because they had already signed her future away.

"Karrine, do you remember this place?"

She tried to shove her feeling aside, grateful for her sister's distraction so she didn't notice Karrine's turmoil. Celine had a look of awe in her eyes and she made herself focus on the good memories, pointing them out to her sister as they walked through the house.

"In the living room, over there is where Mom and Dad sat me down to tell me that I was going to have a new brother or sister." She smiled at the memory of her six-year-old self, nearly bouncing in delight at the news before she turned Celine back towards the foyer. "And that's where I was standing when they first brought you home."

"Really?" Celine grinned up at her, "You remember that?"

"Of course I do," she grinned at her little sister, "It was the best day of my life."

The teenager grinned but it only held her attention for a moment, "Tell me more."

So she did, walking around the house and passing on tidbits of a past that her sister was too young to remember and she had not thought about in years. She didn't even notice the way Steffan followed them around, smiling when they laughed but never taking his eyes off of Karrine as he watched her with a concerned expression.

*

Steffan stepped into the living room and leaned against the wall, taking a moment to just watch his new wife. Karrine was curled up in a chair staring at the wall but obviously not seeing any of the pictures hanging there. Solo had disappeared, probably having followed Celine into the spare room to sleep with the teenager there. He had a feeling his dog had found a new master to love.

Finally stepping inside, he went to sit down in his own chair but let Karrine have her silence, it had been a long day for her. After visiting her childhood home, they had gone to see the other house her family had offered. Although it was still a nice, large home Celine hadn't seemed very interested in it. He was leaving the decision up to the girls but he had a feeling that in the end, Karrine would do what her sister wanted, no matter the cost to herself.

"You don't have to sit there in silence you know," Karrine finally spoke, not bothering to look at him. "I'm not so fragile that if you ask me a question I'll fall apart."

Raising an eyebrow at the harsh tone he made sure his own voice was even, "I didn't think you would break but I also was not sure if you would want to talk or not."

She sighed a bone-weary sound that seemed to make her sink further into her chair. "I don't know what there is to say."

He felt the burden of those words grip his heart and he leaned back in his own chair, begging God to give him the right words to help his wife. He stayed quiet for a few more moments before finally deciding what to say. "I guess we should talk about the houses."

"Yeah," she sounded resigned but she finally turned to look at him, "I guess we should."

When she didn't say anything else he picked up the conversation again, "Celine really seemed to like the house where you two lived before but you did not seem as excited."

"Too many memories," she admitted and he frowned.

"I thought you had good memories in Yagos."

"I did," she shrugged. "Until I found out almost everything my parents ever told me was a lie since they'd signed a marriage contract for me but never bothered to tell me about it in twenty-one years. It's a little hard not to be angry with them."

He couldn't help but feel the sting of her words. Steffan understood why she was upset. He, on the other hand, had always prayed that God would use their arranged marriage for his glory, but Karrine's stubborn refusal to accept it was making him doubt that would ever happen. Ignoring her bitterness, he stayed focused on the conversation.

"What about the other house?"

"It's nice," she admitted. "But Celine has her heart set on living in our old house. With everything else she's had to go through I don't want to tell her no, not about this. If that makes sense. What do you think?"

He could not stop his smile, not just about the fact that she was asking his opinion, but about her obvious love for her sister and her unselfishness. Celine was not the only one who had been through so much lately, Karrine had too, even more than her sister had. Karrine was the one now responsible for a teenager and married to a stranger but that never occurred to her, she only thought of what was best for Celine.

"Yeah, it does make sense and I agree. She has her heart set on it so we may as well pick that one. We can call your family in the morning and let them know. Will you want to fly back to Colorado to get your things packed up or just have your family ship them over?" Her eyes widened at the thought and he instantly regretted his words. "I'm sorry I didn't mean to push."

"No, it's not your fault," she offered him a polite smile that was anything but reassuring. "I just hadn't thought about it. Somehow packing makes this all more . . ."

"Real?" He offered and she nodded.

"Yeah, I guess so." Karrine let her head fall back against the chair, "I think we should fly back though. Celine told all her friends good-bye thinking we would be gone for a few weeks, not moving across the world. She will want to spend some time with them."

"Which reminds me, we also need to talk about enrolling her in school," he reminded her, hating the way she closed her eyes as if the weight of the world was resting on her shoulders. "But we can talk about that after we get moved into the new house." He hesitated, not sure what the protocol was about taking trips together or alone. "Do you want me to go back to Colorado with you?"

Karrine frowned, apparently not having thought about the possibility of him going with them. "I figured you'd need to be here. I know you've taken some time off work with our . . . wedding and all."

Not wanting to think about the fact that she could hardly even mention their wedding he instead focused on his company that he had been neglecting. "You are right, I should probably focus on work. But I could get away for a few days if you wanted me to, I mean."

Instead of answering Karrine just got to her feet, "I don't know, we can talk about it later. Right now, I should go to bed, it's been a long day."

Standing, also he frowned at her, "Are you sure you want to sleep on the air mattress? You could take my bed and I could crash on the couch until we move into a new house. I really would not mind."

She rewarded him with a smile but shook her head, "You'll sleep better in your own bed and I don't mind the air mattress. Thank you though."

He thought about kissing her cheek, or just giving her a hug but neither seemed right so instead he just shoved his hands in his pockets and nodded, "All right, good night Karrine. I hope you sleep well."

"Thank you," she smiled as she turned to head out of the room then glanced back over her shoulder. "As long as your dog doesn't decide to try to sleep on the mattress with me, I'm sure I'll be fine."

"He is not allowed on the beds."

She chuckled, "Oh yeah? Don't look in on Celine then. She's crashing in the spare bedroom and Solo seems quite comfortable sprawled out on the twin bed with her."

Steffan grimaced at the information, "I did not want to know that."

Karrine just smiled, "Good night Steffan."

He smiled, realizing she had finally called him by his name, "Good night Karrine."

*

"Hey, you awake?"

"Um . . ." Celine rolled over in bed and looked at her. "Sort of."

"Did you sleep well?"

"Okay, I guess," the teenager sat up and accepted the cup of tea her sister offered, scooting over so Karrine could sit backward on the bed, facing her while they talked. "You?"

"All right I suppose, thankfully the air mattress didn't lose too much air overnight so that helped." She took a sip of her own coffee that she'd brought in, "But I had a lot on my mind."

"Yeah?" The girl pushed herself up, accepting Karrine's help in repositioning the pillows so she could sit up. "Like what?"

"Oh, like what house we're going to live in," Karrine shifted to get more comfortable on the narrow mattress, keeping one leg on the ground to steady herself. "And how we need to go back to Colorado and pack up our things, what school you're going to go to, where or even if I'm going to work. All of it I guess."

Celine frowned, "Yeah, I guess you have a lot to deal with huh?"

"That's part of the job Cina."

"What job?"

Karrine smiled, "Being an adult."

"Yeah, I guess so," Celine yawned and took another sip of her tea. "Are you going to work at Papa's company?"

"I don't know," she admitted. "What do you think?"

"You're asking me," Celine frowned at her. "I'm just a kid Krin, what does it matter what I think?"

"It matters to me, Cina. I really want to know what you think. I mean have you thought about it? About if you want to work at Papa's company after school."

"Not really," Celine sighed. "Do I have to decide right now?"

"No," Karrine shook her head. "You don't even have to decide this year or next Cina, you've got plenty of time. But what about the other stuff? We're going to need to talk about what you want to do in Colorado, who you want to see. And . . . we need to talk about you starting school here in Yagos."

Celine sighed and let her head fall back against the pillows. "How about the house? Do I get a say in where we live?"

Even knowing what her sister's answer would be she nodded, "Sure, which house do you want to live in?"

"The one we grew up in. Is that okay?"

"Yeah," Karrine smiled. "Of course it is. Steffan agreed to make the arrangements for us, I'll let him know."

"Really?" Celine's excited grin made it all worth it as she gave Karrine a one-armed hug, taking care not to spill their drinks. "Thanks, Krin."

"Sure kid," she smiled as she pushed herself off the mattress. "Now, are you going to get up or sleep the day away?"

"Hmmm . . ." Celine groaned good-naturedly but set the tea on the nightstand and flipped back the covers. "I guess I'm getting up."

"Good," Karrine smiled at her. "Because we have some plane tickets to book."

*

"Hello Mrs. Coren," Steffan gave the secretary a tired smile. "How are you today?"

"You are late," she gave him a scolding look but her lips twitched a little. "But since you did just get married a couple of days ago, I suppose we can let it slide this time."

Grinning at that he tried to perfect a serious look when he nodded, "Well thank you, Mrs. Coren, I appreciate your leniency. Actually, I need a favor. Karrine and her sister, Celine, are going to have to fly back to Colorado."

"You've scared her away already?" Keith Arlow, Sailor IT's vice president, and Steffan's right-hand man smirked as he walked up just then. "That was fast."

"Ha-ha, no, they are heading home to pack up their things and have them shipped to our new house. Karrine said she could take care of the tickets, but she has a lot on her plate today. They are going to visit their Dad's old company today and spend another day with their Uncle Kenneth before he heads home. And if my email is any indication, then I am drowning in work so could you please help me out with this?"

"Of course I will," Mrs. Coren offered him one of her rare smiles. "Just give me the information and I'll take care of it. Will you be going with them?"

"Not this time, thank you. I will send her a text to let her know you are handling it." Smiling his thanks, he opened his office door and waited for Keith to precede him in. "All right Keith, let's take a look at those reports."

*

"So this is it?" Celine's voice was hushed, more like they were in a church than a business office.

"I guess so," Karrine shrugged, looking around the huge building and listening to the sharp click of her heels against the tile.

"Can I help you, ladies?" The receptionist smiled at them as they approached the desk.

"Um . . . maybe, I probably should have called," Karrine frowned at her but the woman just smiled, a slightly confused expression on her face as she waited for an explanation. "I'm Karrine Sandor and this is my sister Celine, our father wa-"

"Your father was Hamilton Sandor," the woman smiled at them, her eyes bright with unshed tears. "And your mother was Brandaliyn, I was so sorry to hear about her accident."

Surprised not only by the sincerity of her words but the emotion behind them, Karrine hesitated, "Thank you."

The woman blew out a breath and wiped away a tear, "I'm sorry girls; I'm not normally so emotional! It's just that we've all been waiting so long to meet you!"

Karrine glanced at her sister, not sure how to respond, "I'm sorry, who has been waiting to meet us exactly?"

"All of us," the receptionist picked up the phone and spoke a few words too softly for either of them to hear. She hung up the phone after just a moment and smiled at the girls, "Let's go, there are a lot of people who'd like to tell you hello."

Celine gave her sister a concerned look and Karrine put an arm around her shoulders, trying to offer reassurance as much as protection against whatever it was they were about to face. Following the receptionist up the stairs to the second-floor conference room where a large group had gathered.

Smiling the receptionist ushered them inside where a gray-haired man wearing a business suit and a huge smile stepped forward to greet them. "Karrine and Celine Sandor! I cannot tell you how long we have been waiting to see you, girls, again!"

"Um . . ." feeling her manners and training kick in Karrine forced herself to smile at the man, "Thank you."

His grin only grew as he looked between them, "You have no idea who I am, do you?"

Karrine smiled guiltily, "I'm sorry, but no."

"My name is Richard Black; I have been managing Sandor Enterprises since you girls moved to the States with your Mum." He hesitated as if waiting for them to comment, when they didn't, he just smiled, "Your father was one of my best friends."

Not sure what to say Karrine just smiled at him, "It's nice to meet you, Mr. Black."

"Likewise, girls," he smiled and turned back to the group. "For years we have all run this company, waiting until you girls came of age so you could take your place in the family company if you like that is. Either way, we are all very excited to meet you." He motioned to the room at large, backing away as people came up and started greeting them, regaling them with stories of their father and talking about how excited they were to finally meet Hamilton's girls.

Chapter 10

"Karrine? Celine? Are you home?" Steffan called out as he let himself into the apartment.

"In the kitchen," Karrine called back, "We have company."

"We do?" He frowned at the information.

"I don't know if we qualify but we are here."

He smiled at Cam and Kennedy as he walked in to find his best friend, his sister, and his wife in the kitchen with Solo happily lapping up attention from all of them. "This is quite the party, where is Celine?"

"She just left to take a phone call," Karrine smiled in his general direction without actually looking him in the eye. "She'll be right back."

"All right," not sure how to continue the conversation, he turned his attention to Cam and Kennedy. "What are you two doing here?"

Cam grinned, "Wait, I need a reason to come see my best friend now? Karrine didn't tell me I needed a reason. Karrine, do I need a reason to come by?"

His wife smiled as she turned to check on dinner, "I think it's safer to stay out of this one."

"Smart plan," Kennedy approved. "Steffan, I'm surprised Mrs. Coren actually let you leave work since you took time off."

"There was a debate," he teased his sister. "How's school?"

"Good and that's actually why I'm here."

"Hey Karrine, what time does our flight get in?" Celine poked her head into the kitchen and smiled at him. "Oh, hi Steffan, I didn't realize you were home."

"Hi Celine," he smiled at his sister-in-law. "How are you?"

"Good," she grinned and held up the phone. "Just talking to Karra, I'll be right back."

"Flight gets in at four, Cina," Karrine told her, "And dinner will be ready in about ten minutes."

"I guess that answers whether or not you got the tickets."

"Yes," she again smiled towards him without looking at him, "Thank you for arranging that. It was a busy day."

Glad to be of help he grabbed the plates out of the cupboard. "I'll help set the table. Kennedy, what were you saying about school?"

"I came by to tell Karrine and Cina some information about McCarthy Hall in case that's where she ends up going." His sister smiled up at him as she followed him around the table, placing the silverware. "Cam's here because Mum and Dad had a dinner to go to and my car's in the shop so I called him to ask if he could bring me over."

"You could have called me," he pointed out.

Kennedy shrugged, "Yes, but he is as much like my brother as you are. I knew you were at work and if he had been busy he would have said so. Besides," she grinned at him and lowered her voice, "We both wanted to see how things were going."

Steffan forced himself to smile but was spared from replying when Celine carried in the mashed potatoes.

*

"You sure you have everything you need?" Steffan asked again as he carried Karrine and Celine's bags over to the security line.

"I'm sure," Karrine smiled but couldn't quite meet his gaze. It was too strange, this relationship she suddenly found herself in, married to a man who was little more than a stranger. Celine liked him and he treated her the same way he treated his own sister, Kennedy. But things were still strange between the two of them. They got along but it was like neither of them was sure how to move forward.

"You will call me when you land, just so I know you got there okay?"

"Of course," this time she looked up at him and saw him smiling back. She wanted to say something, she genuinely thought he was a nice guy and she knew nothing that had happened was his fault. He wasn't the one who had lied to her all her life or came up with the guardianship clause that had forced her into the marriage. But despite all of her training in polite conversation she had absolutely no idea what to say to her husband.

"Have fun Karrine," he spoke before she could. "And try to relax, you deserve a break."

She smiled a little and when he reached out to squeeze her hand she squeezed back, letting the gesture speak for itself.

"Celine, take care of your sister for me," Steffan smiled at the teenager and gave her a quick hug. "And have fun with your friends."

"I will," she hugged him back with the easy affection Karrine both admired and envied. "As long as you take care of Solo while we're gone."

Steffan grinned as he nodded, "Absolutely."

"Oh, so my equivalent is a dog?" Karrine couldn't resist teasing her little sister.

"He's a really cool dog," Celine laughed but edged towards the security line, showing her impatience to get the trip started.

"We should get going," smiling at Steffan one more time she picked up her bag. "See you in a couple of weeks."

Steffan raised a hand as they moved away, echoing her words, "See you then."

The line moved quickly as they went through the x-ray machines and had their bags inspected. At the end when they got to the other side she glanced back and was surprised, and pleased, to see Steffan still standing there, waiting to wave one more time.

*

Steffan had gone back to his office after he had taken the girls to the airport, thinking to take advantage of the time alone to get some work done. Instead, he found himself staring blankly at the computer screen, thinking more about his new family than the work he was supposed to be doing.

Glancing at the clock he almost groaned when he realized he had been sitting there for over an hour. Tapping his fingers against his desk for a moment he considered his options for a moment. A second later he pushed back his chair and grabbed his jacket.

"I am going out Mrs. Coren. If anything comes up, I'll be on my cell phone." He didn't stick around to wait for her response but headed out the door. He bypassed the parking lot; his destination wasn't very far away and the chilly weather would help him focus on the short walk.

It was only a few blocks to his father's office. At one time Sailor IT had been in the same building, but last year when he took over, he'd moved his headquarters to its own space. Owning a floor wasn't nearly as glamorous as owning the whole building, but he'd bought that floor with his own money, earned from the business and made every square inch a reminder of their success.

"Steffan," Roy, the head of security who had been there for years, smiled when he walked inside. "This is a surprise. Your Dad didn't tell me you were coming by, so did he forget, or did you not tell him?"

"He did not know," Steffan confirmed the information. "It was a spur of the moment decision. Is he here?"

"He is," Roy buzzed him through. "So where's that pretty wife of yours? I was sorry I didn't get a chance to meet her at the wedding but you two were pretty swamped trying to greet everyone."

"Thank you for coming, Roy. I will try to bring Karrine to the next company party so you and your wife can meet her."

"We'll look forward to it," Roy smiled and picked up the phone to tell them he was on his way up.

His dad's businesses had always had a strong emphasis on communications and by the time he stepped off the elevator, Charlie was waiting.

"Well Steffan, this is a surprise. Did Karrine and Celine get off okay?"

"Yeah, Karrine texted me just before they stepped on the plane and promised to call when they landed."

"Glad to hear it," Charlie led him to his office, telling his secretary to hold his calls and closing the door behind them. "What's going on, Son?"

Not sure how to sort out his emotions or explain what he was thinking he started to pace. From the chair across from his father's desk, over to the couch in the corner and back again. He knew his father was a busy man who had probably pushed aside at least one meeting and a few phone calls and emails when his son had shown up unannounced but Charlie showed no signs of impatience; he just leaned back in his chair with his arms folded over his chest as he waited for Steffan to explain himself.

"I have known about Karrine for my whole life. I have prayed for her for years. I have cared about her on some level for most of my life but now I find myself with this family and none of it is the way I thought it would be. I mean, my wife will not even use my name most of the time, she hardly looks at me, and we are suddenly supposed to raise a teenager, yet both of them are still grieving the death of their mother who passed away just over a month ago! How am I supposed to deal with any of this Dad? How do I help them?"

"How do *you* deal with it? How do *you* help them, Steffan? I think you're asking the wrong questions. You've been praying for Karrine all these years, but have you been praying for her recently? Since you met her? Since the wedding? Have you prayed for Celine? Have you asked for God's help in getting them through this grieving process? Or have you been so busy trying to do things the way you think they need to be done that you forgot about the rest."

Frustrated he stopped pacing and looked at his Dad, "In my head I know you are right, but I want to do more than just pray for them. Karrine is finally here, part of my life, I don't want to just pray for her anymore, I want to actually help her, learn about who she is and start our lives together. I suppose I cannot expect it all to happen at once, but I guess I thought we would at least be on a first-name basis almost three weeks after we met."

Charlie chuckled and sat forward, "Steffan, you're still looking at things from the wrong perspective. Prayer is not the least of the things that you can do for your wife, it is the best thing you can do for her. And for Celine. You know God can reach people no matter where they are, even when the people closest to them can't come anywhere close. Give Karrine some time, and give yourself time also. Don't try to rush things. As you said, she is still grieving and she is trying to figure out how to raise Celine too. That's a lot for anyone to handle."

"I know you are right but . . ."

"But you're impatient and you want results now instead of waiting until later," Charlie smiled at him. "Steffan, I understand how you're feeling but that is really the best advice I can give you. Well," he shrugged, "That and a lot of handball. Exercise will help you think. You can't force her to confide in you, so you may as well distract yourself until she's ready to do that on her own."

Knowing that he had gotten the answers he had come for he let out a long breath and looked at his Dad, "What meetings am I keeping you from?"

Charlie glanced at his watch, "The Board assembled about three minutes ago."

Steffan smiled and grabbed his jacket, "Then give them my apologies, and thank you for the advice, Dad. Somehow I doubt it will be the last time."

"Anytime, Son," Charlie walked with him to the door but waited a moment before he opened it, "Just so you know your Mother and I are praying for you and your family."

He smiled, "I have to admit Dad, that still sounds really weird but I appreciate the prayers."

"Good, because they are not going to stop, but if you need anything . . ."

"I know where to find you." He hugged his Dad, "I'd better get back to work before Mrs. Coren decides to fire me."

Charlie chuckled at that, "You do know you're still the boss don't you?"

Steffan grinned, "Do you want to try telling her that?"

*

Karrine's eyes opened the moment she felt the plane touch down on the tarmac. She smiled when she realized her little sister had fallen sound asleep. She didn't wake her up right away, waiting until the plane taxied to the airport and people started to disembark before she reached over to shake her sister's shoulder.

"Celine, honey, time to wake up."

"What?" Celine blinked several times, rubbing at her eyes and yawning as she sat up to stretch. "Are we there yet?"

"Yeah Cina, we just touched down in Denver."

Celine smiled and stretched her arms up above her head as she yawned. "Cool."

"Yeah," Karrine smiled at her sister. "Cool." Standing she reached out to grab her carry-on bag and handed Celine hers. "Come on kid, let's go home."

*

"Uncle Andy," she walked into his embrace and let herself be held for a long moment. It had been less than a week since they had seen each other but something about physically being back in Colorado made it feel like it had been forever.

"Hey Krin," he pulled back and smiled down at her. "It's really good to see you kid."

"Yeah," she cleared her throat and had to look away to get control of her emotions. "So what are the chances of me getting to go to the gym at some point today?"

Andy laughed and put an arm around her shoulders, signaling Luke and Celine that it was time to head out. "Let's focus on getting you home to see the family before we talk about climbing. Mer and Don couldn't get out of the office but we're having a big family dinner tonight. They also offered to have you swing by the office, you know everyone there would love to see you, but they'll also understand if it's too much."

She thought about it, weighing the pros and cons of going to her Mom's old office. "How many of them know? About Yagos and Steffan?"

Andy reached out to grab her left hand, holding it up to examine the wedding ring she wore there, "About this? Everyone Krin, we couldn't exactly keep it a secret. You and Cina went to Yagos for a visit and then they heard you weren't coming home. What did you want us to say?"

"Krin can I go see Karra? I told her I'd call her once I knew when we could meet up."

Looking to Uncle Andy she shrugged, "What do you think?"

He smiled, "Sure Cina, we can drop you off on the way. Krin you want to head to the office or the gym or somewhere else? Luke, are you staying at Karra's or heading home?"

Karrine perked up at the information, amused at the way her

younger cousin blushed. "I'll head home; Karra and Cina will want to catch up."

"True, it'll be hard to talk about you if you are there," Celine teased him.

"On second thought maybe I should stay," Luke told this dad

"No way!"

Karrine laughed at their bantering as she pulled out her phone to turn it back on. As they made it to the luggage carousel she stepped away, flipping through her contact list to find Steffan's cell number and pushing the call button, glad she had added international calling to both her and Celine's phones when they'd left for their trip to Yagos.

"If you're calling Steffan, tell him I say hi," Celine called over her shoulder. Karrine nodded in acknowledgment just as his voicemail picked up.

"Hey, it's Karrine. Cina and I just landed in Denver and she says hi. Well, I guess you're busy so I'll talk to you later. Bye now." She hung up and drummed her fingers against her leg, wondering where her husband was and what he was doing right then that prevented him from answering the phone call he had requested.

*

Steffan walked out of the board meeting that had gone far longer than he had intended. As a general rule, he liked running his own business but there were some parts, such as his bi-monthly board meeting, he would rather avoid but as his Dad, one of the board members liked to remind him it was all part of the job.

"Mr. Black is waiting in your office Steffan," Mrs. Coren told him.

He frowned, "Did we have an appointment?"

"No," that was the only answer she gave him.

Walking into his office he smiled at the manager of Sandor Shipping, "Mr. Black, it is good to see you."

"Steffan," the man smiled and shook his hand. "Sorry for the ambush but I was hoping you had a few minutes?"

"Of course," rather than sit behind his desk he sat in the chair next to Richard Black's, getting the sense this wasn't about business. "What can I do for you, sir?"

"Well, actually I want to talk to you about Karrine."

Not really surprised he leaned back in his chair, "What about her?"

"Well, you know she and Celine came to the offices," when he nodded Mr. Black continued, "Steffan, I may be out of line here but Hamilton's dream was always for his girls to take over the family business. Ever since he died that is what we have been waiting for. Now I know Celine is still young but I was wondering, does Karrine have any intention of working in the business?"

He had always liked Richard Black, the man was what his dad called a straight arrow but he wasn't sure how to handle this conversation. "Why?"

Mr. Black blinked at him, "Excuse me?"

Shifting in his chair he tried to remain relaxed, "Mr. Black,

Karrine is my wife and I am now one of Celine's guardians. Now Sandor Shipping is our top client, but my family is my first priority, so I need to ask. Do you feel threatened by the thought of the girls joining the business or is this simple curiosity?"

"I'm not feeling threatened Steffan," Mr. Black smiled at the idea. "But I admit I am glad to see how protective you are of Hamilton's girls. Hamilton Sandor was one of my best friends, Steffan and as I said, his dream was always to see the girls take over the business. Ever since he died all I have wanted is for his dream to come true but I also want to make sure the girls are not pushed into something they do not want. That is why I came to talk to you instead of them, but I do apologize for not making myself clear right away."

He considered that for a moment, feeling a little like he was drowning. He barely knew his wife and yet, here was his biggest client asking for advice as to what Karrine might be thinking. There was no good answer. "I honestly do not know what Karrine will decide. She is in Colorado right now, packing up her things, and we have not had time to discuss it Mr. Black."

"I see," the older man looked disappointed as he prepared to stand.

"I am sorry sir," Steffan sighed. "I wish I had a better answer for you."

"Don't be," he stood and placed a hand on Steffan's shoulder to keep him seated. "Just let the girls know if they do want a place at the business, in whatever role, we would love to have them but if not we understand. They already have a lot to deal with, no one at Sandor Shipping wants to add to their burden."

After he left, Steffan sat there for a long time considering the enigma that was his wife, and the very complicated life she had landed herself in, wondering how long it would take until he started to unravel the mystery of Karrine Sandor Dalton.

Chapter 11

Karrine smiled as she walked through the offices her family had occupied for as long as she could remember. Tracing her finger along the wood paneling she found an odd sense of comfort in the familiar touch. From the time they had moved to the States, she could remember coming to these offices. Taking time visiting various family members, having the secretaries, and other staff who worked in the law offices sneak her candy. Then spending hours playing hide and go seek with her sister and cousins when they tagged along to work with their parents and thought no one was looking.

"Karrine Sandor." The voice pulled her out of her memories and back to the present as she smiled at Grant Lentz.

"Grant, it's nice to see you," she gave the man a polite smile as he leaned in to kiss her cheek. They had grown up together though they had never been close. He had always had a crush on her, but she had never reciprocated the feelings. "How have you been?"

"Not as good as you, apparently, is it true you got married?" Grant's eyes were kind but she could see the curiosity and surprise there too, he was too polite to ask her flat out if she was insane but he had no problem insinuating it.

She winced as she thought about Steffan, the husband she barely knew, "It's true."

"Really? So that's the reason you always turned me down when I asked you out, you were in love with some guy on the other side of the world?" Grant was teasing but she thought there was a little bit of hurt lurking behind those words.

"Sorry, no, I didn't know Steffan until I got to Yagos," she regretted the words almost as soon as she said them.

"You married a guy you had just met?" Grant's eyes widened at the information, "That doesn't sound like you."

"Karrine," Uncle Donovan stepped into the hallway and smiled at her. "There you are. Andy told me you were coming by." He glanced over at Grant and raised a brow, "Sorry, am I interrupting something?"

"Of course not Uncle Don," Karrine smiled and leaned into his hug. "Grant and I were just catching up. Do you have time for lunch?"

"I wish I did kiddo but that's actually why I was looking for you," she recognized the sympathetic and disappointed look on her Uncle's face.

"Something came up?"

"I'm afraid so," he shrugged. "Same with your Aunt Meredith and Tessa but I promise that we will all be home for dinner at your grandparents', the whole family will be there."

"I would expect nothing less," she teased as her uncle hugged her again before heading back to his office. Turning back to Grant she shrugged, "Well I guess that means I'm heading home to start packing. It was good to see you, Grant."

"Well hey," Grant moved quickly to walk backward in front of her as she headed towards the elevator, "I've got some free time, why don't you let me buy you lunch and you can explain about this sudden marriage."

She hesitated but before she could answer Tessa came running down the hall without any shoes, "Oh good you're still here! Dad said you were on your way out. Hi Grant, sorry to interrupt?"

"No problem Tessa," Grant smiled but stepped into the elevator, "I'll just wait in the lobby."

Tessa barely waited until the elevator doors closed before frowning at Karrine, "You're going out with Grant?"

Karrine smiled at the concern in her cousin's tone, "Not the way you're thinking. He invited me to lunch to catch up, that's all."

Tessa frowned at her, "I don't know Krin, I mean you know Grant's always had a crush on you. What would Steffan say?"

She felt anger mixed with defensiveness boiling up and glared at her best friend, "Oh you mean the husband I barely know who insisted I call when I landed, but then didn't bother to answer his phone? I don't know Tessa, what do *you* think he would say?"

"Okay," Tessa held her hands up in surrender, "It's your call. Just be careful, okay?" Tessa leaned forward to hug her. "Take my car so if something happens you can get home without having to wait for rideshare or rely on Grant. Oh, and Krin? I'm glad you're home, even if it's only for a couple of weeks."

Knowing her anger was misdirected she returned the embrace and took the keys, "I'll see you at dinner."

"I love you Krin."

She stepped into the elevator and pushed the button for the lobby, "I love you too."

Once she was downstairs she found Grant waiting for her. "Are you ready?"

Deciding right then, that her new husband had no control over her and ignoring the well-meaning warning of her cousin she nodded, "Yeah, let's go."

*

"So you're really married?"

Grant hardly waited for them to be seated at the table in the restaurant before he peppered her with questions. Karrine pushed aside her uncomfortableness and tried not to compare this lunch to the one she had with Steffan not that many weeks ago in Yagos.

"I really am."

"How did it happen?" Grant did nothing to try to disguise his curiosity. She was tired, lonely, and irritated with her family for being busy and with Steffan for not picking up his phone. Maybe that was what caused her to spill the whole story but before she knew it, she was sharing all the details from the arranged marriage to her frustration of Steffan not answering his phone when she and Celine landed.

"I'm sorry," she apologized when she finished her rant.

"For what?" Grant asked, seeming genuinely surprised at her apology.

"You asked me to lunch to catch up, not to listen to me complain about the mess my parents left for me."

"You sound like you're more upset with your parents than with getting married."

She frowned at his conclusion, not really sure she wanted to talk about her parents right then. "Enough about me," she took a drink of her water. "Tell me what's been going on with you?"

"Oh you know, mostly work." Grant smiled but didn't seem inclined to share much more than that.

Unable to resist teasing him Karrine smiled, "No interesting girlfriends to talk about?"

Grant smiled but this time it didn't quite reach his eyes, "Oh you know how it is, you find a nice girl, and she ends up going on vacation and getting married. Hard to build a relationship if that keeps happening."

Suddenly wishing she'd listened to Tessa's warnings she made a show of checking her watch. "Wow, I didn't realize how late it was, I should probably get home Grant, I have a ton of packing to do before Cina and I head back."

"Oh, of course," he looked a little startled at the sudden suggestion but since they had already finished their food he didn't have much of an argument. He motioned for the waitress and asked for the check. Just a few minutes later they were on their way back to the parking lot. She was suddenly relieved that she had borrowed Tessa's car.

"Thank you, Grant, I enjoyed this," she unlocked the car, but when she smiled back at him he leaned forward, pressing his lips to hers and causing her to pull back in surprise. His hand wrapped around her back to keep her in place and prolong the kiss. Her hand practically took on a life of its own as she reached out and slapped him hard across the face. "Grant! I'm married!"

"But not happily," he objected, "Come on Karrine, can you really tell me you love your husband?" He demanded as he leaned forward to try to kiss her again. "You've fulfilled the contract, you can keep Celine. Just end this charade and come back home. I'll help you! You don't love him."

Beyond angry, she glared at him, "That really isn't the point and you know it just as well as I do. What I feel isn't important, Steffan is still my husband and you had no right to kiss me!"

She climbed into the car and pulled the door shut hard behind her, backing out with barely a glance over her shoulder to make sure Grant was out of the way, she peeled out of the parking lot and headed home, hoping to put the whole incident out of her mind.

*

"Hey, it's Karrine. Cina and I just landed in Denver and she says hi. Well, I guess you're busy so I'll talk to you later. Bye now."

The voicemail made him sigh. Karrine did not sound happy. He hadn't even thought about keeping his phone turned on during the board meeting so he did not miss her call. Especially since he had been so insistent they call the minute they landed he could

hardly blame his wife for being upset with him. Dialing her number, he waited with impatience when the call went to her voicemail.

"Hey Karrine, this is Steffan. I am sorry I missed your call earlier, I was in a meeting. Anyway, I'm glad you and Celine made it safely and I hope you have fun with your family. I guess I will talk to you more when you figure out when you are coming home. Be safe."

Grabbing his keys he considered going home before he tossed them back down and picked up his phone again. A moment later Cam answered.

"Haddon."

"Hey, Cam."

"Hey Steffan, what's up?" His friend answered immediately.

"I was hoping you could do me a favor. You know the girls are in Colorado, packing up their things so I am going to stay at the office for a while and try to get some work done."

"You want me to pick up Solo?" Cam didn't wait for an answer, "Do you want me to bring him to you at the office or keep him with me. Or I could always drop him off with your parents if that would be better."

"Would you please bring him to me," Steffan requested. "I have food here for him so it is probably the easiest."

"I'll bring him by," Cam hesitated. "Are you holding up all right?"

Steffan frowned even though his friend could not see him. "I insisted Karrine call me when their plane landed and then I missed her call."

"Ouch, did you get a hold of her?"

"Nope, I guess I will have to wait until she gets back home."

Cam barely paused, "Well, no one ever said marriage would be easy."

Keeping in mind his friend's own past he decided not to comment. "Thanks for picking Solo up, I appreciate the help."

"Sure, I'll be there in a bit." Cam hung up without a good-bye and Steffan lowered his head, taking some time to pray, not just for his wife and his new sister-in-law, but also for his best friend and for whatever God had in store for Cam's future. Not to mention his own.

*

"All right, what's wrong?" Tessa demanded the moment she walked into the living room of the house Karrine had once shared with her mother and sister.

"Why would you say something's wrong?"

Tessa pursed her lips and gave her an impatient look even as she picked up a box and started packing things away. "Let's think about that, yesterday you went to lunch with a guy who's been in love with you for years, then last night at the family dinner you barely said two words to anyone. This morning you started packing before dawn but didn't go to see anyone in the family for breakfast, even though I know there's no food in this house. Now you're throwing stuff in that box with enough anger you're going to break something," she grabbed a snow globe out of Karrine's hand and wrapped it carefully before she actually did break it. "So, what's wrong?"

"You were right," Karrine picked up a photo to pack then just set it back down and looked at her cousin. "How did I not see it?"

"All right back up," Tessa took her by the hands and led her over to sit on the couch. "Start from the beginning and tell me what happened."

It didn't take long to detail the events, she did nothing to spare herself but repeated in vivid detail how she had ranted against her parents, the circumstances, and her new husband. She launched into an explanation of how uncomfortable things had gotten when Grant started making insinuations about having been in love with her, finally ending it all with the fated kiss and slap in the parking lot before she had come home. By the time she finished, Tessa had her head in her hands.

"You slapped him?"

"What was I supposed to do?" She demanded, jumping up again to finish packing the bookshelf and resisting the urge to throw the book in her hand against the wall. "I'm married and he kissed me!" Across the room, her phone buzzed and she glared at it. When Tessa started to reach for it she held up a hand to stop her, "Don't. It's Grant, he's been texting and calling since I left yesterday, trying to apologize, while still insisting he can help me with a divorce. He keeps asking if he can see me to explain and so on."

Tessa's blue eyes narrowed at the news, she purposefully moved away from the couch and grabbed Karrine's phone up off the table. Pushing a few buttons, she held the phone up to her ear. Karrine listened to the one-sided conversation in a mixture of admiration and horror.

"Stop calling her Grant. Stop texting her. She doesn't want to hear from you. She's married, you need to leave her alone, understand?" Tessa paused for a moment apparently listening to whatever Grant had to say and her voice softened a little when she spoke again. "I'll see you at work."

"What did he say?" Karrine asked, not sure if she really wanted to know.

Tessa didn't answer but set the phone on a side table, "So rather than figure out how to pack the whole house why don't we figure out what you want and hire a moving company. Anything you don't want can be donated."

"I suppose that would make it easier . . ."

"It would," her cousin agreed, "Unless there's some other reason you're trying to prolong packing all of this."

Sitting back on the couch Karrine let her head fall back and closed her eyes, desperately trying to hold back the tears. "I've been struggling with being married to a stranger before this mess Tessa, how am I going to face Steffan now?"

*

Five Days Later

"Hello, is anyone home?" Steffan called out as he walked into his parent's house, letting Solo run inside in front of him.

"In here," his Dad called back from the living room. When he came around the corner he found his parents, sister, and Cam all waiting for him. "Welcome back to the land of the living Son."

"Thanks," Steffan smiled at them. "I see I am the last to arrive."

"Last or not we're happy to see you," his mother assured him, lifting her face for him to kiss her cheek in greeting. "No one has even heard from you since the girls have been in Colorado."

"I know, sorry," he sat down next to his sister on the couch, leaning over to kiss her cheek also. "Things have just been so hectic the last few weeks that I really needed a few uninterrupted days to catch up on work."

"How are the girls doing in Colorado? Are they coming back soon?" Kennedy asked.

Steffan shrugged his jacket off and laid it over the arm of the couch, "I am not sure, I haven't had a chance to speak to either of them."

"Are you serious?" Kennedy's eyes were wide and he smirked at his little sister.

"Yes, I am. They've been busy and so have I." He frowned when he realized the rest of the people in the room looked just as shocked at his words. "Karrine said she would email me when she figured out when they were coming home."

"Let me make sure I understand," his Dad leaned forward as he spoke, "Your wife has been on the other side of the world for almost a week and you haven't spoken to her since she left?"

Still confused he nodded, "Well yes. I mean, Karrine called me and left a voicemail saying they had landed but I was in a board meeting and missed the call. I called her back and left a message, but she did not answer, and she has not tried to call back. Why are you all looking at me like I'm crazy?"

"Steffan, I don't know much about marriage," Kennedy told him with a shake of her head, "But even I know that's not normal."

"Nothing about our marriage is normal," he retorted. His parents exchanged a look as if trying to decide if they should talk to him or not. Tired and losing patience he ran a hand through his hair, "What Mum and Dad? Just say what you're thinking."

"Steffan I admit your marriage is anything but normal," his mum started slowly but she broke off and looked at her husband.

Charlie picked up where his wife left off, "The problem Son, is that you don't seem to be working towards *making* it normal."

Cam shifted in his seat and Steffan glanced over at him, well aware of how his friend's past would make this conversation uncomfortable. "On that note, how long until dinner?"

His parents exchanged another look but his mum stood, "I will go check."

Once she was gone, he turned to look at his sister. "So kid, how are things at university?"

*

Three Days Later

The week flew by far too fast for Karrine's peace of mind. Before she knew it the house had been cleared out, everything they wanted to keep was packed and ready to be shipped out to Yagos, everything else had been donated, given away or sent to an auction house to be sold.

Celine had been spending more and more time with her friends as the week went on, barely wanting to come home for family dinner most nights. The last few days she had even been making noises about wanting to stay in Colorado, maybe move in with someone in the family or one of her friends instead of going back to Yagos. When Karrine failed to reply Celine hadn't pushed and she hoped her sister would let the issue drop.

"Krin, I'm heading out," Celine called out early that morning. Sitting in the living room of her Aunt Jules and Uncle Andy's home she resisted the urge to roll her eyes.

"Have you even had breakfast?"

The teenager stuck her head in the room, an irritated expression on her face she knew better than to voice. "I'll get something at Karra's."

"Fine, but I want you home for dinner tonight, the whole family is getting together before we fly out tomorrow."

"But it's our last night!" Celine objected.

"Exactly," Karrine narrowed her eyes at her little sister. "Which is why we will be spending it with our family. Now go have fun with your friends unless you want to keep arguing and spend the day at home too."

Celine muttered something under her breath, too quiet for her to understand and stormed out of the room, slamming the door shut behind her. Karrine sighed and rubbed her temple.

"You're doing a good job with her."

Jumping a little she offered Uncle Andy a weary smile. "I really wish I could believe that."

"You can, or at least you should," her Uncle came to sit beside her. "I know it hasn't been easy for either of you Karrine, but I have to admit I'm glad you're not alone in this mess."

Nodding slowly she tried to keep the weariness out of her voice, "I know you're all there for us, but considering we live across the world from each other it makes things a little more complicated Uncle Andy."

"We are always here for you Karrine, but I wasn't talking about our family," he paused only a beat, "I was talking about your husband."

The anger she had been suppressing for the last week surged to the surface and since it was just Uncle Andy with her she didn't bother to try to hide it. "My husband? Oh, you mean the one who insisted I call when I landed then was too busy to answer his phone and when he did return the call it was in the middle of the night and he left me a voicemail!"

Andy didn't seem too upset by the information, "And did you try calling him back?"

Staring at her laptop screen she shrugged, "It was late in Yagos by the time I got the message. I sent him an email when we finalized our return flight. He emailed back to confirm, but that's the only communication I've had with him since we've been here Uncle Andy. What kind of loving husband does that sound like?"

"What kind of loving wife does it make you sound like, that you haven't tried calling him again?"

Exhausted and frustrated she blinked back tears but refused to meet her Uncle's gaze, "I didn't want this marriage, Uncle Andy. It wasn't my choice. Don't I get points for not trying to get out of it?"

"I know, but you're in it now kiddo. It's not enough to just say 'you're not trying to get out of it' it's time you start making the best of it."

*

"What are you still doing here?"

Steffan looked up from his monitor to see Cam leaning against the doorframe to his office. Blinking a few times to clear his vision he frowned at his friend, "Better question; what are you doing here?"

"It's your last day on your own and you want to spend it working? What kind of friend would I be if I let that happen?"

Looking back at his screen he tried to focus on the report he was reviewing from the accounting department. "The kind that remembers I have my own business which hasn't been getting enough attention since I got married to a woman who's a guardian for a teenager."

"Aren't you both Celine's guardians?" Cam sat down across from his desk.

"Legally, no." He sat back and finally looked at his friend, still processing the information he had just learned a few hours ago. He'd called his lawyer after the girls had left, asked him to update his living will and deal with any other ramification from his sudden marriage and new family. When the lawyer had called back to ask if he would be petitioning the court for joint custody of Celine, Steffan had been shocked. "I assumed my marriage to Karrine meant shared guardianship of her sister but apparently it does not."

"Have you told Karrine?"

"No," he looked away, focusing on his computer again. "I still haven't talked to her. She sent me an email to confirm their flight for tomorrow but she has been busy, trying to get their old house packed up and arrange for things to be shipped or sold as needed."

"And you've been so busy here you couldn't call?"

He ignored the censure in Cam's voice if anyone had room to criticize it was Cam, but he was not up to listening to it. "They will be home tomorrow and we'll have to find a school for Celine, I found some options." He picked up a file from his desk and handed it over. "Some of them have boarding options but I do not think it's a good idea, not after everything she's already been through, but it isn't really up to me."

"Legally, no, but does that really matter?"

Exhausted he rubbed the back of his neck and glared at his friend, "Get to the point Cam."

"You may not legally be her guardian, but you are married to her legal guardian. So . . . are you going to let a technicality stop you or are you going to step up and be the man she needs in her life, be a father, brother, friend, or sometimes all three?"

Steffan felt the hit, let himself absorb it then met Cam's gaze head-on without his expression ever changing. "Are you finished?" He didn't wait for an answer, "Because, I really need to get this work done before my family comes home tomorrow. See I don't just have a wife, there's a teenage girl I am responsible for also."

"Yep," Cam stood and let the smile spread across his face, "I'm done. I picked up Solo earlier, I'll drop him off before work tomorrow so he's home to greet your girls when they get back."

He didn't bother to reply but turned back to his report, really hoping he would be able to finish his work and still get home at a decent hour.

*

"Call me when you get there, I promise I'll answer," Tessa smiled when she said it but it didn't reach her eyes and Karrine knew her cousin was struggling as much as she was with saying good-bye this time.

"Bad joke Tessa," Karrine tried to smile but couldn't force herself to. Glancing over her shoulder she saw the sullen Celine standing nearby, pouting, but out of earshot. "I still don't know if I'm going to tell him what happened or not. I mean things were complicated enough and now with Celine deciding she wants to stay here instead of going back to Yagos . . . I just don't know if adding any more turmoil is a good idea right now. I mean it's not like anything happened right?"

Tessa just shrugged, "I wish I had the answers Krin. Just be careful okay? And seriously, call me when you land."

"I will," Karrine hugged her one more time. "Love you Cuz."

"Yeah, I love you too."

They managed to go through security and board the plane without an incident, but Celine refused to speak any more than she absolutely had to. By the time she got on the plane, she was exhausted. Making sure her sister was settled with her earbuds securely in her ears she closed her eyes and willed all of the problems out of her mind so she could try and get some sleep.

Chapter 12

Steffan waited at the airport terminal, wondering if the flowers he had bought for the girls were overkill. An older woman standing nearby smiled at him.

"Waiting for your sweetheart young man?" She asked, her flawless English laced with a French accent.

"My wife," he hesitated before adding, "and my sister-in-law."

"Oh," she frowned a little at the explanation but didn't ask questions.

Feeling like he should explain he shrugged, "She lives with us, but they have been visiting their family for the past week and a half."

"So you bought flowers? That is so sweet!"

He could not help but grin at her excitement, "Well my sister-in-law would probably prefer seeing my dog to flowers but I did not think bringing him to the airport was such a wonderful idea."

She smiled sweetly, "I am sure they will both just be glad to see you."

Steffan nodded just as people started to come through security muttering loud enough for her to hear, although that hadn't been his intention, "Let's hope so."

Again the woman frowned but a young family caught her attention just then and she smiled in delight as two young children ran towards her, cries of *"Grand-maman!"* filling the air. Embracing the children, she spoke to them in rapid-fire French, embracing a young woman who looked like her and then hugging a man who looked a little more reserved than the rest of his family. Realizing he was still standing there she looked up at him and smiled, "I hope you enjoy your reunion as much as I am enjoying mine."

"Merci," he nodded, and she smiled again as she moved away with her family. Moving his attention back to the stream of people, wondering how far back the girls had sat. His heartbeat kicked up a notch when he saw Karrine step through the crowd, even from a distance he could see the exhaustion and tension on her face and instantly he felt concerned, and a fair amount of guilt. He wished he had called her while she was gone. It was obvious something had happened on her trip, maybe if he had bothered to check on her he would have been able to help her through it.

Shifting his gaze he saw Celine trailing behind her sister. In the short time, he had known the teenager he had never seen her look so angry, and immediately he felt the concern mix in with a good dose of dread. He had a bad feeling that whatever had happened to make Celine so mad had a lot to do with why his wife looked so tense. Which meant, one way or the other, he needed to have a long talk with his family, and hopefully figure out how to resolve whatever had happened in Colorado.

"Karrine," he smiled once his wife got close enough and leaned forward to kiss her cheek, ignoring the way she tensed at the contact. Handing her the larger bouquet of flowers he tried to joke, "You know we are really going to have to come up with a nickname for you, saying Karrine and Celine all the time is too long and similar."

"So come up with a nickname for Celine," she suggested, flicking a hand at her younger sister. "I like my name."

Resisting the urge to smile he turned as the teenager approached and presented the flowers to her with a flourish. "Welcome home Miss Celine."

She didn't even smile but pursed her lips, "This isn't my home!"

Karrine sighed loudly and glared at her sister, "Don't start Celine. We literally just stepped off the plane, just tell Steffan thank you for the flowers, okay?"

"All right," Steffan drew out the words and reached out to take their bags from them. "Do you have any more luggage?"

"No, we left everything else at the house to be shipped back." Karrine told him, "Thank you for arranging that by the way."

Not sure why he was surprised at how reserved she was he nodded, "Not a problem. I am sure you two are exhausted, why don't we head home or would you rather get something to eat first?"

Karrine hesitated before nodding, "I could eat. Where were you thinking?"

"Whatever sounds good, would you rather dine in somewhere or just head home and get something there?"

They both looked at Celine but the teenager had already turned her attention back to her phone, her fingers flying over the keyboard. Apparently not wanting to try to get an answer from her, Karrine shrugged. "If it's not too much trouble I think I'd rather just pick something up and take it home."

Steffan nodded and turned away before she could see his smile at the way she said home. "All right, let's go home."

*

Steffan tried to start a conversation once they were at the car but Celine was keeping up her pouting in silence and Karrine was too tired to give him more than one or two-word answers. They picked something up at a café where Steffan had called in an order before they left the airport, but they ended up eating the food in the car instead of waiting until they arrived home. Even if she had been more awake she wasn't sure she would have answered, she was still angry he hadn't once bothered to call her the whole time they were gone. Eventually, he gave up and the rest of the drive was made in silence.

Solo jumped up and down, barking a greeting when they got inside but even the sight of the dog barely got a smile at Celine. Without a word to anyone she grabbed her bag and marched up the stairs to the room, she had claimed when they first looked at the house, the same room she had slept in when she was a baby.

With a shake of her head and a tired sigh, Karrine shrugged, "I'm sorry, she's mad because I wouldn't let her even talk about the possibility of staying in Colorado."

Her exhaustion kept her from noticing the panic on her new husband's face and how he took a moment before he carefully answered, "She wanted to move back to Colorado?"

"Yeah. Now she's angry because not only didn't I let her stay, but I wouldn't even think about it."

"Do you want to move back?"

Surprised by the question she turned away so he wouldn't see the conflict on her face, "I think Celine and I both need a change, living in Yagos will probably be good for us." Not wanting to talk about it anymore she grabbed her own suitcase. "I'm going up to my old room, I thought I'd just sleep in there, did you pick a room yet?"

Steffan cleared his throat, "Um . . . yes, what might have been a guest room down the other hall."

"Okay," without looking at him she headed for the stairs. "Good night then."

"Good night Karrine, sleep well."

She didn't turn around or she might have noticed how he watched her as she walked upstairs or how he stayed in the living room for over an hour, thinking about the changes in his life and the conflict in his new little family and praying God would show him some way to fix it; before it tore them all apart.

*

Karrine woke out of a deep sleep to a strange sense of dèjá vu. Everything around her seemed strange and yet somehow familiar. The big wooden bed had a pink comforter with a white lace border, a pink and white canopy hanging from the ceiling and coming down to surround her. Lacy curtains hanging on either side of the window that overlooked a forestry area with strange-looking trees that didn't seem like anything she had seen in Colorado.

Trying to clear her foggy mind she rubbed the heels of her hands against her eyes catching sight of the ring on her left hand. A silver band with a ring of diamonds inlaid around the top half. It was beautiful in its simplicity and the sight of it brought everything flooding back.

In an onslaught of memories, she remembered her Mother's accident, and her decision to bring Celine to Yagos to give her sister some space from her grief. Meeting Steffan, learning about the marriage contract, the sting of her parents' lies and betrayal, and the rushed wedding. The trip back home to pack things up, the horrible mess with Grant, Celine wanting to stay in Colorado, and finally the anger with her new husband about how he had ignored her the whole time she was gone.

Everything blurred together, overwhelming her with the emotions and causing hot tears to well up in her eyes. Even if she wanted to, there was no energy to try to stop them. Exhausted and drained even after a good night's rest she curled up on her bed, wrapped her arms around a pillow, and cried herself back to sleep.

When she woke again the room seemed brighter and she remembered her window faced west so it didn't get the early morning sun but she could always enjoy the sunset from the window seat. When she was little, she would curl up against her Mom's side on that very seat while she listened to bedtime stories.

Not wanting to dwell on the memories she pushed them aside and started searching for her clothes, wishing she had bothered to unpack the night before so the sweater she pulled out would not look quite so wrinkled. Placing it in the bathroom she turned the shower on, hoping the steam would at least get the worst of it out.

By the time she was finally feeling ready to face the day it was nearly one in the afternoon. She smelled something cooking as she walked downstairs. Curious she headed into the kitchen to find out what it was.

"Hey, good morning," Steffan turned and greeted her when she walked inside. "Your timing is impeccable, I have brunch just about ready." He spread out his hand to indicate the fresh fruit on the counter. "The quiche will be done in just a minute too."

Not sure what to think of the scene in front of her she just stared at him in surprise, "You cook?"

Steffan shot her an amused smile. "I am twenty-three years old Karrine, how do you think I have managed to feed myself all these years?"

"Of course, I'm sorry, it's just . . . at home, I did most of the cooking."

The timer beeped and he turned to pull the quiche out of the oven. "I figured you two would be pretty tired today, I did not want you to have to worry about finding food when you got up."

Sliding onto the stool she nodded, "Thank you, that was very," she hesitated, searching for the right word, "considerate of you."

"Well, we have a lot of decisions to make today, this was the least I could do."

Not sure she wanted to get into a conversation about their future she searched for a distraction as she decided which fruit she wanted to eat and Steffan dished her up some quiche. "Don't you have to go to work today?"

"I went in for a couple of hours this morning, but I got enough done while you were gone that I can take the afternoon off. If something comes up they can call me."

Accepting the reality she nodded, "Well, we already have a house so I guess that was the first big decision right?"

"Yep, the next is a school for Celine."

"How do we decide?"

"One moment," he left the room only to return a moment later with a file in hand. "I have done a lot of research and this is what I've learned." He hesitated, "Should we wait until Celine can talk with us?"

"No," she rejected the idea immediately. "First we will narrow it down, then we can talk to her about it."

They fell into silence as she quietly ate and read over the files, including detailed notes he had made. Steffan cleaned up the kitchen around her then sat down to work on his own laptop, patiently waiting for her to finish. About halfway through she looked up with a frown, "By the way, where is Celine anyway? Have you seen her yet this morning?"

"She came down about twenty minutes before you did, ate some fruit, and then headed back to her room. She said she was tired and was going back to sleep."

"Bratty teenagers," Karrine mumbled under her breath then went back to her reading.

A half-hour later she set aside the last file, Steffan shut the laptop lid and smiled at her.

"So, what do you think?"

Moving the files around Karrine pulled three out and set them on top, "These would be my top choices. I have no idea what they cost or anything else but from the notes you made and all the information here, these would be my choices. They are close enough she can live here, thank you for listing the commute times by the way. With everything else going on I just don't think boarding school is a good idea."

"I agree but I wanted to give you the option."

"Thank you." Karrine pursed her lips when Steffan only nodded. Reaching out she touched his hand, "Seriously, thank you."

Giving her a brief smile, he nodded. "You're welcome. So let's talk about these schools."

Chapter 13

<u>One Week Later</u>

"I don't want to go to school!" Celine's voice carried from the upstairs hallway down into the kitchen making Steffan rub his forehead. In the week since the girls had come back from Colorado, there had been nothing but fighting in their household. For the most part, he tried to stay out of it, give Celine her space and charm her out of her bad mood by bribing her to take Solo out for walks or setting it up with her Aunt Fern to go horseback riding but now reality had set in as Celine's first day at her new school rolled around.

"Celine you are going, and you are going to wear the same uniform every other girl wears so just get dressed and don't argue with me."

"You can't make me go!"

"Yes Celine, I can," Karrine's voice hardened a little. "I'm your guardian, deal with it. Now get dressed!"

Footsteps on the stairs warned him to wipe the smile off his face and pour a cup of coffee for his wife. "Good morning Karrine. I would ask how you are, but I think I already know."

She cringed at his response, "You heard all that?"

"It was hard not to," he admitted, fixing her the plate of fruit, yogurt, and the toast with jam he had learned she preferred in the mornings she didn't drink a protein shake. "How are you holding up?"

Karrine set her coffee down with a humorless laugh, "Oh I'm great, I mean my whole life has turned into a war zone but other than that everything's absolutely fantastic."

Steffan forced himself to smile before he turned away, hoping she wouldn't see him cringe as her words sent a punch straight to his gut. Here he was trying to make their marriage work, praying they might actually be able to make a real life together despite the chaos that had ruled in their lives since they had met, and now Karrine only saw it as a war zone.

Knowing better than to dwell on things he could not control or fix he took another drink of his own coffee and turned back to his wife. "So, what are your plans for the day?"

"Actually, I'm planning on going into my Dad's office today. I think I'd like to spend some time there, get a handle on how things work even if I don't decide to take an active role in the company."

"I think that makes sense," he agreed, glad to see she had made her decision and was not just going to ignore her family's company.

Her head snapped up and her eyes narrowed a little, "I'm so glad you agree."

Not sure what he had done to deserve her sarcasm he chose to just ignore it and picked up the notepad he had left on the counter. "I am planning on going to the store after work to pick up some groceries, is there anything specific you would like me to pick up?"

*

Karrine wasn't sure what to think of her new husband. He cooked for her, tried to charm Celine out of her bad moods, asked about her day, and was even going to the grocery store after work but when she was in Colorado he had never once bothered to call. The contradictions were hard for her to accept.

It had been a busy morning. She had dropped Celine off for her first day of school, filled out some necessary paperwork to get her registered, and had a private meeting with the headmaster to explain the circumstances that had brought them to Yagos. The kind man, a friend of Steffan's family, had agreed to keep an eye on Celine, knowing it was likely to be a tough adjustment for the teenager.

Yet the whole time, in the back of her mind, was her confusion about Steffan. More than any other time in her life she found herself wanting to curl up under her blankets and stay there until everything in her life went back to normal. Not that she had any idea what normal was anymore.

Grateful for the Bluetooth enabled speaker in the car that her aunt was letting her borrow she voice dialed her cousin.

"Krin, are you okay?" Tessa's worried voice made her cringe.

"Sorry, forgot about the time difference. What time is it there?"

"It's four, I'm still at work. Are you okay?"

"I don't want to distract you if you're busy."

"Eh," her cousin ignored the out she offered. "I've got a few minutes, what's going on?"

Taking a deep breath she let it out loudly. "Well . . . since you asked, I took Celine to her first day of school, oh and she hates me. My husband," she spat out the word with a heavy layer of sarcasm, "Apparently thinks he can make up for anything by acting like a perfect gentleman whenever we're home and ignoring me when we're not and now I'm on my way to a company that used to be owned by a man who sold me off like livestock in a marriage contract. How's your life?"

"So things with Steffan still aren't so great huh?"

"Not great would imply they'd ever been good," she corrected. "I don't even know him, Tessa, how are we supposed to build a relationship from that?"

"Well, to start with, you could try being honest with each other. Have you told him what happened with Grant?"

"Why?" She didn't wait for her cousin to answer the rhetorical question. "There's no point because nothing happened and nothing's going to."

"I get what you're saying Krin, really I do, but are you sure this is the best plan?"

"Positive, can we talk about something else now?"

Tessa sighed, conveying without words her disapproval but she gave in, "Tell me about your Dad's company."

*

Steffan laid his hand on the open Bible on his desk, not seeing the words in the Psalms but just staring off into space as he took a few moments to pray for his new family. Every day he prayed for Karrine and Celine but even though it had only been a few weeks he was not sure it was doing any good.

"Why is this so hard God?"

As if on cue there was a knock on his door before Cam entered. His best friend looked at the Bible sitting on his desk then closed the door again before coming to collapse in a chair across from him.

"Things not going well at home?"

"You think the only time I read my Bible is when life is tough?"

"I think when you look this upset and your hand is on your Bible like that, it's probably because your new wife and sister are not adjusting very well."

Giving up he leaned back in his chair and closed his eyes, "This is not how I expected things to turn out."

Cam chuckled under his breath, "Tell me about it."

Wincing at his own insensitivity he opened his eyes again, "I'm sorry, I really do not mean to complain."

"You don't have to apologize to me, Steffan. If there's anyone who knows at all what you're going through, it's me, stop worrying about offending me, and just talk to me when you need to. All right?"

Steffan took a moment to consider his friend, trying to decide if he should take him at his word, before finally accepting he didn't have much choice. "Celine wants to move back to Colorado."

"And Karrine?"

"She says it will be a good move for them to live in Yagos, away from the memories but . . . ."

"But what?"

He shrugged, "But I am wondering if it's just a matter of time before she wants to go home too."

"Okay, so say she does, she decides to move home and packs up her little sister and moves back to the land of the Rocky Mountains. What are you going to do about it?"

Steffan frowned, not sure where his friend was going with the conversation but getting the uncomfortable feeling he was not going to like it. "What can I do?"

"Come on Steffan, that's not an answer," Cam pushed, leaning forward and resting his forearms on the desk, his hazel eyes intense and serious, a rare look for him. "What would you do?"

"Try to convince her to stay I guess. What other option do I have?"

Cam pushed his chair back and stood, "Ephesians five."

"I know the verses!" He called out but Cam was already gone so he flipped the pages in his Bible, rereading the passage he knew so well. When he got to the part about how husbands were to love their wives as Christ loved the church and gave up His life for it he frowned, he knew this had to be what Cam was talking about, but there was no new information. Closing the Bible, he leaned back in his chair, not sure what he was supposed to have learned, still having no idea what to do with his new wife.

*

Two Months Later

"How was school, Cina?"

Celine climbed into the car and threw her backpack in the back, slouching down in the seat and staring out the window without answering. Karrine sighed but didn't push. Sometimes it was easier when the teenager just took up the silent treatment instead of screaming about how much she hated their new life.

The thirty-minute drive back to the house passed in intense silence, but as they drove she got more and more wound up. It had been two months of walking on eggshells in their home. She and Steffan didn't live together, they simply existed around each other. Celine spent more time with the dog or on the phone than she did with either of them. Other than when someone was driving her to and from school or forcing her to come down for meals she avoided them as much as possible.

Her anger grew with each passing mile and by the time they arrived back at the house she was at her breaking point. Turning the car off she turned in her seat, "Celine, we can't keep doing this. Our life is here in Yagos now, you need to start accepting that. I'm tired of living in silence so if you have something to say then you may as well say it because ignoring me isn't going to fly anymore."

"Can I go in now?"

Resisting the urge to strangle her little sister she grabbed the keys out of the ignition and pushed her own car door open. "Come on Cina, you really have nothing to say to me? Can't you at least tell me how school is going?"

"How's school going?" Celine shoved open the door and threw her backpack onto the ground. "I hate it! That's how it's going. I hate every moment I have to spend at that place!"

"What are you talking about? It's a great school," she leaned down and picked up her sister's backpack, hanging it on the coatrack so no one would trip over it. "What could you possibly hate about it?"

"I don't have any friends there Krin, all of my friends are back home in Denver. Our lives are in Denver."

"Our lives are here Celine and like I said in the car you need to accept that."

"I don't want to accept it! I hate this place and I hate you!"

"That is enough Celine," Steffan's voice stopped the teenager's tantrum cold. "Your sister and I have worked hard to make this life work for you and I am sorry you do not like it, but you are not a child and you will not act like one in this house. If you have a problem at school then you can come to us and tell us what is going on so together we can try to come up with a solution, but I will not tolerate you screaming at Karrine, do you understand?"

"Me?" Celine put her hands on her hips, "What about you two? You don't even talk to each other. You call this a marriage? I call it delusions of grandeur! Maybe you should put us all out of our misery and get divorced so Krin and I can go back to our lives in

Colorado and you won't have this ridiculous marriage and custody of a teenager hanging over your head anymore!"

"Go to your room!" Steffan pointed towards the stairs, "You can come back down when you're ready to act like a civilized human being again."

Karrine watched her sister march up the stairs, Solo trailing behind her with his head hung low and tail tucked between his legs. She turned to her husband as he rubbed his eyes, the stress showing on his face. "How dare you."

"What?" Steffan raised his gaze to meet hers.

"How dare you yell at her like that! She's just a scared little girl who's having a hard time adjusting and instead of trying to help her you just made it worse."

"Karrine, I will not tolerate anyone, including Celine, yelling at my wife like that."

"Wife?" She scoffed at the word, "We're hardly a traditional married couple Steffan, it's not like I need you coming to my defense!"

Walking to the kitchen he helped himself to a glass of water, "Our marriage may not be traditional, but you are still my wife. If Celine is angry then she is always welcome to come to talk to me, or you, but that is no excuse for her screaming at you that way."

"She's just a kid."

He slammed the glass on the counter and turned to face her, "She is a teenager and she is well on her way to becoming an adult, it is time she starts acting like it and you start treating her like one!"

Karrine crossed her arms over her chest, "You're not her father!"

"And you are not her mother."

"I'm her guardian!"

"And I am not," he nodded, "At least not legally, I know. What I am is your husband and I still get a say in the rules we make."

Surprised at the information he had no legal hold over Celine but too caught up the in the argument to comment she glared at him and rocked back on her heels, "Says who?"

"Seriously?" He walked back to the entryway to retrieve his briefcase, "This must be where your sister learns her behavior from. Says who, Karrine? Says me, says the vows we made before our families and God. Like it or not we're in this marriage and Celine is our responsibility so even though I am not her guardian I am still going to insist she treat my wife with respect—she, and you, are just going to have to deal with that."

Karrine glared at his retreating back as he headed down the hall to his office, closing the door softly behind him. Snatching her keys up and marching outside she slammed the door behind her. She needed to climb.

*

They were driving him crazy.

Steffan tossed his briefcase onto the forest green wingback chair Kennedy had convinced him he needed when they had moved to the new house. His office was the only room in the house that was truly decorated, he had assumed Karrine and Celine would want to do the rest themselves but even after two months of living in their new home they had barely done more than provide the basics. Collapsing behind his desk he leaned back and closed his eyes, not sure if he should be thankful or worried about the silence that had settled over the house. A car starting drew his attention the window and he saw Karrine's car tear out of the driveway like bats from hell were after it.

"What is the point of fighting for a marriage if I'm the only one who's invested in it?"

The sharp ring of his cell phone broke the resounding quiet that echoed in the wake of his question.

Grabbing his phone he noted the name. Dad.

"Not really the Father I was hoping would answer," he muttered as he pushed the button to accept the call. "Hi, Dad."

"Hi Son, how are you?"

Wondering if there was an honest way to answer without telling his father that his wife had just left and his new sister-in-law wanted nothing more than to go back to Colorado far away from him, he took a moment to try to formulate an answer.

"I'll take it from your silence that life hasn't gotten any easier lately?"

The dam that had been keeping his emotions bottled up showed its first crack. "Dad, life was easier when I knew I had a fiancée out there somewhere, who I would eventually meet and marry but until then I could just keep living my life, building my company, and the only person I came home to at night was Solo. Ever since the Sandor girls came to Yagos life has been a lot more complicated and not one second of it has been easy."

"Maybe that's the start of your problem Steffan."

"What? Karrine and Celine being in Yagos? I don't think there is a way to get out of them being here." His voice dripped with sarcasm, but he didn't care, "The whole marriage thing makes it a little difficult."

"Marriage isn't your problem Steffan, and having a teenager to care for isn't it either."

"Yeah?" He tipped his head back to stare at the ceiling, wondering for the tenth time why people thought putting textured paint over natural wood was a good idea. "Then what is?"

"You didn't call them Karrine and Celine, or your wife and sister, or ward or whatever else."

"She is not my ward," he wasn't sure why it mattered but suddenly he felt the burden of sharing the news. "Karrine is Celine's guardian, but I'm not. I have no say in what happens to her."

His dad didn't even hesitate, "Maybe not legally Steffan, but that doesn't mean you don't have a responsibility to that little girl. In her short life, she's lost both parents, moved across the world, technically twice. She's said good-bye to everything and everyone she knows and has accepted a new man in her sister's life who, instead of saying 'Let me be here for you' is saying, 'You're not my responsibility'. That's not the man your mother and I raised you to be."

Springing out of the chair he paced over to the window, staring out at the empty spot where Karrine's car had been. "What am I supposed to do about it? I cannot change the legalities of this mess."

"Stop making excuses," Charlie's tone reminded him of being in trouble as a teenager and knowing it would be better to shut-up and listen because no amount of fast-talking charm would get him out of whatever punishment was coming. "Karrine and Celine are not a mess to clean-up. They're your family. You may not be able to change the paperwork but you can still step up and do the job. She's a little girl who needs someone Steffan, imagine if it were Kennedy. Wouldn't you want someone to take care of her?"

The thought of his little sister being put in Celine's shoes was like a knife in his heart and he rubbed his hand over the area as if to take away the physical pain.

"Karrine's no better, she's barely twenty-one and has no parents," Charlie didn't give him a chance to breathe before continuing the verbal assault. "She's responsible for her sister and has left her family and all her loved ones behind in Colorado. She feels like her whole life has been a lie and I'm willing to bet, based on things I've seen recently and conversations I've had, she has no concept of God being involved in her daily life. You need to step-up and show Christ to that girl, not just as a believer but as her husband."

"It's not that simple Dad, the girls are stubborn and they do not want anything to do with me."

"The Sandor girls, that's what you called them right?"

He could sense the trap but had no idea how to avoid stepping directly into it, "Yeah."

"But they're not Steffan. Not anymore. Karrine's last name is Dalton, not Sandor. How can you ask either girl to start accepting this new life if you've had twenty-three years to prepare for it and yet you haven't even been able to start using your wife's new last name?"

Leaning his head against the window he relished the feel of the cool glass against his flushed skin, "This is not all my fault."

"I didn't say it was, I said you were the one who needs to start fixing it. All you can do is be responsible for yourself son, but maybe if you take the first step and live the example then the rest of your family will find it a little easier to follow in your footsteps."

Clicking the phone closed Charlie let out a deep breath and looked at his wife who was sitting on the couch next to him.

"Do you think I was too harsh?"

"No," Genève reached out to take his hand. "I think you said exactly what God laid on your heart. What Steffan does with that . . . well, that is up to him."

"And the girls?"

His wife of twenty-six years snuggled closer to lean her head on his shoulder. "It is like you always say Charlie, all we can do is pray and lead by example. If we keep accepting them as part of our family and drawing them in, maybe someday they will start to see themselves that way."

Chapter 14

Sweat trickled into her eyes causing them to burn. She blinked rapidly so she could see where her next handhold was. Her muscles spasming, warning her she was pushing herself too much, her body would not hold up under the assault for much longer but she ignored the signs. All she wanted was to clear her mind, push herself to the point where she wouldn't have to think any more about the voices ringing in her head.

"I hate you!" She didn't think she would ever be able to erase Celine's vicious words from her memory.

She's a teenager. Teenagers say stupid things. Lifting her left foot, she made sure the slight ledge was strong enough to hold her before lifting herself up, changing handgrips, and securing another carabiner. *So why doesn't that make me feel better?*

"Like it or not we're in this marriage," Steffan's words came back to haunt her, zinging around in her head like a ping-pong ball followed by the conversation with her uncle a few months before.

"I didn't want this marriage, Uncle Andy. It wasn't my choice."

"I know, but you're in it now kiddo. It's time you start making the best of it."

She definitely hadn't been doing her part to make the best of it.

And why should I? Steffan was the one who knew about the contract all this time, he could've come looking for me, but he never even bothered to so much as look up a picture of me in all these years. He should be the one trying to fix this, not me.

Another step up with her right leg and she turned back to look at the view, amazed by the beauty of her new home. With spring now upon them the days, and the light, were staying longer but still fading quicker than she liked, making it harder to see but she was not ready to stop climbing, not yet. The clouds had rolled in, turning the blue sky gray as if to match her mood. Rolling hills and fields were a far cry from the mountains of Colorado but there was a beauty here that spoke to her heart.

The light green grass, the strange but fascinating trees, and the indescribable essence that filled the air. It was a strange combination of mystery and familiarity as if the land itself was welcoming her back to her childhood home.

"You should probably start heading back down, it's going to be dark soon."

Karrine turned at the unfamiliar voice, resenting the disruption of her reverie. The two climbers, a man, and a woman were probably ten years older than herself. They were well outfitted with worn but sturdy climbing shoes, helmets, and heavy-duty ropes. They were obviously well-experienced climbers and they were giving her that patient, concerned look she wasn't used to getting from anyone outside of her family and, at least lately, Steffan's parents.

"I'll go soon."

"Just be careful honey," the woman cautioned her. "It can be dangerous to still be climbing at dark, especially on your own."

"I know what I'm doing."

The couple exchanged a look but didn't push the issue and the man finally smiled, "As long as you're sure. We can wait for you if you want. Make sure you get down okay?"

"That's not necessary." She turned her attention back to the rock face and started looking for her next handhold. The couple bid her good-bye, but she didn't respond as she went back to her struggle to tune out the world and just climb.

A way up she started looking for the next piton to clip onto, but the dimming light made it hard to see. Spotting one to her left she tried to stretch over but it was too far away. Her legs were sore, her hands were getting sweaty, so she stuck them in her chalk bag.

"Come on Karrine, just a little bit further, you can rest at the top." She muttered to herself, "You're never going to be tired enough to get everyone out of your head if you stop now."

Climbing sideways she positioned herself until she was close enough to reach the piton. Shaking out her arm she took a second to catch her breath, keeping her body close to the rock to conserve her energy. The light was fading faster than she had thought but she was determined to keep going. Stretching out her left arm she went to clip the carabiner but she had misjudged the distance, and before she could secure the rope her weight shifted, throwing her off balance. Her legs couldn't support her, and her right knee buckled, slamming into the rock face, and causing her foot to slip. One moment she was secure in the position, the next her harness was constricting on her legs and waist and she didn't even have a chance to scream as the rope tightened, keeping her from falling to her death but twisting her around until she swung back towards the rock, slamming her head as the world went dark.

"Evan! The girl!"

"Call emergency services," Evan ordered. "I'm climbing up to get her"

"It's too dark, you won't be able to see," Vena argued even as she dug her cell phone out and dialed the number, waiting impatiently for the call to connect.

"I've got to help her," Evan took the time to grab his headlamp out of his bag and secure it to his helmet.

"Just be careful." The operator finally picked up, but she kept her eyes glued to her husband as he climbed as quickly as he could to try to help the unconscious girl dangling from her rope. She finished giving them the information about where they were and what had happened, "Please, you have to hurry."

"I'm already dispatching help ma'am," the man calmly assured her. "They're on their way."

"Is she going to be okay?"

"We're going to do everything we can for her," the paramedic assured Vena as he and his partner got the unconscious climber loaded onto a backboard. "You and your husband getting her help so quickly may have saved her life."

"Let's hope so," Evan wrapped his arm around his wife as they watched the young woman being loaded up to be taken to the hospital, "Let's pray so."

*

She should have been home by now.

Steffan grabbed the pan off the stovetop and slammed it onto the granite countertop, getting some perverse pleasure out of the loud clang. Pulling plates down as loudly as he could he let the cupboard door slam closed before jerking open the silverware drawer to retrieve the utensils. His wife's temper tantrum had gone on long enough. They were going to have a serious talk when she got home about the fact that mature adults did not just take off without so much as telling someone where they were going, and then stay away for hours on end.

A little voice in his head suggested maybe his anger had more to do with the residing sting from his Dad's earlier phone call but he ignored that. It was Karrine's behavior that was unacceptable, not his.

Yes, he had known about the marriage long before Karrine had, and he had been given practically his whole life to prepare but it wasn't his fault the Sandor family had kept the marriage contract a secret.

"Stop making excuses."

His dad's rebuke had him clenching his hand around the glass he had just pulled out of the dishwasher but the feel of the cool glass against his skin reminded him not to squeeze too hard. No use having to make a trip to the hospital for stitches because he was mad at his wife.

Wife.

Sometimes the word still caught him off guard, even when he least expected it. Karrine was not just a random woman living in a house with him. She was his wife. They didn't sleep in the same room, or know each other's schedules or even share more than polite small talk most days, but that did not change the facts. Before God and man, they had exchanged vows and promised to love, cherish, protect, and care for each other until death parted them. He had just never expected it to be this hard.

Setting aside the dinner preparations he grabbed his phone and quickly scrolled through the contacts, leaning his elbows on the counter as he waited for the call to connect.

"Shouldn't you be spending time with your family?"

Thinking better of the idea of having this conversation standing in the kitchen where anyone could walk in he headed to the back door, stepping out into the cold night. "We haven't even had dinner yet."

"Really? It's late. Is everything okay?"

How to answer that question? Nothing was okay, not really, but Cam did not need a dissertation on the troubles in his life and Steffan didn't have the time to give one. "When you realized life with Mabel wasn't going to be what you had planned on how did you learn to accept her?"

Silence rang out on the other end but he waited, hoping his friend would answer once he collected his thoughts. This was unchartered territory for them—Cam's former fiancée wasn't a subject they talked about. Ever. But this time it was necessary, if there was anyone on this earth who would be able to help him figure out the new situation he found himself in, it was Cam.

"I had to learn what may be one of the hardest but simplest truths of my entire life."

"And what is that?" He walked into the grass, wondering if they were going to have to hire a groundskeeper come spring to keep the lawn up or if he would be able to handle it himself. Considering his work schedule that currently didn't seem possible.

"Love is a choice. There are feelings and emotions and a lot of other stuff that goes into it, but at the end and beginning of every day and each moment in between, you can choose to love. Sometimes it's easy, like with your family, but it's not always. I think though, it's during those moments, the moments when you chose to love even when it's hard, that you really start to see people through Christ's eyes."

There was an opening here and he wanted to take it, push the issue of Christ and His love but he knew Cam well enough to hear the edge of defensiveness to his words. He was expecting Steffan to try to walk through that door and he was dreading it.

Swallowing his own words, he started back for the door. "Okay. Thanks, Cam."

There was a second's pause like Cam had to adjust his thought process. "What are you going to do?"

His hand closed over the doorknob as a plan started to form in his head. "I am going to put the dinner I made in the fridge and make cheeseburgers, then I am going to Google how to make homemade French fries."

To Cam's credit, he didn't laugh, "Sounds like a good place to start."

*

"Do we have a name?" The doctor came alongside the gurney, getting the details from the paramedics without glancing up from the woman lying unconscious on the wheeled bed.

"Haven't had time to look for any identification," the senior medic replied. "Witnesses said she was alone, said she was an experienced climber but in the dark, she must have misjudged her handholds or something."

"Or she wasn't as experienced as she thought," the nurse commented. "It wouldn't be the first time we've treated someone who thought they knew what they were doing."

The paramedic replied but the doctor ignored them both, focusing on the condition of the girl as he officially took over her care. The circumstances did not matter. She was a patient, and someone out there would be missing her. His job was to make sure she was able to go home to them.

"All right people, let's get ready to move her, and someone find me a name for her."

"Already on it, doctor," one of the nurses replied as she went through the bag that had been brought in, looking for some sort of identification. "Doctor."

He didn't bother to look at her, "What is it?"

"She's an American."

Glancing up he saw the passport in her hand but only gave a curt nod. "Someone call the Embassy. Let them know we have one of theirs here."

*

"Celine," Steffan knocked on the teenager's door, hearing muffled sounds from the other side before she opened it.

"Is Krin home yet?"

"Not yet, but I made dinner. Should I bring it up here or do you want to eat downstairs?"

A furrow appeared between her eyes as she studied him with suspicion, "Krin doesn't like it when I eat in my room."

"True," he had to be careful here, he didn't want to undermine Karrine's authority, but he also needed a place to start if he was going to begin building a relationship with his sister-in-law. "But as long as we don't make it a habit and we make sure not to leave a mess I think it will be all right. Just this once."

She seemed to consider that for a long moment before stepping out of the room, patting her leg to beckon Solo to join them. "Can we eat in the living room instead? We could watch a movie or something."

It was on the tip of his tongue to ask if she had homework, but he stifled the question, there would be time enough for that later, this was more important. "We can but first we need to talk. Is that okay?"

Her steps faltered a bit as they walked side by side towards the stairs but she nodded. Leaving it at that he proceeded her down into the kitchen so he could load everything onto a tray. Celine's eyes widened a bit as she caught sight of the food.

"Are those cheeseburgers?"

A small sense of triumph welled up in him but he controlled it before his smile could show on his face, "They are. I would have made fries too, but we don't own a deep fryer and it takes too long in the oven."

"Why'd you make them at all?"

Ah, the question of the hour. Walking to the fridge he retrieved two sodas to add to the tray. "That is actually one of the things I want to talk to you about. I owe you an apology, Celine."

Crossing her arms over her chest she glared at him, "What'd you do?"

"It is more about what I didn't do. I never took the time to really stop and think how hard this has all been on you. Moving here, especially so soon after losing your mum, having to leave all your friends and your family in Colorado and start over here. Your sister and I getting married . . ." he stopped when he saw her swipe a hand under her eyes. "Celine?"

"It's not your fault," she shrugged, losing all bravado and looking like a lost little girl. "It's Mom. I miss her, but Karrine never wants to talk about her."

Empathy washed over him along with a fair heaping of guilt, this was one more thing he hadn't thought about. Of course, she missed her Mum, but Karrine was still so angry about the marriage contract that she had never even thought about talking to her sister about their shared loss. In fact, she had probably shut her down every time Celine tried to bring it up. Walking around the island he put both hands on the girl's shoulders like he would with Kennedy.

"I am so sorry, Cina. I never thought about that before. And as much as I wish I could, I can never give you back what you have lost." He took a second to choose his next words knowing they needed to be the right ones. "But maybe we could make a deal that can help us both out."

Her eyes narrowed again, replacing the sadness with suspicion, "What kind of deal?"

He smiled down at her, "The kind that says I promise, whenever you need a friend, or you want to talk about your mum, or your dad, or your life in Colorado, I will make time for you. I'll always make time to listen and talk with you. Deal?"

"What do I have to do?"

"Be a teenager," he smiled before adding, "And give your sister a break. She's trying. We both are, but neither of us has ever been guardians before. Maybe you could go easy on us?"

Mischief danced in her eyes as she stared back, "Probably not."

Laughing he took a chance and leaned in to hug her, "Fair enough, I suppose I did ask for that. Are you ready to eat?"

"As long as I get to pick the movie!"

He started to reply but his phone rang, and he grabbed it as Celine danced out of the room, announcing her triumph, "No romances!"

"No guarantees!"

With a chuckle, he accepted the call, "Steffan Dalton."

"Steffan, this is Ambassador Wiggins from the United States Embassy."

Straightening he moved to lean against the back of a stool, wondering why the U.S. Ambassador to Yagos was calling him at nearly, he glanced at the clock on the oven, nine o'clock at night. He knew the man, both through social circles and because of his business. It was amazing the people you got to know when you began working in the import-export world.

"Good evening Ambassador, how may I help you this evening?"

"Actually Steffan, it's about your wife."

Immediately the anger he had felt earlier was replaced with fear and he reached out to grab the granite island, "Karrine. Is she alright?"

"I'm afraid there's been an accident. She's in the hospital."

The ambassador kept talking but he only heard bits and pieces. Rock-climbing—good Samaritans—Mercy National—sorry. None of it made sense. It felt like he was drowning—fear, guilt, confusion, it was all washing over him in waves. He needed more facts but he was not sure he wanted to ask for them. Through the emotion, one thought pushed itself to the surface.

Celine.

Steffan did not remember thanking the Ambassador or hanging up the phone but he found himself standing in the doorway to the living room, looking at the teenager as she munched away on her cheeseburger and searched for a movie. Glancing up she grinned at him.

"Hey, I found a few options bu—Steffan? What is it?" She set the plate aside but didn't stand, instead she crossed her arms as if to protect herself from whatever was coming next, breaking his heart even more. "What's wrong?"

"Your sister. There's been an accident."

"No," she was already shaking her head as her eyes filled with tears, "No. She can't be dead! I can't lose her too!"

"She is not dead," he crossed the room and sat down on the couch beside her just as she flung herself at him, the sobs already overtaking her. Praying he was telling her the truth he rubbed his hand up and down her back. "She is not dead Cina but she's in the hospital. There was some sort of accident, I don't know the details yet."

"I can't lose her."

The words were muffled but he heard them clearly enough and he closed his eyes, wrapping his arms a little tighter around her as if to give her strength that he wasn't sure he possessed. "I know." They sat there for another moment, but he gently pushed her back and stood, pulling her up with him. "We need to go to the hospital; do you need to get anything to take with you?"

"No," she was still crying but she allowed him to lead her out of the room, stopping long enough to find his keys and wallet, and making sure Celine had her coat. Solo whined and tried to push his way outside when they opened the door. He started to scold the dog and put him back in the house but seeing the way the dog stayed by Celine's side he relented, he opened the back door of the car and waited while both girl and dog slipped inside.

Chapter 15

The ride to the hospital was both the longest and shortest of Steffan's life. He felt anything but prepared as he and Celine walked inside Mercy National Hospital, but she was gripping his hand as if her life depended on it. He determined at that moment to be strong for her, and his wife. No matter what they were about to face.

The first person he saw was a man sitting behind a plastic window, looking bored, so he walked up. "I am looking for my wife, Karrine Dalton," he paused. Had Karrine changed any of her paperwork to her married name? Probably not since they hadn't even discussed citizenship. That was probably why the American ambassador had called instead of the local police. Pushing aside the errant thoughts he tried to focus. "It may be under Karrine Sandor."

"How do you spell that?"

Celine shifted her feet impatiently at the question but stayed quiet. Steffan wanted to reach through the window and shove the guy out of the way so he could find the information himself. Instead, he carefully spelled out his wife's name and waited the painstaking long moments of explaining his relationship to

Karrine, again, until he was finally rewarded with the information of where they could wait until a doctor could come out and see them.

The elevator ride was silent and he was glad they didn't have any background music playing like so many places did. The waiting room wasn't very big but large enough that the few people inside were able to spread out and have their own space. The walls were sparse, with neutral pictures of flowers and mountains hung at intervals against the white background. Gray plastic chairs looked uncomfortable at best and a few blue couches were too basic to add much color to the sterile room. Harsh fluorescent lights showed the stains on the gray flooring and emphasized how pale Celine was as tears continued to roll down her cheeks. Leading her to a set of chairs with a good line of sight to the door he waited for her to sit down before starting to pace, keeping an eye on the doorway so he would know the moment the doctor walked in.

The first time a woman in a white coat walked in he stopped but she walked past him to a young couple who was waiting on the opposite side of the room, speaking to them for a few moments before leading them away. Twenty minutes later a nurse came to the door and he stilled again.

"Is the family of Leeland Parks here?"

A teenager and an older man both stood, and she motioned for them to join her. Steffan started pacing again.

More people came into the waiting room, some looked scared, some sad and a few just seemed numb as if they didn't know how to react. Nurses and doctors came in and out, but no one seemed to have information about Karrine.

Finally, after more than an hour of pacing, he sat down next to Celine, noting for the first time that the teenager had managed to pull her knees up close and rest her head on her wadded up coat so she could doze off. Considering the emotional rollercoaster of the day she had endured, and the ridiculously long wait they were facing he was glad she was getting some rest.

For the first time since the ambassador's call, he realized he hadn't prayed. A few short pleas in the car about not letting Celine lose someone else, about clearing the traffic so they could get there safely, and even a muttered word here and there about sending someone in with information, but he had not really poured out his thoughts and fears to his Heavenly Father.

Propping elbows on his knees he clasped his hands and started to do just that. It was a struggle to put his emotions into coherent words and he finally gave up. He just mentally reciting Scripture verses he had memorized over the years and thinking about all the stories in the Bible of sick people being healed. His mind tried to remind him of the people that he had known over the years who hadn't been healed, despite earnest prayers, but he ignored those thoughts, knowing he needed to try to stay positive for Celine's sake if nothing else.

"What are you doing?"

"Praying," Steffan opened his eyes and tried to smile as the teenager disentangled herself from the chair so she could stretch. "Did you sleep all right?"

"Not really." She shrugged, "Does it help?"

Surprised by the question he took a second to answer, "Prayer? Yeah, it does."

"How or why?"

Wondering how much Celine really knew about Christianity, despite her sister's claim to faith, he searched for the right words. "Because I know that no matter what is going on in life God is always there to listen and He understands exactly what I am going through."

Celine looked skeptical but just nodded, "I'm thirsty. Do you think there's a place to get some water around here?"

"We can probably ask at the nurse's station," he stood too but she waved him off.

"I can go myself, you should wait here in case someone comes in about Karrine while I'm gone."

Reluctant to let her go alone despite the fact she was a teenager and plenty old enough he nodded, "Okay. Come right back."

With a roll of her eyes, she headed to the door and he sat back down, staring at the doorway again as if willing someone, anyone, to come in and tell him what was going on with his wife.

"It never gets easier whether they're four or forty," the old man who was sitting along the opposite wall moved closer when Steffan glanced over at him. "I have three kids myself, eight grandkids, and two great-grandkids on the way."

Not sure why this man had decided to talk to him, he reminded himself to be polite to this elderly man. He could tell he was American from his accent. "That is quite the family."

"Sure is, and they're wonderful, every one of them. Crazy and loud, mercy are they loud! But they're still wonderful. How 'bout you? Is the girl yours?"

Confused he glanced towards the door where the man pointed as understanding dawned, "Not exactly, she is my sister-in-law."

"Ah, well sometimes they're no better. My wife's little brother was more like one of our own kids most days. Still, it never gets easier. Once a kid gets in your heart they just never let go, even when it's hard. And then one day you look back and realize you never want them to."

"Karrine Sandor's family?" A doctor appeared at the door and he stood but as much as he wanted to know what was going on with his wife, he took the time to turn back and offer his hand to the man.

"Thank you, sir, you are correct. She is in my heart."

"She'll make you proud son," the man got to his feet and shook his hand, his grip still strong despite his age. "She'll make you angry and she'll make you sad, but she'll also make you proud. So, you make sure you do the same for her, ya hear?"

"Thank you, sir," he saw Celine return out of the corner of his eye and let go of the man's hand, but as he approached the doctor the man's words stayed in his mind, like water absorbing into the dry ground of his heart. This was part of choosing to love. No matter what happened with Karrine and what the doctors had to say, Celine was not only his responsibility but a person God had put into his life to shape and mold her as she moved into adulthood. It might be the most important task he had ever been given.

"Are you Karrine Sandor's family?" The doctor asked as he approached, just as Celine came back and joined them.

"I am her husband, Steffan Dalton," he explained, "This is her sister, Celine."

"Fine," the doctor looked tired but he motioned for them to move over to the side where they could talk. "Your wife was in a rock-climbing accident. From what I've been told she had an accident while she was climbing."

"That doesn't sound like Krin."

The doctor glanced at Celine, "It was dark, maybe she slipped—the point is something happened. Her rope caught her but she was thrown into the rock face. She suffered a concussion, a dislocated shoulder, broken leg, fractured hip, and her rib broke and punctured a lung."

"Will she be okay?" He felt Celine grab his hand and he wondered if she was trying to offer strength or seeking it herself.

"I don't know," the doctor admitted. "We've done everything we can, but your wife is currently under medical sedation. The next forty-eight hours are critical."

"Can we see her?"

The man looked hesitant but after glancing between the two of them he finally nodded, "Yes but just for a moment. Even though she's unconscious we don't need people in there overwhelming her." The doctor looked at them both and softened his tone, "Besides, you two look like you could use some rest of your own. You should both go home and try to sleep. This is not going to be a short road to recovery."

"I'm not going anywhere!" Celine objected but Steffan just put a hand on her shoulder to calm her.

"And I'm not going to make you, but we did leave Solo in the car. If both of us are going to stay here then we will have to call someone to come pick him up." His head started to pound as he thought of all the people he needed to contact. None of the family knew of Karrine's accident. He'd been so focused on just getting to the hospital and then waiting for information that he hadn't even thought about calling them.

"Why don't I take you to see Ms. Sandor," the doctor interrupted. "Maybe then you can figure out who you need to contact and how to move forward. It may be easier if you have family members take shifts here at the hospital with her."

"Thank you, Doctor," Steffan kept one hand on Celine's shoulder as they followed the doctor down the white-walled hallway, not so much to lead her as to offer his support.

His thoughts whirled as he tried to mentally make a list of everyone he needed to contact. There was his family, hers, Celine's school to tell them she wouldn't be in the next day, and so on. *Do I even have a number for her family in Colorado?*

Too caught up in his lists and thoughts he almost ran into the doctor when he suddenly stopped in front of an open door with a closed curtain. "I need to warn you before we go in that she's in very serious condition. She's hooked up to several monitors, I.V.'s and so on. I don't want it to scare you when you see her."

He was addressing both of them but Steffan's only concern was for Celine. After everyone the teenager had lost, he hated the idea of her seeing her sister lying unconscious in a hospital bed.

"Are you sure you want to go in Cina?"

She glanced up, trying to appear brave in spite of the tears spilling down her cheeks again. "She's my sister. I can't just not see her. She'd be there for me."

It was tempting to take the decision out of her hands and banish her to the waiting room in an attempt to protect her, but he stopped himself, knowing she needed to be the one to make this decision, so he nodded permission at the doctor. The man reached up to draw back the curtain and Steffan's breath froze in his lungs. Celine made a whimpering noise and ran to Karrine's side, looking up at the doctor.

"Can I touch her? Can I hold her hand?"

"Go ahead, just be gentle, and make sure it's her right hand, her left side sustained most of the injuries."

"Karrine," Celine took her hand, crying quietly as she murmured to her big sister, begging her to wake up.

Steffan couldn't tear his gaze away. Karrine's blonde hair was barely visible beneath the bandages wrapped around her head. Her left leg was in a cast and pulled up off the bed, suspended over her body, presumably to keep it from moving. Her arm was bandaged, and monitors and tubes seemed to be coming out of her from all directions. The fact that Celine found room to stand next to her was something of a miracle.

"How did this happen?" His voice was so quiet he was surprised the doctor heard him, much less bothered to answer.

"The truth is I don't know. She really is quite lucky to be alive."

Lucky? He wanted to argue—this wasn't what luck looked like, but he couldn't find the words.

"If she hadn't been wearing a helmet then the impact probably would've killed her."

"I don't understand how this happened," he turned his back on the room, it was too painful to see Karrine like this. "Is she going to live?"

"It's too early to say," the doctor put a hand on Steffan's shoulder. "You really should call someone, it always helps to have loved ones here when you're dealing with a tragedy like this."

"Right, okay." Blindly he dug out his cell phone as he tried to decide who to call. What loved ones was he supposed to contact for his wife? Most of her family lived on the other side of the world and it wasn't like they had any mutual friends to contact. They hardly knew each other after all.

What would he do if someone needed to make medical decisions for her? He couldn't tell them what her wishes would be, they had never talked about it. They had never talked about anything. Celine might know but he could not – would not force the teenager to make those kinds of decisions. She had been through so much already, he was the adult, and, guardian or not, he needed to be the one taking care of Celine, and Karrine. His dad was right, they were his family and right now his family needed him. He was just going to have to pray that he had the strength to be there for them. That was the only way any of them were going to survive this ordeal.

Please God let Karrine survive.

"Is there someone I can call for you?"

He had not realized until that moment that the doctor was still there, apparently concerned about leaving him. Gathering his wits he forced himself to shake his head and hold up his phone, "No, thanks. I can handle it."

Giving a nod the doctor walked away and with a heavy heart, he went to his contacts list, selecting the button for Cam. Maybe his best friend should not be his first call, but it was the middle of the night. If he was going to be there for Celine, stay with Karrine, and contact everyone, he was going to need reinforcements.

*

"I'll stay here and keep an eye on Celine, you should start calling people."

Steffan nodded, knowing his friend was right. Cam had come to the hospital after his call and picked up Solo so he wasn't left in the car any longer. Then he had come back to see what else he could do. He had brought coffee and dinner since neither Steffan nor Celine had finished their burgers, not that either of them was able to eat, but the caffeine had helped some. Finally, he had distracted the distraught teenager by having her go through Karrine's phone so they could make a list of numbers for Steffan to start on.

"Have I said thank you?"

"Doesn't matter, I wouldn't be anywhere else. You should start with Karrine's family in the States so they can make arrangements to get here right away. Everyone else is already in Yagos."

"Yeah, okay," taking another long taste of his coffee he glanced at Celine who had fallen asleep again, her jacket acting as a blanket. "I am going to head outside, I do not want to wake her up."

"She's going to be okay you know."

"Who?" Steffan turned tired eyes on his friend but in his mind, he was picturing Karrine, stretched out on the hospital bed hooked up to countless machines and paler than he had ever seen her. "Karrine or Cina? Because right now I am not sure either of them will ever be okay again."

"Keep your faith, it's the only way you're going to get through this. I should know."

Not sure what to say to that he just nodded and walked out of the room. The hospital was cool and he wished he had asked Cam to bring him a jacket. The hallways were lined with color-coded strips of tape, telling him what turns he needed to take to make it to the main lobby, and finally, he found the exit. He was not sure what time it was but it was still dark and even colder outside than in, so he figured it was sometime in the middle of the night. Pulling out his phone he dialed the first number and waited for it to pick up.

"Hello?"

"Tessa? This is Steffan Dalton," he hesitated before adding, "Karrine's husband."

"I know who you are Steffan," she informed him. "Is everything okay? It must be the middle of the night over there!"

"Uh, no," he scuffed his shoe against the ground and wondered how to break the news, "It's not."

"It's not the middle of the night?" She sounded more amused than anything and he hated the fact that he was going to ruin her good mood with his next words.

"No. It is the middle of the night, but everything is not okay."

There was a long pause and he heard what sounded like a door being shut, "What is it? Celine? I know she's been having a tough time. Did something happen with her? Is she okay?"

"Celine is fine Tessa," he took a deep breath and begged God for the words.

"Okay . . ." she drew out the word. "Then what is it?"

"It's Karrine, she was in an accident." He plunged ahead before she could ask any questions, "She was rock-climbing and it was getting dark, they think she slipped but they're keeping her medically sedated so we don't know for sure. We are at the hospital and-"

"I'm on my way."

"Wh-what?" He wasn't sure he had heard her correctly.

"I'm on my way," she repeated. "If you will call Aunt Jules and Uncle Andy, I'll tell my parents and grandparents. I'll let you know when I'll be arriving. What hospital is it?"

He gave her the necessary information then added, "Thank you, Tessa."

"She's my best friend Steffan, and my cousin. You couldn't keep me away if you tried."

Hanging up the phone he gave himself a moment to breathe

and prayed for strength before he dialed the next number on the list.

*

Steffan woke up slowly as if he were trying to surface from deep underwater—things registered one at a time. First, the pain and the odd angle of his neck, next, the light that was bright enough to be noticed even with his eyes closed, finally the fact that he was sitting, not lying down. Blinking, he tried to orient himself in the strange surroundings, when his gaze fell on Celine, curled up in a chair next to him he remembered the circumstances that had brought them to the hospital the night before.

"You're awake," Cam handed him a cup of coffee, keeping his voice low so as not to disturb the slumbering teenager. "How'd you sleep?"

"Fine, I guess. Any word?"

"I would've woken you if there was."

Not having a reply to that he just nodded, "How long has she been out?"

"Celine? Almost an hour, she dozed on and off for a bit but kept waking up to ask if there was any news. I promised her I'd wake her up if there was any change, I think once she finally accepted that would have to be good enough, she was able to really rest."

"Good," he rubbed a hand over his tired eyes. "This has been really hard for her."

"For both of you," Cam corrected, "It is your wife in that hospital bed after all."

With his defenses down and the slumbering teenager not at risk of overhearing Steffan was freer with his responses then he would have been otherwise, "Wife in name only. The only time we have ever so much as kissed was at our wedding."

Cam's lips twisted, "In name only can have more power than you would think. And not being intimate doesn't mean there aren't emotions involved, even if it's only a one-sided commitment."

"How did you do it for so long," he asked the question that had been burning in his mind for years. "I know you said you chose to love her and be faithful but how did you stay sane with all of that?"

"It doesn't matter," Cam ignored the question with just a roll of his shoulders, "It's not the same situation as what you have. You and Karrine have had a rough start but she's still here and when she wakes up you have a chance to make this work. Don't waste that opportunity, if you do, you'll both regret it for the rest of your lives."

Glancing at Celine he studied her even breathing for a long moment before voicing the fear that had settled in his heart since the Ambassador's phone call, "What if she doesn't wake up?"

*

Five Days Later

"We're going to try to bring your wife out of the sedation now that the swelling in her brain has gone down."

Steffan glanced back at the assorted family members sitting in the waiting room, talking quietly while they waited for him to come to relay the information. Celine had her head together with Kennedy as the older teenager tried to distract her. Tessa was talking with his parents while Cam spoke with Andy, the only other member of Karrine's extended family currently at the hospital. Others had come and gone in shifts over the last few days.

"What are her chances, Doctor? Honestly." He looked back at the man whose kind eyes had too many shadows in them. "Is my wife going to die?"

The doctor stuck his hands in his lab coat and looked at the ground as if considering whether or not to answer. "Honestly there are no guarantees, I think she has a good chance, but when and if she wakes up she has a very long road ahead of her and it is going to be the hardest thing she has ever done in her life."

Thinking of what he knew of Karrine's life up until now he shook his head, "You do not know what she's been through. She can do this."

"I think you're right Mr. Dalton," the doctor agreed after a moment. "She's a fighter or she wouldn't have made it this far, but I need to caution you about the emotional toll that recovery and rehabilitation can take on a patient. It may not be a question of whether or not she *can* do this but whether or not she will."

Again Steffan looked over his shoulder at the people that had gathered and prayed his next words would be true, "She has tons of family cheering her on. If they have any say in it, she will make a full recovery and probably do it in record time too."

The doctor smiled just as his name was called over the intercom, "I hope you're right Mr. Dalton, excuse me, I'll send someone down to explain about the process more in a while so we can get the necessary paperwork out of the way."

"Any news?" Celine asked as soon as he came back in. Regaining his seat next to her Steffan made sure his focus was solely on the teenager but spoke loud enough to include the other people in the room who were waiting for his explanation.

"The doctors want to try to start bringing her out of the sedation today."

"Try?" Tessa interrupted, "Is there some reason it won't work?"

He glanced over at her, recognizing the family resemblance in the straight posture, crossed arms, and slightly defiant expression on her face. "Karrine has a long road ahead of her, a lot of what happens from here on out is going to be up to her."

"You're saying she may not want to wake up?" Celine asked, refocusing his attention on her and reminding him that she had to be his first priority right now, come what may.

Praying for the right words he did his best to smile, "One thing I know about your sister is that she loves you more than anything in this world and she will do whatever it takes to make sure she gets to watch you grow up. Of that, I have no doubt."

Several echoes of agreement came from the others before conversation resumed and Steffan leaned back in his chair, content to let the noise flow around him. When the nurse came to get him, Andy stood also and followed him out of the room. Not sure what to think he kept one eye on his wife's uncle, who gave him some space, while the nurse explained what they were going to do and had him sign the proper paperwork. By the time all was said and done, Andy was still there, apparently waiting to talk to him.

"Is there something on your mind sir?"

With a nod of his head, Andy indicated they should walk down the hallway, going several feet before beginning to speak. "You told Celine Krin would do everything she could to wake up so she can watch her grow up."

Confused by the statement he nodded, "And she would. Do you not agree?"

"Absolutely, Karrine would do anything for her sister. But my question is, is her sister the only reason she has to wake up?"

Uncomfortable with the question he pulled on the neck of his shirt, wondering how a collarless t-shirt could suddenly seem so suffocating. "Of course not, she has lots of people who care about her."

"That's not what I'm asking and you know it," Andy's tone stayed friendly but held a note of steel, warning that he expected an answer and he was not going to walk away without one.

Weighing the options in his mind Steffan finally relented. Hedging around this topic would only prolong the conversation and he needed to get back to the waiting room in case the doctors came to talk to him. "You know the circumstances under which Karrine and I got married. I guess I am not really sure what kind of answer you are expecting me to give you here."

"A truthful one, you've been married for a couple of months now. I was hoping you would have at least started to make things work. Is there any indication that you two are going to be able to have a happy marriage?"

The same question he had been asking himself since before their wedding day but somehow talking about this with Karrine's uncle felt wrong—like a betrayal of some kind and although he wasn't sure how he felt about his wife exactly, he knew he did not want to hurt her. "Honestly sir, I am not sure how that is any of your business."

"It's my business because she's my niece and I want her to be happy," he replied frankly.

Steffan turned that over in his brain, "So do I, which is why I am going to have to decline to answer. Karrine may not be awake right now but if she was then I doubt she would approve of us talking about her this way."

Andy stopped in the hallway and pinned him against the sterile, white wall with a hard stare. Steffan forced himself to stand his ground, staring back. Finally, Andy smiled, "Well, maybe there's hope for your marriage after all. Come on, let's head back before anyone comes looking for us."

Suddenly exhausted from all the emotions of the last few days he could do little more than a nod and follow Karrine's Uncle back towards the waiting room to wait for someone to take them up to Karrine's room.

Chapter 16

Something was wrong. Karrine's mind struggled to assimilate the information as things began to register. A far away, but insistent noise that sounded like the beeping of a machine. A low murmur that could have been voices. Everything was dark, oppressing darkness that went beyond physical light and seemed to penetrate to even the deepest recess of her mind. She tried to push through it but she couldn't seem to find the light.

"Is she waking up?" The man's deep voice seemed familiar but she could not place it.

"Give her some time." This voice seemed different, authoritative, and unfamiliar.

"How long is this supposed to take?" The familiar voice spoke again with impatience, and maybe some worry in his tone.

I'm right here! I can hear you! She wanted to shout but she couldn't get her voice to work.

"Doctor," this was a female speaking, but who was she talking to? Why was there a doctor there? Was she sick? The woman said something else that didn't make any sense to Karrine, something about monitors and medication.

She tried to open her eyes, to see if they were talking about her or someone else. To try to sort out what they were saying, but her eyelids felt so heavy and they wouldn't open no matter how much she tried to force them too. She felt herself slipping now, back into the darkness. She tried to fight it, to speak or blink, anything to let them know she could hear them but it was so hard and she was so tired. Finally, she just let herself sink back into the abyss.

"I'm sorry Mr. Dalton," the doctor put his hand on Steffan's shoulder.

"I do not understand, I thought she was supposed to wake up now." He tried to keep his frustration under control but knew that some of it leaked into his voice. He just wanted this nightmare to be over.

"We've weaned her off the medication that was keeping her sedated and there were spikes on the monitor suggesting she was waking up but we can't force it. She has to wake up on her own. Until she does . . . well, the only thing we can do is wait."

"All we have done is wait!"

"And we'll have to wait some more," Dr. Wageoner said patiently. "We can't force her to wake up if she's not ready. And even if we could that might do more damage than good."

The neurologist's explanation allowed him just enough emotional distance to get his temper back under control and he rubbed the back of his neck, staring at the tiled floor as he nodded. "Yeah, okay, okay, I understand. Do you know when she might wake up?"

Dr. Wageoner gave him a sympathetic look, "Unfortunately there's no way to tell, she could wake up in an hour or never. It's all up to her now."

Steffan stared at his wife. Even unconscious and still bandaged up from her accident she was stunning. Tessa had combed her hair out so it lay around her face and she looked completely at peace in the hospital bed, an expression he had never seen on her face in the short time they had known each other.

Seeming to sense his shift in mood, the doctor and nurse both slipped out with a murmur of being back later to check on Karrine. Sitting down hard in the chair next to her bed he reached out and took his wife's hand—a liberty he doubted he would have taken if she had been awake.

"Please wake up sweetheart, I know this marriage is anything but conventional but I am still hoping we can work it out. I'm not asking for you to wake up for that though. You have got a whole family out there in the waiting room just waiting, praying, and hoping you'll open those beautiful brown eyes and come back to them. Not the least of which is Celine. She is trying so hard to be strong Krin but she needs her big sister. She needs *you*. I am doing the best I can for her and so are our families, but you are the one she really needs. If she loses you, after everything else she has been through . . ." he shook his head, unwilling to finish the thought. "Just wake up Krin, for her sake if nothing else. Please, just wake up."

Bowing his head he took some long moments to pray, begging God to heal his wife and give him a second chance to be a good husband. He wanted to stay, holding her hand, waiting for her eyes to flicker, and laying his burden at the feet of the Lord, but the two families in the waiting room still needed an update.

Feeling far older than twenty-three he pushed himself out of the chair and leaned over his wife, brushing a kiss across her forehead and squeezing her hand one last time. Turning towards the door he paused at a sound that sounded like a rustle of sheets but when he looked back, Karrine was as still as ever.

Brushing it off as wishful thinking he headed out the door.

*

Three Days Later

"All right Steffan, what's so important that we had to leave the hospital to have this conversation?" Donovan Franklin sat down in the chair across from his desk. "And why are we meeting in your office instead of at your house?"

"The office is closer to the hospital in case anything happens," he explained, coming around to sit in the chair next to his wife's uncle. "And I did not want to talk where we could be overheard. I need your help on a legal issue."

Don's chin lowered just a bit and he pinned Steffan with a hard glare, "You in some kind of trouble son?"

If he hadn't been so stressed he might have smiled at the question, "No sir. It's about Celine. I found out a while back that because of the way the marriage contract was written I'm not Celine's legal guardian, only Karrine is."

"That's right," Don drew his words out slowly, "I haven't thought about it but I remember now. It was done to protect Celine. Since we didn't know what kind of man you would become there was a clause that would prevent Karrine from having to go through with the marriage and this clause that you wouldn't have any legal control over Celine. Of course, none of us could have predicted Brandi's death or that you would even be placed in this position."

"Understood, but with Karrine's accident I'm worried what would happen to Celine if something should happen to her sister."

Don crossed one knee over the other and settled back into the wooden padded chair, "And you think you have a solution?"

"I think she should stay here," he silently thanked God that his voice had not wavered but Don's stern gaze had him tacking on a prayer for the right words to convince this man he was the best guardian for the teenager. "Sir, when Karrine and I got married I knew I was taking on Celine as my sister but also my responsibility, and together we would be raising her. I believe God put me in that position for a reason. More than anything I want Karrine to wake up and not have any of this be an issue, but I have to face the reality that, as much as I want it to, that might not be the outcome. Or if she does wake up she may not be in any condition to raise a teenager."

"So you're saying there's a possibility that your wife could be brain-damaged. You think taking on the responsibility not only for her but also the responsibility of raising a teenager, and running your own business, plus keeping an eye on the girls' assets seems like a good plan for your life? You would be giving up everything Steffan. That's a tough decision for someone as young as yourself.

We're not just talking about a few months here; we could be talking about the rest of your life."

He hesitated, up until now he had tried to avoid thinking too deeply of the possibility of Karrine being brain-damaged but what if she was? Could he handle taking care of her and raising Celine? Plus keep his business running? How would he find the time? Just the thought of it was overwhelming.

Love is a choice.

Anchoring his elbows on his legs he leaned forward and looked Don in the eye, "Sir, Karrine and I made vows to love, cherish, and care for each other in sickness and in health. No matter the outcome, if she wakes up, I will be by her side every step of the way. I also made a promise to Celine that I would be there for her. I will not turn my back on her now. If it means hiring someone to run my business or figuring out how to work from home then fine, that's what I will do. But I will not have Celine's life upturned again and send her away as if she is not wanted here. She is my family, my responsibility, and I will keep my promise to her, no matter what."

"You can still be there for her from afar," Don countered. "Colorado has been her home since she was a baby. We're her family too and it's not as if you would be sending her to strangers."

For a moment he tried to imagine letting Celine move back to America, she had said she wanted to at one point. Would it be better for her?

Finally, he sat back against his chair. "I guess we would have to talk about it. If the best thing for Celine and Karrine was to go back to Colorado then I could either move the company or sell it so we were closer to their family, your family."

"But your family is here."

"Karrine and Celine are my family now," Steffan contradicted, feeling the reality of that finally start to set in. "My parents and sister would understand that I need to do what is best for them. If that's moving to Colorado then so be it, but I don't see any situation where sending Celine away is what would be best for her."

Don uncrossed his legs and stood, "I agree. I'm glad to hear you've thought through this and obviously prayed about it. I'll look into the contract and do some research, I'm not very familiar with Yagos family law, our firm's specialty is international business, but I'm sure we can get the correct paperwork into place to have you appointed as Celine's guardian too, so no matter what happens to Karrine, now or in the future, Celine's guardianship is settled."

Reaching out a hand he finally felt like he could take a breath, "Thank you, sir."

"Thank you, Steffan, thank you for loving our girls. I know the feelings might not be there yet but the actions are and sometimes that's more important than anything else. You really are the man our family has prayed you would be."

The words made him stop, not sure he had heard correctly. "You prayed for me?"

Don's eyes grew moist and he brought up his other hand to put it over their clasped ones. "Every day since we learned about the marriage contract. And we haven't stopped since the wedding."

Taken aback he opened his mouth but no words came. Finally, he just nodded, completely at a loss for words.

Apparently understanding, Don just released his hand and took a step back, "I'm sure you're drowning in work from having to take so much time off. If you need to take care of some of it we can cover things at the hospital."

Steffan glanced around his office, the desk was overflowing, the monitor was covered in notes and his email would probably take a week to clear out his inbox. It would be so much easier to just stay here for a while and numb his emotions.

You need to show Christ to that girl, not just as a believer but as her husband.

His Dad's words came back to him and he walked around his desk to retrieve his laptop. "I'll bring this with me, anything I am not able to do from the hospital can wait until Karrine is out of the woods. Family comes first."

Don's eyes lit with approval as he nodded, "Then we'd better head back over there I guess."

*

The microwave was beeping. At least she thought it was the microwave, Celine must have been heating something up, but why wasn't she getting it out? Maybe it was the washer. Or the doorbell? Perhaps it was her alarm.

She flung out a hand, trying to reach it so she could shut off the irritating sound, but her hand didn't connect with the alarm clock.

Had she rolled on the bed and was further away from the clock then she'd thought?

"Doctor, she's moving again."

"Ms. Sandor? Can you hear us? Karrine? Where's her husband?"

Husband? She frowned at the thought, trying to figure out what the strangers were talking about? Whose husband were they talking about? And why was there a doctor in her bedroom? The darkness started to overwhelm her again and she could feel herself being pulled back asleep but this time she fought it with everything she had.

"I don't know if he's back but her sister's here. Should I get her?"

Celine. Wherever she was Celine was there, that was good. Now she just needed to open her eyes. Something had obviously happened, even if she couldn't remember the details she needed to wake up and make sure Celine was all right.

"Check for her husband first, she needs someone with her but her sister's young, I don't want her in here if something happens."

"Yes, Doctor."

If something happens? That didn't sound good. She needed to wake up but her eyes felt so heavy. *Help me, God.* The prayer was a desperate cry for help but it must have worked because suddenly she felt her eyes flicker open just a tiny bit to find a middle-aged man in dark blue scrubs and a white lab coat staring down at her.

"Well, it's nice to finally see the color of your eyes, Ms. Sandor. It's been a while."

She opened her mouth to reply but her mouth felt dry and her lips cracked when she moved them making it difficult to speak. The door opened again and she glanced over to see a nurse walk in with a handsome man right behind her. Relief showed on his face as memories assaulted her.

Steffan. Her husband. This was the man they had been talking about. But that still didn't explain how she had ended up in a hospital. At least she was assuming it was a hospital room she was in.

"Karrine," Steffan moved to her side and reached out like he was going to touch her face but hesitated and took her hand instead. "I am so glad you are awake. You had us all worried."

Moving her lips again she tried to find her voice. The nurse, seeming to understand her dilemma, grabbed a glass of water off a nearby tray, and helped her take a drink through the straw.

"Take it slow, you've been through a lot. You don't want to overwhelm your system."

"Don't try to talk," Steffan added his own words of caution to the nurse's. "Right now, it is just enough that you're awake."

Ignoring his advice she took a moment to gather her energy before finally croaking out, "What . . . happened?"

He glanced at the doctor as if wanting someone else to explain but after a second he looked down into her eyes again and squeezed her hand. "You were in a rock-climbing accident. They had to put you under medical sedation until you were stable."

Rock-climbing accident? Her mind tried to assimilate the information as bits and pieces started coming back to her. She had picked Celine up from school and then they were fighting. Steffan had interrupted. She had yelled at him and he had yelled back. She had stormed out of the house and then . . . that was it. That was all she could remember.

"Karrine?" Steffan was staring at her with a worried expression marring his handsome features. Had she ever noticed how handsome he was before? He had a strong jaw, and his eyes, a beautiful chocolate color, but there were deep circles under them that she didn't think had been there before. A closer examination showed frown lines on his forehead and he looked like he might have lost a few pounds from his already lean physique. What had happened to him? Had this all been because of her accident? Did he really care that much?

Too rattled to try to sort through those questions and not brave enough to voice them she focused on gathering information. "How long?"

Steffan's lips turned down at the corner as if he didn't want to answer but after a moment he did. "It has been eight days."

Eight days! A jolt shot through her at the answer and for the first time, she realized her leg was in a cast and elevated. Her arm, similarly, was in a sling. She had yet to register the pain and could only assume it was from whatever pain medication they had her on. Judging from the injuries she could see the coma had probably been a blessing to keep the pain at bay and give her body a chance to heal but it made her wonder—how bad had the accident been to cause so much injury?

Celine. If she had been in a coma for so long her sister had to be out of her mind with worry. The teenager had been through so much in her short life the last thing she should have to deal with was this mess.

"I need to see Celine." She told Steffan, but already she could feel herself starting to get tired again. It had taken so much energy for her to wake up now she was quickly fading but she desperately wanted to stay awake long enough to see her little sister and assure her she was okay. She owed Celine that much.

"I will get her now," he reassured her. "Can you stay awake that long?"

It was too hard to answer so she just nodded, sending an aching pain through her entire body at the motion. She welcomed the pain, using it to keep her awake for just a little bit longer.

"Karrine?" Only a moment later Celine hesitated at the door, looking so young and vulnerable that it broke her heart. Gathering what little strength she had left she managed to smile.

"Hey sweetie, what are you doing all the way over there? Come give me a hug."

That was all the encouragement the teenager needed to fly across the room and give her sister an exuberant, but gentle, thanks to Steffan's reminder, hug. "I was so scared you weren't going to wake up."

Emotion clogged the back of her throat making it hard to speak but she stroked Celine's hair and forced the words out anyway. "I'm awake now, let's focus on that. I'm not going anywhere, okay?"

Celine sat back and studied her intently as if trying to reassure herself that everything was, indeed, right with the world again before she finally nodded. "Steffan prayed for you."

Not sure what to do with the information she glanced at her husband but he didn't meet her gaze. What was that about? Instead, he put a hand on Celine's shoulder.

"We should let your sister get some more rest. Why don't we tell the others the good news?"

Karrine expected her sister to argue but she just nodded and gave her one more hug before standing. "I'm so glad you're awake."

"Me too."

Steffan waited for Celine to leave then turned back to her, "Do you need anything before I go? Some more water?"

It was then she realized that both the nurse and the doctor had left the room at some point, leaving her alone with her husband but she was too tired to be uncomfortable. Shaking her head she let herself relax against the pillows, hoping the pain would recede again and let her sleep. Already the exhaustion was pulling at her. "No, thank you for taking care of Celine and . . . for being here."

She thought she heard him reply, something like, "You are my wife Karrine, I wouldn't be anywhere else," but sleep came up to claim her and she couldn't quite be sure if it was real or just a dream.

Chapter 17

Two Weeks Later

"What are you doing here already?"

Steffan looked up with blurry eyes as he tried to focus in on the frowning face of his secretary. Glancing at the clock on the computer screen he groaned out loud, "I am not sure if you can still count it as 'already'. I never went home."

"What? What about Celine? When I left you said you were going to have dinner with her tonight after you took her to see Karrine at the hospital."

"I did," he rubbed his tired eyes and wondered how many cups of coffee was considered to be too much to be healthy. Deciding he had already far surpassed the limit he threw caution to the wind and walked out to make a fresh pot, Mrs. Coren trailing behind, waiting for an explanation. "Tessa picked Celine up from school then took her to see her sister before bringing her here. I took her out to dinner then dropped her off at home, then swung by the hospital to check on Karrine before coming back to the office to do some more work. I am still at least a week behind even after working all night."

"And you think neglecting your family will help you catch up on work Steffan Dalton?" She took on that scolding tone she had used when he was a kid and she had caught him racing with Cam down the hallways of his Dad's office. "It won't. It will just mean you have to play catch up at home too and that will be far more complicated than taking care of things here at the office."

"Getting too far behind in work and losing clients so my company goes bankrupt, and I am not being able to provide for my family will make things far more complicated too," he retorted as he searched drawers trying to find the blasted coffee filters. He had managed to find them a couple of hours ago when he made the last pot. So where were they now?

"There is no danger of that happening and you know it," she pushed him out of the way and reached over to grab the filters from the top of the microwave, had he left them there? Deftly she added the proper scoops and filled the pot with water while she lectured him. "Your clients know you and they know you will follow through. You have created a good team here who would have no problem stepping up to share the burden, you just have to learn to utilize them better. You're a married man now Steffan, you can't be staying at the office all night."

"My wife is not even home, she doesn't even know I was here all night." He knew the argument was a mistake the moment he saw the glitter of triumph in her eyes but it was too late to take them back now.

"Exactly my point. She may not be home but you also have a teenage girl to think about and she is aware that you weren't home last night. How do you think Celine must have felt when her cousin had to take her to school this morning? Hmm? Her sister's in the hospital and her brother-in-law is burying himself in work. That's no way for that girl to grow up. If you want her to feel loved you have to be there for her like your parents were for you. No matter how busy they got."

Her argument hit its mark. The night of Karrine's accident he had promised to be there for Celine, and to be fair he had made an effort. Their relationship was flourishing and even he and Karrine were starting to communicate more. He visited the hospital every day and though she always seemed a little surprised to see him she always greeted him with a smile. They talked mostly about her recovery and Celine. It wasn't much but it was better than where they had been. Maybe, just maybe, they were on their way to having a real relationship but not if he managed to mess it up by staying at the office at all hours.

"All right, you win. I will finish up what absolutely cannot wait then see if Keith can take on some of the work so I can take the afternoon off and spend it with my wife before I pick Celine up from school. Agreed?"

Never one to give too much ground, Mrs. Coren just harrumphed and marched back to her desk, grumbling all the way about insolent kids who thought they were far more grown-up then they were. Shaking his head indulgently he poured himself a cup of coffee and took a grateful sip before heading back to his own desk to try to get as much done in as short a time as possible.

*

"I'm so glad you're here," Karrine smiled when Tessa muted the T.V. and repositioned herself in what looked to be a very uncomfortable hospital chair.

"I wouldn't be anywhere else." She had repeated that same sentence probably a dozen times each day but Karrine still felt the need to thank her cousin for flying across the globe to be at her bedside. Not to mention taking extended time off from work to stay while she recovered. "The moment Steffan called me I started looking at tickets. I was even willing to fly coach," Tessa made a face, and Karrine giggled, enjoying the moment almost enough to not regret the pain.

"Now that would be torture."

"Tell me about it," Tessa gave a dramatic sigh before straightening in her chair. "But you know I'm not the only one who's stayed at your bedside Krin."

Thinking about her husband she fiddled with the thin brown hospital blanket, staring at the worn fabric intently. "I know."

"He cares about you." Tessa waited a moment but when Karrine didn't reply she pushed a little further. "And I think you're starting to care about him too, am I wrong?"

It took everything in her to gather up the courage to shake her head, "No, you're not. I just . . . I'm not sure what to do about it?"

"Well, you could start by getting to know him."

Get to know him. She turned that idea over in her head for a long moment. It seemed so simple but weren't you supposed to get to know each other while you were dating? Not after you'd been married for, she did some quick math, two and a half months? "How are you supposed to get to know someone you're already married to?"

"Dad says that you should never stop getting to know your spouse," Tessa countered earning her a glare from her cousin.

"You hate it when he says that."

"Because the only relationships I have ever been in have ended horribly," Tessa countered. "That doesn't mean that he's not right."

Picking at the blanket Karrine gave a noncommittal shrug, "I wouldn't even know where to start. He's so different than me Tessa. He even wants us to go to church every week even though it's almost an hour away. Who does that?" When her cousin just gave her an amused look Karrine rolled her eyes, "Okay, yeah, your family always goes to church too I guess but you know my Mom never liked it if Celine or I went. I mean she didn't come right out and say we couldn't go but just about."

"Your Mom's not here anymore," Tessa put her hand on top of Karrine's to take the sting out of her words. "I know it's not easy to accept but maybe you should start by going to church with him. Learning more about his faith seems like it would be a good way to start getting to know your husband."

A brief knock on the door saved her from answering and she almost welcomed the thought of another nurse coming to check her vitals. "Come in!"

Instead of hospital personnel walking through the door, Karrine startled when she saw Grant Lentz walk into her room. Tessa was the first to break from her shock and she stood to confront him, hands on her hips like a warrior preparing for battle.

"What are you doing here Grant?"

"Karrine, I need to talk to you." He ignored Tessa and looked past her at Karrine, his eyes pleading with her to give him a chance.

"There's nothing to talk about."

"Please, Karrine just give me a few minutes," he pleaded.

"She has nothing to say to you," Tessa stepped in front of him as if to block his view.

"Well then she can listen," Grant sounded as close to despair as she had ever heard him. "Please Karrine, just hear me out. I flew across the world just so we could talk face to face."

*

Steffan felt rather good about his decision to go visit Karrine in the hospital. Since she had woken up from her coma there had been a definite change in their relationship. It was subtle but it was there. A softening that actually gave him hope that they could somehow make their relationship work.

He even stopped at the gift shop to buy her a bouquet of flowers, choosing a pretty bunch with all sorts of different colors he thought would make her smile. At the last moment, he also grabbed a soft white teddy bear, earning a smile from the lady working the cash register. With a light heart, he navigated his way through the halls that were becoming all too familiar as he headed towards his wife's private room, greeting doctors, nurses, and patients alike with a friendly smile.

Just as he turned the corner to her room raised voices made him frown. His steps slowed a little as he tried to place where they were coming from, he had no desire to interrupt someone's argument accidentally but as he got closer to his wife's room he realized the argument was coming from there. Stopping just outside the door he tried to decipher who was talking.

He recognized Tessa's voice, she sounded angry as she told someone that they shouldn't be there. Steffan tensed, wondering what in the world was going on. Karrine's voice was softer and he couldn't quite make out her words though her tone sounded just as tense as her cousin's. A third voice entered the mix, a man he was certain he had never heard before, pleaded that Steffan's wife just give him a few minutes. Who was this guy?

"Karrine, I need to apologize. I should never have kissed you."

Steffan had never known what pure jealousy felt like until that moment, around him everything faded, and all of his senses focused on what was happening on the other side of that door. Unable to wait for a second longer he jerked the door open and stormed inside. Karrine and Tessa both gasped but he ignored the women and focused on the stranger whose wide eyes were filled with guilt and trepidation at his entrance. If he had been in a more generous mood he would have given the guy some credit for standing his ground but he was feeling anything but generous right then.

"I think it is time you left." It was a miracle his voice remained as steady as it did. His hands were fisted at his side and his jaw was starting to ache from being clenched so hard.

"Please, you must be Karrine's husband, just let me explain."

He almost laughed, almost. Explain? This idiot wanted to explain how he had kissed another man's wife? To the other man!

He was asking for a black eye and if he didn't leave the room soon Steffan was going to oblige.

"Leave. Now."

"Grant, you need to go," Tessa stepped in, coming towards them but apparently smart enough not to get too close.

"Are you sure?" Grant glanced at her then back to Steffan as if he was concerned about her and Karrine's safety. Steffan had not known he could get any angrier but the other man's reluctance to leave certainly pushed him over the edge and he barely kept himself from taking a swing at the smaller man.

"I'm sure. We'll be fine," Tessa insisted. "Just go."

Apparently not smart enough to follow a simple instruction Grant just glanced at Karrine one more time, "I really am sorry." He looked like he wanted to say more but another glance at Steffan had him scooting towards the door. "See ya, Tessa."

Steffan waited only until the door closed behind him before he slammed the flowers and teddy bear on the nearest table and glared at his wife. Her expressive eyes were wide with fear, shame, and guilt. Tears were threatening to spill over onto her too-pale cheeks. It was the sight of those tears that did him in and he knew, no matter how mad he was, he couldn't stay and watch her tears fall. Instead, without saying a word, he turned and marched back out of the room.

*

The phrase 'echoed with silence' had never held such significance for Karrine until that moment. Both she and Tessa stayed riveted in place, unsure of what to say or how to react.

Never, from the time she left Colorado to return to Yagos, had she imagined there would ever be any kind of confrontation between Steffan and Grant. Or what she was supposed to do if the two ever did come face to face.

"Are you okay?"

Unable to help herself Karrine glared at her cousin, "All that schooling and the best thing you can come up with is 'are you okay'? I thought you were supposed to be an eloquent lawyer."

"It is a lot easier to be eloquent writing briefs than it is watching a scene from some soap opera play out in real life, especially when my cousin is the leading lady. What am I supposed to say in this situation?"

"I have no idea," Karrine pulled up her good hand to wipe away the tears that were escaping down her cheeks, just then noticing her hand was trembling. "I have no idea what you're supposed to say or what I'm supposed to do or how Steffan's supposed to act. I have no idea about any of it. How can I? This," she indicated the room at large, "Was never supposed to happen."

Crossing her arms tight against her middle so she could grab her elbows Tessa studied her with a quiet, intense stare, "Do you mean your accident? Or the scene between Grant and Steffan just now?"

Giving a little shrug Karrine gave up on stemming the tears and let them fall freely, settling her gaze on the bouquet of flowers Steffan had slammed down before leaving. The happy colors seemed to mock her and the mess she had made of her life. "Any of it, all of it. I don't know any more Tessa but it's not like this is the first thing to go wrong. Ever since I came to Yagos things have been a mess. Meeting Steffan, the marriage contract, getting married. Right up to Grant kissing me and then him coming to Yagos. It all feels like a giant mistake." She fell silent for a moment as she thought back over the last few months of her life. "You know before I got married Aunt Jules told me that God had a plan for all this. Even if I couldn't see it then." She huffed out a laugh and turned her gaze on her cousin, "Some plan, huh?"

She had expected Tessa to agree with her but instead, her cousin pulled the chair close to the bed and leaned back, a thoughtful expression on her face. Karrine had seen that look a thousand times before and it rarely meant that she was going to like what her cousin would say next. Turning her gaze to the window did nothing to stall her cousin from pushing the issue.

"You think Aunt Jules was wrong?"

Bitterness and anger rose up inside her, threatening to spew like molten lava out of a volcano but she bit it back, not wanting her cousin to endure the brunt of her temper. "I don't see how she could be right. What possible plan could God have that would include all of this?"

"Maybe one to bring you closer to Him," Tessa spoke quietly but without hesitation, causing Karrine to take notice of her cousin's conviction.

"You sound like Uncle Andy," her words were spoken without malice and Tessa seemed to brighten a little at the observation.

"Actually, I've been going to church with them lately. So have Mom and Dad, to be fair they started going first but that's not really the point."

"Since when?" Karrine could not help her curiosity. Even though she wanted answers about what to do next and why her life was such a mess something about Tessa was different this trip, something that had never been there before. She had noticed it ever since she woke up from her coma but had chalked it up to her imagination, or her own relief at Tessa being there to help with Celine while she was in the hospital. Now that they had started talking about it, she couldn't seem to let the conversation go, despite the disaster that had just happened.

"Pretty much since you left," Tessa shifted in her chair as if to get comfortable before giving up with a sigh and just leaning back. "I was bored and lonely, so I called Ben to see if he wanted to hang out one Saturday and we ended up doing a movie marathon. It was late so I just stayed at their house and then went to church with them the next morning. That's when I found out Mom and Dad had been going there also."

"They were going before I left?" Karrine asked, surprised she hadn't noticed a change in her aunt and uncle's routine. They were a close family and everyone normally got together for Sunday night dinners at her grandparents' house.

"I was surprised too," Tessa admitted. "I had no idea they'd switched churches. To be fair, it's not like you and I were around most Sunday mornings anyway. We were normally either gone or sleeping in and since Mom and Dad have always gone to church somewhere . . ." she shrugged, "I guess I just didn't notice."

"Why didn't they say anything?"

"I asked them that same question but they said they were waiting for me to show an interest in God again because they didn't want to push. When I went that Sunday the pastor was talking about God's plan for peoples' lives and how it's not just a vague plan but one that's detailed and mapped out for each individual person."

Cynicism colored her words as she rolled her eyes, "What does that even mean? 'God's got a plan.' It's just something people say to make themselves feel better. I know He created everything but why would he actually care about each person's life? Doesn't that seem a little hard to believe?"

"I thought so too," Tessa admitted, not seeming at all bothered by Karrine's cynicism. "Until I started reading the Bible."

Her head was starting to hurt from trying to follow the roundabout conversation and she told her cousin as much.

"Think about it this way," Tessa suggested, "Jesus came to die on the cross and save us from our sins, right? Three days later He rose again and if we accept Him and ask forgiveness, He saves us. We both know that and believe it."

"Of course," Karrine readily agreed. "But what does that have to do with me being forced into an arranged marriage?"

"Everything. If Jesus just wanted to save us from our sins and not be involved in our everyday life, why would He come as a baby?" Tessa leaned forward in her chair, growing more passionate with each word. "Why would He bother to grow up and go through all the pain of a human existence? And why would He bother to have twelve disciples that He trained, and lived with and taught every day for years? What would be the purpose of that?"

Unsure how to answer and not entirely comfortable with the questions Karrine shifted a little, trying to ignore the pain that jolted through her at the movement. It must be time for more pain medicine. Realizing her cousin was still waiting for an answer she tried to focus on the question, "I don't know, I guess so the disciples could tell other people about him?"

"Yes, but why would He do that if He didn't want people to know Him? I mean really know Him, not just know about Him. And why would He want people to know Him if He didn't care about each and every one of them?"

Reaching for her medication button she shifted in her bed again, "The medicine's wearing off. I'd better take some more, and you know it always puts me to sleep. You don't have to stay if you don't want to."

Tessa looked like she wanted to protest but instead, she smiled and got up from her seat, "I could use something to eat. I'll just head to the cafeteria." A shadow passed over her face, "I should probably call Grant too. Is there anything I should tell him?"

"Tell him to go home," she spoke firmly even as her face heated at the memory of Steffan coming in as Grant was trying to apologize. "I don't even know why he's here in the first place."

Tessa opened her mouth as if to say something but apparently thought twice and instead, she just nodded before slipping out of the room. Karrine hit the button for more meds but then just lay there for a long time, her mind whirling with all the questions Tessa had just challenged her with. Was it possible God had done more than just create the earth? That he might really care for individual lives and not just the human race as a whole? And if so, how did her messed-up life fit into his plan?

*

Steffan was fuming. As soon as he left the hospital he headed to his car but he was too angry to drive. He needed to be moving, doing something other than sitting still. Grabbing the gym bag from inside he slung it over his shoulder. Thankfully the city of Teller was laid out so everything was relatively central to each other. His gym was an easy walk of twenty minutes away. He made it in ten before sending Cam a text to meet him there.

He needed to talk to someone. His parents would tell him to go back, listen to Karrine, get the whole story, and then work it out. They wouldn't understand. If he walked back into her hospital room right then his temper would take over, he would end up saying something that he would regret later. She might deserve it but there was still Celine to think about.

Celine. He had forgotten that he needed to pick her up in, he checked his watch, just over two hours. That should give him enough time to get his temper a little more under control. As long as Cam showed up soon.

"All right, I'm here," Cam announced as he walked into the handball court about thirty minutes later. "Why am I here in the middle of the afternoon when we should both be working? Or at least I should be working, and you should be at the hospital with your wife?"

Tossing him the ball Steffan ignored the question, "Let's play."

And they did. For over an hour before Cam finally collapsed on the ground, "I'm out. I don't know what happened to you, but I don't have the same adrenaline to keep me playing any longer."

Knowing he needed to talk to someone and without much time left before he needed to pick Celine up, Steffan dropped down beside him and rested his forearms on his knees. "Karrine cheated on me." For a long moment, they sat there in silence before he finally looked at his friend. He expected to see outrage, even betrayal on Cam's face just like he was feeling but instead, the other man was just staring at him impassively. "What? You don't have anything to say about that? You? Of all people?"

"I'm waiting for the rest of the story."

"What rest of the story?" Pushing himself to his feet Steffan paced around, throwing the ball against the wall with all his might and trying to release the tension in his shoulders. "That is all there is to the story. I went to her hospital room and walked in right as some guy was apologizing to her for kissing her. What more do you need to know?"

"Oh well, if that's what happened," Cam let the sarcasm drip off his words as they trailed off and he pushed to his feet, anger sparking from his eyes. "Did you ask her about it? How do you even know this happened after you were married? Who is the guy? Maybe he's an ex who didn't know she was married or here's a question, did she kiss him back? Steffan, there's a lot more here to find out before you can declare that she's cheating on you."

Temper flaring he whirled to face his friend, "I thought you of all people would understand."

"That's because you're an idiot." Cam didn't even pause when Steffan's hands fisted at his sides. "What? You want to hit me? Fine, do it. But hear me out first. Karrine isn't Mabel. Stop expecting your wife to be like my former fiancée, she's not the same person. You can't compare the two. Mabel was a mess from day one. Karrine? She's a sweet girl who got put in a bad situation and is struggling to make the best of it for her sister's sake. A sister that you love too, by the way. If you can love and accept Celine, maybe it's time you actually give your wife a chance at being part of your life too." Without waiting for a reply Cam turned and started heading towards the door.

"Where are you going?" Steffan called after him but Cam didn't even slow down.

"Back to work, some of us don't sign our own paychecks!"

Turning back to the court Steffan picked up the ball just to throw it against the wall again, trying to get rid of his anger as Cam's words sank in. Was it possible this whole time he had kept a wall around his heart? Unwilling to let Karrine close for fear she would turn out like Cam's former fiancée? But even if that was the case there was still the issue about the man in her hospital room that had to be dealt with. Now if he could only figure out how.

Insert chapter two text here. Insert chapter two text here. Insert chapter two text here. Insert chapter two text here. Insert chapter two text here. Insert chapter two text here. Insert chapter two text here. Insert chapter two text here. Insert chapter two text here. Insert chapter two text here. Insert chapter two text here. Insert chapter two text here. Insert chapter two text here.

Chapter 18

Karrine clicked her nails against the bed rail as she waited for the international phone call to connect.

"Well, this is a surprise. How are you feeling sweetheart?"

"If Mom was so against the marriage contract why didn't she tell me about it? She could've tried to get me to marry someone else and that would've nullified the contract. Or she could've just told me to never come to Yagos. Instead, she planned to bring me here herself and practically force me into a marriage, just like Dad was going to."

She knew her uncle well enough to understand the silence on the other end of the line wasn't a reprimand at her lack of manners or shock at the accusations, but rather a sign of him thinking through his words before he answered. Still, it made her want to squirm in her seat with impatience. The only thing that kept her from doing so was the promise of pain at the slightest movement.

"I imagine she didn't try harder to get you out of it for the same reason you went through with it. Celine."

The thought of her baby sister sent a tendril of guilt wrapping around her heart. "I thought I was protecting Cina by marrying

Steffan but what if I just end up causing her more pain? Divorce is never easy for anyone to go through, but I can't imagine how Celine would handle it after everything else she's been through."

"And has it come to that Karrine?" Uncle Andy's quiet voice carried only compassion over the phone line without the condemnation that had been apparent in Steffan's eyes. "Is your marriage really over? Or does it just seem hopeless?"

"I don't know," she admitted in a voice so soft she wasn't sure he would be able to hear her. "I'm so confused Uncle Andy. I just don't know what to do." With a heavy heart and overflowing of tears, she explained the whole mess to her uncle, sparing no detail, even though she knew full well how bad it made her look. When she was done there was still one question burning in her heart but she wasn't sure she had the strength to voice it.

"What else? I can practically hear those gears turning in your mind like you're trying to decide if your rope is going to hold you up."

His gentle teasing and favorite analogy snapped the last bit of resistance she had been clinging to. "Right before our wedding Aunt Jules said that God had a plan in all of this, but I don't see what it could possibly be. What good can come out of an arranged, broken, marriage and the hurt that is no doubt going to come to Celine if we divorce? Or worse, if we don't divorce but just live in the same house without speaking to each other for the rest of our lives. You always say God is good but what kind of good God would orchestrate this catastrophe?"

"You know Krin," her uncle gave a heavy sigh and she could almost see him giving her a patient but weary smile, "Ever since you were just a little girl you always asked some of the hardest questions."

"You're changing the subject," she couldn't keep the hurt from slipping into her voice at his avoidance of the question. If anyone was going to answer the hard questions it was going to be Uncle Andy but now even he was ignoring her.

"No, I'm not. I'm making an observation but I have every intention of answering you although I'll admit I'm praying for wisdom as I do because this isn't a simple yes or no conundrum we're dealing with here."

Impatience filled her and she started to click her nails again, glad he wasn't there to see her irritation, otherwise, he would no doubt tease her about it and delay the answer even further.

"I think the answer is simpler than you realize Karrine. I think God, in His mighty wisdom, has allowed all these things to happen, including your accident, to bring you to exactly the spot you are now."

"A hospital bed?"

A low chuckle filtered across the phone lines, "No. Questioning your faith and trying to decide if God is just a casual observer of your life or if you're ready to truly give everything over to Him, to let Him be the Lord and Savior of every aspect of your life."

"But I'm already a Christian," frustration was mounting the longer he talked. She wanted answers, not a sermon, but her uncle didn't seem willing to back down.

"You accepted Christ and asked for forgiveness of your sins when you were little, that's true," he agreed, "but it's more than that. It's about *living* your life for Him. About spending every day getting to know Him better and becoming more and more like Him. We weren't made to just spend each day wandering through life aimlessly but to spend our time and everything we do praising and glorifying the Lord with each task as well as with our thoughts and words."

Deep down something inside her clicked, like a door that had remained shut and locked all these years finally creaked open, just a tiny bit. It was like the gentlest wind stirred in her heart whispering words of comfort and peace and leaving her with a desire to know more, to understand where the whisper came from and what it was saying.

"Is any of this making sense to you?"

Her uncle's voice brought her back to her surroundings, reminding her he was still on the phone and she frowned. "I don't know. I think I'm going to rest now. I'll call you later?"

If he was at all surprised by her abrupt ending to their phone call he didn't give any indication but instead just accepted it with a quiet, "I'm always here if you need to talk. I love you."

"I love you too." Disconnecting the call she leaned back against her pillows but her mind was whirring too fast to let her rest. Pressing the call button, she waited for a nurse to answer before making her strange request. "Is there any chance someone has a Bible I could borrow?"

*

In the end, he called Tessa. She was the only one he could think of that could help him solve the predicament he found himself in.

It had taken some fast talking and serious convincing to get his wife's cousin to explain who the man in Karrine's hospital room was, and more importantly, set up a meeting with him but she finally had. Though only under the condition that she could come along.

He had argued, saying she needed to stay with Karrine, and someone had to pick Celine up from school but Tessa had refused to give in. Finally, he had been the one to cave. The meeting would take place the next day. Karrine's aunt Fern would stay with her so Tessa could join him. She refused to even give him the name of the café where they would be going so he wouldn't be able to get there on his own.

Although it was not his ideal plan he had to admit he understood Tessa's stance. Grant Lentz worked for her family's law firm and as such, she didn't want him to 'get beat up even if he is an idiot and probably deserves it' as she had put it; she felt the need to protect Grant because of her family's connections to him. No matter how hard he tried to convince her he just wanted to talk to the man she was not about to back down. Not that he could really blame her. Just thinking of how angry he had been in the hospital and how close he had come to laying the guy flat out made him think maybe Tessa was right to show up to the meeting.

Still, it meant a restless night of hanging out with Celine, trying to get some work done from home and answering her incessant questions about how Karrine was and when she might be able to come home. Eventually, she had given up on talking to him and gone up to her room to call her best friend in Colorado instead. Pushing aside the guilt he felt at semi-ignoring her he just focused on getting through the night.

The next day came in equal parts of far too quickly and far too slowly in his opinion. He made it to the office after dropping Celine off and was able to reschedule his day in order to accommodate the meeting. Mrs. Coren didn't seem impressed when he said he was leaving after lunch but she gave little more than a 'humph' of acknowledgment.

Pulling into the hospital parking lot he looked up at the huge building that had become so familiar to him lately but this time he didn't go inside. In his heart, he knew avoiding his wife was not the way to make a marriage work, but he could not seem to bring himself to get out of the car. Instead, he sent Tessa a text, letting her know he was waiting for her. Less than five minutes later she was slipping inside the car.

"What did you tell Karrine?"

"The truth." Tessa shrugged as he pulled back onto the road. "Well not the whole truth, and I don't like having to lie to my cousin by the way."

"You just said you told her the truth. Is that not, by definition, not a lie?"

"A lie of omission is still a lie even if it's a half-truth," she sounded like she was quoting someone but he didn't bother to ask who. "I told her that her aunt was coming to stay with her so I could take care of some business. She assumed I meant for the firm and I didn't correct her. Satisfied?"

Instead of answering he focused on the red light, they were stopped at, "Which way?"

It didn't take long to reach the small café that Tessa had picked for their meeting. As he parked he saw that Grant Lentz was already there. Instinctively he tensed when the other man waved a hand in greeting as they got out of the car.

Glancing up at him Tessa frowned, "Are you sure you are going to be okay with this?"

"I promise not to hit him," was the best promise he could give. With a not quite satisfied expression she nodded and together they headed toward the table. This time of day there weren't many people around and being seated on the patio gave them quite a bit of privacy.

Tessa perched on the very edge of her seat as if she was afraid of getting too comfortable while she made the introductions. "Grant Lentz, this is Steffan Dalton, Karrine's husband. Steffan, meet Grant, he grew up with Karrine and I and has worked for my family's law firm since he was an intern going to law school. Shall we sit?"

"Tessa said you asked to talk with me," Grant fiddled with his silverware, glancing up but not quite meeting his eyes. "I'm happy to hear you out but first I want to apologize."

"You can apologize after you explain," Steffan ignored Tessa's kick under the table at his impolite command. "I want to know what I walked in on yesterday and why you were apologizing for kissing my wife."

"Karrine didn't tell you?" Now Grant did look at him but a low mutter sounded strangely like a growl from Tessa had him retracting the question. "I'm sorry, it's none of my business." He hesitated but when Steffan did not correct him he cleared his throat. "I guess I should explain that for several years I would ask Karrine out, she always turned me down but I kind of had it in my head she'd agree eventually."

He was not at all sure how he was supposed to react to this stranger telling him he had essentially been in love with Steffan's wife for years, whether or not she had ever returned the affection. Instead of trying to figure it out, he just nodded to indicate Grant should continue.

"Anyway, when she came back to Colorado a few months back I asked her to go to lunch with me. I had heard about the wedding but I couldn't quite believe it. As she told me about you I could tell she wasn't in love." He held up a hand when Tessa would have interrupted. "I know that's no excuse but when I walked her to the car, I kissed her."

His jaw clenched and he would no doubt end up with holes in his tongue from biting it so hard to keep his thoughts to himself but a quick prayer for strength and he was able to nod for Grant to continue.

"She pushed me away immediately." Grant smiled in an embarrassed sort of way, "She actually did more than that, she slapped me. And by the time she drove away I was already regretting what I'd done. I tried to call and apologize but she wouldn't answer."

"Rightfully so," Tessa inserted.

"True," he agreed. "After a couple of days, I stopped trying to contact her but then I heard about the accident. I wanted to check on her but maybe the worst mistake of that day was that I lost our friendship. So, when this opportunity came up to come search for an office for the law firm here in Yagos I immediately volunteered. With Tessa here and so much of the family having taken time off to be here for Karrine no one else was really in a position to come instead."

"Mom and Dad don't know about what happened," Tessa explained but he wasn't sure if it was for his benefit or for Grant's. "They never would've let you come if they did."

"I figured and I also knew there was a good chance Karrine would throw me out the moment she saw me but I had to try. I couldn't let things go without apologizing for what I did," he leaned forward and looked directly at Steffan. "But I swear to you, the last thing I wanted to do was cause problems between the two of you."

As angry as he was at this man, not to mention Karrine, he couldn't help but believe him. Satisfied that he had heard the whole story he pushed back his chair and made as if to stand. "Thank you for telling me. I appreciate your apology."

Grant stood also and held out a hand, "I really am sorry. I hope at some point in the future we can at least be cordial, if not friends."

It took everything in him to not laugh in Grant's face but instead, he just shook the man's hand and waited for Tessa to stand also. Courtesy and pride in his country forced him to offer a polite parting, "I hope you enjoy the rest of your stay in our country."

"Actually, my flight leaves in a few hours," Grant replied. "But maybe I'll see you next time you come to visit Karrine's family in Colorado."

"I'll talk to you later Grant," Tessa patted his shoulder in a friendly gesture. "Have a safe flight home."

"Thanks, Tessa, and Steffan?"

He faced the man, hoping his impatience did not show on his face. "Yes?"

"Please, tell Karrine how truly sorry I am."

A nod was the most he was willing to offer before he and Tessa headed back to his car. As she climbed in the passenger seat she turned to look at him. "Now what?"

"Now I drop you back off at the hospital." He started the car and hoped she'd drop it but she wasn't one to give up that easily.

"And what are you going to do?"

That was the question of the hour. As he turned onto the road he answered honestly, "I think I need to find somewhere to pray."

*

"You've been quiet today."

Karrine pushed down the guilt that assailed her at her Aunt's remark. The therapist had just arrived for a physical therapy lesson when Tessa had left and Aunt Fern had come to take her place. Afterward, she had slept for a bit. When she woke up her aunt was still there and told her Tessa had stopped in for a moment to check on her before leaving again, apparently, there was still more work to be done. Karrine had just turned on the T.V., in no mood to talk. Her mind was spinning with all the events of the last couple of days, from Grant's appearance, and Steffan's confrontation. To her spiritual state and the conversations, she'd had with Tessa and Uncle Andy. The Bible the nurse had brought her was safely hidden away in a drawer in the nightstand, waiting until she was alone again to bring it back out to read some more.

Turning her eyes to the woman seated in the chair beside her bed she asked the first thing that came to mind. "Are you a Christian Aunt Fern?"

Fern seemed surprised by the question but nodded, "Yes, I am. Why do you ask dear?"

Rather than answer she asked another question, "Was my Dad a Christian?"

A spark of understanding lit in her eyes but Fern didn't ask questions, "Yes, he was."

"Then why would a man who served a God who believes in free will write a marriage contract that would take away mine?"

Fern studied her hands for a moment before answering slowly as if she was choosing her words very carefully. "I don't think that's how your Dad ever saw it, sweetheart. In his mind, he was protecting you. He saw how painful it could be for people as they dated, searching for the right person and he didn't want that for you. So, instead, he picked a good family and signed a marriage contract between you and someone he believed would grow up to love and protect you. For Hamilton, it wasn't about taking away your free will but about protecting you from the world. Can you understand that?"

She wasn't ready to try to understand it much less forgive her father's actions so she just kept asking more questions. "But Mom wouldn't let him sign a contract for Celine right? There's not a second groom hidden away we don't know about?"

Fern's lips twitched at the question but she didn't let the smile grow too far, "No, nothing like that. To be honest with you dear, your father was a very stubborn man."

Memories of the man she had adored assailed her, including ones of Hamilton and Brandaliyn fighting because neither of them was willing to compromise. Even as a child she had understood her parents were both very stubborn people, a trait both she and Celine had inherited. "So was Mom."

"True. And as much as Hamilton believed he was protecting you, Brandaliyn disagreed. I'm not even sure she agreed to the contract but he signed it anyway. To be honest I think he would have done the same for Celine had he not passed away when he did, although he had promised Brandi he wouldn't. Maybe he would've kept that promise, maybe not. I really couldn't say. The one thing I do know Karrine is that your father adored you girls and everything he did, even the marriage contract, he did with your best interests at heart."

Another question had been bothering her since she had come back to Yagos, but it was only now she found the courage to ask it. "I spent a lot of time with you before we moved back to Colorado."

A weary sigh escaped Fern's lips and she made a show of smoothing down her skirt. "And you're wondering why we didn't stay in better contact after you moved home."

Hating how guilty she felt for bringing up what was obviously a painful subject for her aunt she tried to subtly turn the conversation, "I always loved the gifts you sent for my birthday and Christmas."

"Well thank you, dear, but gifts are no substitute for a relationship. The truth is after your father died, your mom, well she was angry. With God, with us, and with anything that reminded her of Hamilton, so she took you girls and she went home. I don't blame her; she was hurting but Grover had just lost his brother and we were hurting too. I guess it started out as just wanting to give her some time and eventually it just became easier not to deal with the emotions that came up every time I called Brandi, so eventually, I just stopped. I'm sorry for that dear, that's no excuse and in the process, I hurt you and lost my chance at watching you girls grow up. I can't tell you how much I regret that. Can you ever forgive me?"

There, lying in a hospital bed with her whole body in pain, Karrine took a deep breath of courage and let go of the anger she hadn't realized she'd been holding onto ever since she was an eight-year-old girl leaving her home and everything she had ever known after her father's death. With a genuine smile, she felt a little piece of her heart start to heal. "Of course, I can."

With tears in her eyes, Fern gave her a gentle hug and for the first time in a long time, Karrine began to feel hope. Letting go of the anger was just the first step in a long journey but she couldn't help but think that the first step was always the hardest. Maybe if she could forgive her aunt after so many years then there was still hope Steffan would forgive her and together they might be able to build a family and provide the support system she had always wanted Celine to have.

Chapter 19

It had been three days since Steffan had seen his wife. He had been avoiding her, there was no way around that fact. Each day when he went home for the evening Celine would tell him about visiting Karrine at the hospital or talking to her on the phone and how well her big sister was doing in physical therapy. Even though the teenager never said it there was always an unspoken question that hung between them. When was he going to visit the woman he had vowed to love and stand by?

Now when he should have been at his office trying to clear off the ever-mounting pile of work on his desk he was sitting in his car staring up at the imposing beige walls of the hospital. He knew he should go inside. Staying in the car only served to prove his cowardice but even as he told his hands to open the door they stayed frozen to the steering wheel, unable to make even the smallest step towards reconciliation.

Leaning forward he rested his head against the steering wheel. "Lord, what do I do? I don't know how to talk to her. I don't even know where to begin. What good does it do to go see her if we just stand there glaring at each other? I am tired of fighting. I just don't have the energy for it anymore."

Come to me, all you who are weary and carry heavy burdens, and I will give you rest.

It did not seem like much of an answer but he knew what needed to be done. Moving as slowly, as a man who knew he faced a horrible yet inescapable fate, he climbed out of the car and made his way into the hospital. Unbidden he compared his mood today to his visit a few days ago. Then he had been happy and hopeful. A change in Karrine had made him think that maybe, just maybe they would be able to turn their marriage into more than just a contract. Today only dread filled his heart as he rode the elevator up to the orthopedic ward on the fifth floor.

Stopping just outside the door he stood there for a few seconds, debating the merits of going in or walking away. If there was one thing he had always prided himself on though, it was facing his problems. As much as he did not want to go in he just couldn't stomach the idea of walking away either.

Tessa's eye widened the moment he stepped through the door and she immediately looked to Karrine. His wife's steady, even, breaths indicated that she was sound asleep. He somehow doubted she would rest quite so well if she knew he was there.

Getting to her feet Tessa kept her voice low as she approached him. "I could use a cup of coffee. Would you like one?"

"No," he declined without even looking at her, his gaze focused on his slumbering wife. Because they had never shared a room he hadn't had much cause to watch her sleep, other than when she was sedated, which did not count. Now he could not help but notice how peaceful she looked, angelic even. It made him realize for the first time how stressed she normally was.

There were only a few times in the months that he had known his wife that she had truly seemed at peace. He realized with a pang of sadness none of those times had been when she had looked at him. Was she really unhappy in their marriage? Or was it just the way it had come about that was still bothering her.

Troubled by the question he went to sit down in the chair Tessa had vacated, noting absently that she had slipped out, apparently making good on her statement to get more coffee. Taking the opportunity of the quiet room he studied his wife's features as he had not had much of a chance to do before. He took in every detail from the way her hair shined as if it had been recently washed to how long her eyelashes were and the paleness of her skin. Weeks in the hospital had faded the tan she had acquired from her rock-climbing adventures.

His heart felt heavy as he watched her, he couldn't even find the words to pray. Instead, he just sat there, trusting that the Lord understood his mixed-up emotions and that He could make sense of them far better than he could at the moment. When Tessa came back a while later, he slipped out of the room without a word.

Once in the car, he headed towards his office with no more peace than he had had when he first left home.

*

It had been a week since Karrine had last laid eyes on her husband. Tessa had told her he had stopped by once while she was sleeping but he had been gone again before she woke up.

The days slipped by, one into the next with only restless nights and family members coming and going to mark their passing.

Three times a day a physical therapist would come for her session. They were working on teaching her to transfer from a bed to a wheelchair as well as gaining stamina just by sitting up. The doctors seemed happy with her progress, her strength as a rock-climber certainly aided the process but it felt impossibly slow, not to mention, painful, to Karrine. She was dreading the pain that would come when she had to start walking again but it would be worth it, especially when they gave her the all-clear to start climbing again. Even now she was fighting the desire to get out there to climb if only to escape the four walls of the hospital.

She spent every free moment reading the Bible she had borrowed. Pouring over the words and studying verses she had heard but never understood the context of. Some things didn't make much sense, but plenty did and for the first time since she was a child, a flame of faith, long-neglected, began to burn brightly once again.

The nurses began chastising her for staying up reading instead of sleeping at night but Karrine hardly cared. She was learning so much. Finally, some of the things that Tessa, Uncle Andy, and even Steffan, had said began to make sense. A picture was forming in her head of a loving father, much like the one she had once had. God also had her best interests at heart but unlike Hamilton Sandor, he never made mistakes or questionable decisions. Not just that but He took those mistakes and worked them together to use them for her good.

When Tessa arrived one morning Karrine was finally ready to talk about what she had discovered. As her cousin slipped into the room Karrine sat up.

"You're awake," Tessa observed as she set her laptop bag down in her chair. She had been doing more and more work each day and Karrine knew it wouldn't be long before she would need to fly home in order to catch up on the things that couldn't be shifted to someone else or done remotely.

"You sound surprised."

"A little," Tessa smiled and set a cup of coffee on the bedside table for her, near her right arm. "You've been sleeping a lot lately."

"Just during the day," she corrected with a wry smile.

"You're not sleeping at night?" Tessa immediately frowned. "Are you in pain? Have you told the nurses?"

"It's not that," she quickly assured her cousin, reaching out for the Bible she had been keeping in a drawer beside her. "I've been up at night because I've been reading this."

Immediately Tessa's eyes brightened and what looked like a spark of hope flickered in them as she reached out for the book. "You've been reading the Bible?"

"After we talked, I called Uncle Andy. I talked to him about God's plans. I also talked to Aunt Fern. She said Dad was trying to do what was best for me, even if no one else agreed he had my best interests at heart."

Sitting down in the chair Tessa pulled it close to the bed, "That's great Krin but I don't understand what your Dad signing a marriage contract for you, has to do with you deciding to read the Bible?"

She couldn't help but laugh, "That's almost exactly what I asked you last week. But as I read I realize that even this marriage contract is part of God's plan. It may not have been the best decision my dad made but God used it for good. I don't know exactly why it happened the way it did although I know people have free will so that must tie in somewhere. Think about it though, by coming to Yagos and having this accident I finally got to the point where I could listen to what you and Uncle Andy have wanted to tell me about God. I was so angry with my parents for lying to me but laying here I've had a lot of time to think. Talking to Aunt Fern I realize now Dad really was trying to protect me, and Mom by not telling me, was trying to do the same thing. She wanted me to have a normal childhood."

"I guess it would've been hard going through school if you knew you were engaged," Tessa said with a twist of her lips.

For the first time in too long Karrine laughed, it made her whole body hurt but it felt good to truly smile, and about her marriage no less. "Yeah, that would've made the search for a prom date more interesting."

The cousins shared a chuckle before Tessa moved on. "So, what does this mean for you and Steffan?"

"Honestly, I have no idea. He's angry and I don't blame him." Her heart ached at the way she had treated Steffan since they had been married. "I've made a lot of mistakes already in our marriage and we have a long way to go. I don't know if he's even willing to give me a second chance, but I do know he cares about Celine and he doesn't believe in divorce. I'm hoping that'll be enough for us to get a fresh start." She sighed and closed her eyes for a brief second, thinking about her husband and the damage she had done.

"Don't give up hope," Tessa squeezed her good shoulder. "God is a God of forgiveness and we'll pray that Steffan is willing to follow His example."

Trying to believe her cousin's words Karrine frowned, "I have to say, I'd feel a lot more hopeful if he'd at least come to visit. How do I make amends if he won't talk to me?"

Picking up Karrine's cell phone Tessa handed it to her, "Last I heard, phone lines still work both ways."

She knew from the look on Tessa's face that her cousin was not going to leave it alone until she called. Her fingers trembled but she managed to find her husband's contact and pushed call. It went straight to voicemail and she frowned. "It's his voicemail, do you think he's ignoring my calls?"

Tessa bit her lip but shrugged, "I don't know. Maybe his phone died?"

Biting her lip Karrine waited for the beep, "Steffan, its Karrine. Could you please call me back? Or just come by the hospital when you get off work? I think we need to talk."

With a heavy heart, she hung up and handed the phone back to Tessa who perched back on her chair. "Well, there's nothing more we can do for now. Tell me more about what you've been reading."

*

"Steffan? Steffan?"

Glancing up his eyes widened when he saw his father standing in his doorway. "Dad, I am so sorry I just did not hear you. When did you get here?"

Charlie Dalton frowned as he made himself comfortable in one of the chairs across from his son's desk. "I must have called your name at least four times. For a moment I thought you had gone deaf."

Recognizing the slight scolding in his father's voice Steffan cringed, "I am sorry. I never heard a thing, I suppose I was distracted."

"I figured that out when you forgot our lunch plans," Charlie said as he leaned back in his chair.

His mind was a blank but he tried not to show it as he discreetly pulled up his calendar on his computer. There it was, with an alarm set to notify him and everything. Looking at his phone he realized the battery had died. "I am so sorry Dad, it was in my calendar but I forgot and my phone died so it didn't remind me." The clock said it was nearly two in the afternoon, "I suppose you've already eaten by now?"

"Yes," Charlie smiled, "When you missed lunch and didn't pick up your phone I decided to surprise Kennedy instead. I was able to catch her between classes but I admit the college dining hall leaves a lot to be desired."

Remembering too well his own college days he made a face, "No argument here, I think I normally went home to eat."

"Speaking of going home," Charlie made a show of leaning back in his chair, interlacing his fingers over his stomach. "Any word on when they might be releasing Karrine?"

A shaft of pain hit him square in the heart, combined with more than a little guilt that it had been over a week since he had last spoken to Karrine's doctors about how she was progressing. "Um… no, I have not heard anymore."

"Haven't heard or haven't asked?" Charlie's perceptive gaze pinned his son in his seat. "What is going on with the two of you? I thought things were going better since she woke up."

"They were," he admitted, leaning his head back and closing his eyes as if he could somehow block out all the pain and frustration of the last week. "I was trying to do what you told me to Dad, put her and Celine first, show them the love of Christ through my actions, but then . . ." he let his voice trail off, not sure how much to say. One part of him wanted to share everything with his Dad, let him feel the same pain and betrayal that Steffan was dealing with but another part of him wondered if Charlie's reactions would be more like Cam's and he wasn't sure he was up for that. "It has been hard," he finally said.

"Marriage is always hard Son. Yours might be harder than others right now but I doubt that it is hopeless. Is it?"

Thinking of Karrine he remembered how she went through with the wedding because she wanted what was best for her sister. He cared about Celine too, loved her like she was his own sister, but was that enough to make their marriage work? "I just don't know Dad."

"Then it seems you have a lot to think about," Charlie got to his feet but waved Steffan off when he would have stood. "I know my way out but Steffan let me just point out one thing. You went to college and started your own business when most people still considered you a child. You have turned your ideas into a thriving company and you are keeping a teenage girl safe and sane while her sister is recovering from major trauma. You have never been afraid of a little hard work, so don't let it stop you from making a go out of what could be the happiest relationship in your life."

It was hard to imagine him and Karrine getting along much less being happy but he nodded, knowing it was expected. "Thanks, Dad."

"I know it may not seem like it right now but remember God put the two of you together for a reason. Do not let difficult circumstances rob you of the blessings He has planned." Charlie smiled, "Oh, and plug your phone in. If your mother can't get a hold of you she'll start to think you've flipped your car upside down in a ditch somewhere."

Laughing at the statement because he knew it was true he got up to hug his father good-bye. "I will do it right now."

After his father left he plugged his phone in and got back to work, trying to force his tired brain to focus on the work that needed to be done. When his phone beeped with a new voicemail he almost ignored it, assuming it was his father's missed call from earlier but instead he reached out, absent-mindedly pushing the buttons to check his messages. The expected message from his father came in and was deleted but a second message started to play and he paused when he heard his wife's voice.

"Steffan, its Karrine. Could you please call me back? Or just come by the hospital when you get off work? I think we need to talk."

Deleting the message, he leaned back in his chair, his concentration ruined yet again. His wife wanted to talk and she had even used his first name when she made the request, but did he want to hear what she had to say?

*

Tessa had just left to pick up Celine so Karrine, physically exhausted from physical therapy and emotionally from the toll of telling her cousin about her newfound faith, could get some much-needed rest. Leaning her head back against the pillows she closed her eyes, letting her mind drift and thanking God for Tessa's presence. When she heard the door open she smiled,

"What'd you do? Forget your car keys?" She teased her cousin. When Tessa didn't laugh in response she opened her eyes and saw her frowning husband standing at the foot of her bed. "Steffan."

"Were you expecting someone else?"

The cold, accusing tone caused her face to heat with embarrassment. She never realized until that moment how much she had always appreciated his laughter, his easy sense of humor, and his lighthearted attitude. "I, um, no, of course not, I jus-

"You called me, remember?" He cut in.

Irritation sparked in her blood and her eyes narrowed a little as she met his glare, "I thought you were Tessa. She just left to pick up Celine and when I heard the door I thought she must have forgotten something. You're not normally off work this early."

Now it was his turn to look embarrassed, "Right. I was at the office but . . ." he let his voice trail off and took a deep breath

269

before looking up at her again. "Your message said you wanted to talk?"

Until that moment she hadn't really thought about what she had to say to her husband. It had taken all her courage just to call him, but now that he was here how was she supposed to explain what had happened with Grant? For a moment she froze, panic set in. Then a small voice reminded her of the verse Tessa had shared with her a little while ago. 'I can do all things through Christ who strengthens me.' Desperately she prayed for the strength to do the impossible—convince her husband that she had made a mistake. "Do you want to sit down?"

He shuffled his feet but shook his head, "No, I am fine."

Taking a deep breath she tried to find the right words before deciding there weren't any 'right' ones, there were just words and she needed to use them. "Steffan, I want to explain what happened the other day when you came in here. The man that was here, Grant, he's a f-"

"You don't have to explain," Steffan cut her off, again, irritating her already frayed nerves.

"I really think I should," she insisted. "It's not what you think."

"Karrine, I know who Grant is."

"Like I said he's a friend from back-" she cut herself off. "Wait, you know? How?"

Gripping the railing at the foot of her bed he shrugged but stared at the wall above her head as if the boring white color was the most fascinating thing in the world, or at least more interesting than she was. "I asked Tessa to set up a meeting. We sat down last week and he told me everything."

"You, he," her mind whirred with the new information as she desperately tried to process what he was saying. "Last week?"

He nodded and said something about Grant apologizing but she barely heard him. She was still trying to understand what had happened. Steffan knew about Grant. Grant had told him what had happened. Tessa had set it up.

Tessa. A familiar sense of betrayal hit her and her eyes burned at the thought her cousin, the one person she trusted more than anyone else had gone behind her back.

"Do not blame Tessa."

Shocked and angry that he had figured out where her mind went so easily she glared at him. "Don't pretend to know what I'm thinking."

"I do know what you are thinking," he corrected, his lips barely curving. "You are about the easiest person to read I have ever met. It's a good thing you didn't decide to become a lawyer like your cousin. You would never be able to keep opposing counsel from figuring out your strategy."

Irritation and jealously roared through her veins and she wished more than anything she could stand up so she didn't feel at such a disadvantage. "Is that all you can talk about now? How wonderful my cousin is?"

"Jealously. Karrine?" Steffan gave her a mocking smile. "Coming from you that is rather amusing, wouldn't you say?"

Immediately she felt convicted of the jealously, she knew Tessa would never intentionally hurt her. And in the time they had known each other Steffan had never done anything to make her question his faithfulness. He had even told her he didn't date growing up because he knew they were engaged. Still, the hurt and irritation, once planted in her mind weren't so easy to dispel. "If Grant told you everything then I guess there's no point in me explaining."

He looked down at her for a long moment, "No, I guess there is not."

As he walked out of the room tears streaked down her cheeks. She couldn't help but feel like she had just made one of the worst mistakes of her life. And this time no one was there to help her know how to fix it.

I will never leave you nor forsake you.

The verse came quick and sure and she closed her eyes, letting the tears fall as she tried to meditate on the Lord. *"Thank you, God, that you're still with me."*

Chapter 20

Steffan knew the moment he walked out of Karrine's hospital room that he was making a mistake, but pride and stubbornness refused to let him turn back. He was halfway down the hall when he spotted a sign he had never noticed before. Following the directions, he slipped inside the dimly lighted chapel and collapsed into a pew. Resting his head in his hands he simply sat in the quiet, trying to push aside his emotions so he could feel God's presence.

"Do you have a loved one who's sick?"

Irritated at the interruption he didn't look up, hoping the chaplain would simply leave him alone but instead he felt the pew shift slightly as the man came to sit beside him. Realizing he wasn't going away Steffan didn't look at him but turned his focus to the cross that hung at the front of the room. "My wife. She is recovering from an accident."

"And you are angry," the man observed. "Tell me, who are you mad at? The person who caused the accident?"

"It was her fault," he muttered, refusing to look at the man.

"What happened?"

Finally glancing over at the man he took a moment to study him. Dressed in slacks and a plain gray dress shirt he was the epitome of a quiet, reassuring man of God but there was a tenacity in his eyes that warned Steffan he would sit there until he got the answers he wanted. Forcing himself to be semi-polite he answered, "She fell." When he saw the chaplain's eyebrows lift he shook his head, realizing how his explanation must have sounded. "Not like that. I did not push her, she was rock-climbing and she fell."

"But you *are* angry. At her for falling or is your anger about something else?"

Expelling a deep breath, he turned sideways to better face the man, "No, not about her falling. We," he took a deep breath, "we have only been married for a few months and . . . things have not exactly been going well."

Smiling the chaplain tipped his head to the side, "I remember my first few months of marriage."

Not up to listening to some platitude about how things would get better he interrupted before the chaplain could go any further. "It was an arranged marriage. We only met a couple of weeks before the wedding."

"My wife and I met on our wedding day," the chaplain said, chuckling when Steffan's eyes widened. "What? You thought you were the only one with an arranged marriage? Surely you know better than that. Your accent tells me you are from Yagos."

"Yes sir," he stared down at his hands. "I've met lots of people who have had arranged marriages and I know they don't always go well but . . ."

"But you were hoping you could make your marriage work and now you are not so sure?"

Not sure what to say all he could do was nod. The chaplain reached over to put a hand on his shoulder. "What's your name son?"

"Steffan."

"Well, Steffan let me tell you a little story. Early in my marriage, I decided I had made the worst mistake of my life. Some things had happened and I was sure we could never make things work. I actually thought about leaving her. Then, by the grace of the Almighty, I met a man who asked me one thing. Do you love your wife?"

Steffan looked up, intrigued, as much by the story as by the reassuring cadence of the man's voice. After weeks of mental and emotional exhaustion, there was something comforting in just having a conversation with a stranger, even if he didn't feel much like talking.

"At first I was angry," the chaplain told him. "I mean I barely knew the woman. How could I love her? Then he got out his Bible and he read me two verses that I had never thought too much about before. The first was Ephesians 5:25 'For husbands, this means love your wives, just as Christ loved the church. He gave Himself up for her . . .' I had heard that verse before and I argued with Him that she wasn't doing her part by submitting to me as the head of the household. He wasn't about to listen though and that is when he shared the second verse. Matthew 5:19 'So if you ignore the least commandment and teach others to do the same, you will be called the least in the Kingdom of Heaven. But anyone who obeys God's laws and teaches them will be called great in the Kingdom of Heaven.'"

The chaplain chuckled again and shook his head, "Now being a Biblical scholar at the time I argued that Paul wrote Ephesians and it was not a command, but the man refused to back down. He pointed out that God commanded man to leave his father and mother and cleave unto his wife. I could add a few more verses in there but I think you get my point. So, let me ask you, Steffan, do you love your wife?"

Rubbing the back of his neck he finally let the last few walls come down around his heart and shrugged. "I am not sure I even know how to answer that. My friend told me love is a choice and I am trying but Karrine and I barely know each other. The only reason she even married me is to retain custody of her sister. What kind of marriage does that give us?"

"You can only have the kind of marriage you choose to make but let me back up. You said you do not know how to love her because you do not know her. So, why don't you get to know her?"

With a heavy heart, he shook his head, "I think it might be too late for that. We both said things an-"

"And you will say and do more things to hurt each other in your lives," the chaplain interrupted. "I can promise you that. The trick is learning to forgive one another and move past it and the only way to do that is to talk to each other. So, I'm assuming she's in the hospital?"

"Yes."

"Good," he gave a decisive nod. "Then go talk to her, apologize for what you said and ask if you two can start over. It will take time but start talking, make it a habit to start getting to know each other, and treat her as if you were dating. Woo your wife Steffan, and each day purpose in your heart to love her. Then stand back and watch God breathe life into your marriage."

It sounded too simple. It was the same thing his Dad and Cam had been telling him to do but it still seemed too easy and he said as much. The chaplain laughed.

"Oh, there will be nothing easy about it, I can promise you that, but it will be wonderful. Why don't you just give it a try? After all, what do you have to lose?"

Feeling slightly insane for taking a stranger's advice he shook the man's hand and retraced his steps towards his wife's hospital room. The door was open and for a moment he stood there, seeing Karrine lying on her back, casts and cords still hooked up to her as quiet sobs overtook her.

Moved by the sight of his wife he walked over to stand next to her bed.

*

Karrine was sure she was dreaming. Steffan was standing at her bedside looking down at her but it couldn't possibly be him because he had left. He had stormed out of her room just before her tears started to fall. So many tears, and for good reason; she had failed at her marriage.

Ever since she was a little girl she had dreamt of her wedding, of the man she would marry, of being loved unconditionally. Of having children and raising them in a home of love and laughter like the one she'd had before her father's death. Then she had come to Yagos and all of her dreams had gone out the window when she learned about the marriage contract.

For a little while there she had thought they had turned the corner. When she had woken up from the medical sedation and learned Steffan had been by her side the whole time she'd finally started to hope. Celine had talked nonstop about how he had been working so hard to be a good big brother. Her aunts and uncles had sung his praises for staying by her side, barely sleeping and making sure everyone else was taken care of. Even Tessa had not had one bad thing to say about him. For the first time since just after their wedding, she had let herself study her husband. She had seen what a compassionate and caring man he was, that he was selfless and how he lived out his faith, something she was only now learning the significance of. She'd started to think he might be someone she could really see herself falling in love with, and then she had messed it all up.

If she had just been honest with him at the beginning none of this would have happened. He had told her, hadn't he? Before their wedding, he'd told her that he would be there for her. He promised that together they would work things out but she had been too stubborn to accept that. She was angry at her parents; she had felt betrayed and abandoned so she had taken it out on Steffan. When he tried to get close, she had pushed him away and now she was paying the consequences.

That was why she knew it had to be a dream. There was no way he would come back and stand by her bedside after everything she had put him through. Maybe they had switched her meds and the new ones were causing some weird side effects or something. She should probably alert the nurse.

"I went to the chapel."

His voice was all too real and she almost reached out to touch him, just to see if he was real or not but she thought better of it and he sank down into the chair, just out of her reach.

"I was not really sure why but now I realize that God led me there for a reason. I was sitting there and this chaplain came up and he asked me if I loved my wife."

Karrine's heart froze. With a sudden burst of clarity, she realized this was no dream, it was an all too real nightmare. He was about to tell her that their marriage was over, and they had never really even given it a chance. She hadn't. He had tried. Her own stubbornness and bitter anger were costing her the chance at her dream.

"He is not the first person to ask me that lately but I finally told him I don't know how to love you. That we don't even know each other so how could I possibly love you?" Steffan met her gaze, "Do you know what he told me?"

All she could do was shake her head. He reached out and gently wiped her cheek, making her realize for the first time that she was still crying.

"He said it was time for us to get to know each other. And if I would commit to choosing to love you God would breathe life into our marriage."

Somehow she found the strength to speak, "What did you say?"

Steffan smiled, "Nothing. I came here. So now I'm asking you Karrine Sandor Dalton, do you think we could start over? Would you be willing to put in the work to get to know each other and learn to love each other so we can make this marriage work?"

More than anything she wanted to accept but fear held her back. Before she could agree she had to say something. "When I first found out about the marriage contract, I was angry. I felt like my parents lied to me my whole life and I felt betrayed. I took out that anger on you and for that I'm sorry." She took a deep breath even though it hurt her ribs to do so. "But."

Steffan felt the air freeze in his lungs. Here he was, taking a chance and pouring his heart out to Karrine, asking her to take a chance with him, on him, and really try to make their marriage work but was she about to reject him?

Belatedly he remembered to pray, asking God to change her heart and committing to do his part to make their marriage work, even if his wife was unwilling to do the same. Remembering a conversation with his Dad, the day of the accident, he recalled Charlie asking him if Karrine and Celine were to move back to Colorado what he would do. Now he knew the answer, he would go too. He may not love his wife, at least not yet, but he was committed to her and to their family. Somehow he was going to make this work, even if it meant leaving everything behind. Just like she had.

"I went through with it for Celine's sake." Karrine started talking again. "Maybe that wasn't the best reason to agree but I did." Biting her lip she looked down and he could see the hesitation on her face.

He wanted to press her but something told him to wait, to let her gather her thoughts before she spoke.

After a moment she looked at him again. "Since I've been awake, Celine's told me how much you've done for her. Even starting the process to become her legal guardian to make sure she'd be taken care of if something were to happen to me. She's really come to love you."

He couldn't help but smile at the thought of the teenager, "The feelings mutual, she is a great kid."

If he thought that would make her happy he was wrong because her frown deepened as she looked down again. "She is. And that's why I need to know, are you agreeing to this marriage because you want it to work or because of my sister?"

He could not have been more shocked if she had suddenly gotten up and started walking. For a long moment, he sat there, trying to assimilate his racing thoughts before his Dad's words hit him again. *'Maybe if you step up and take the first step and live the example then the rest of your family will find it a little easier to follow in your footsteps.'*

Praying for the right words he reached out to take her hand. "I always planned to marry you, I didn't plan to raise your sister. It is true I love Celine and I plan to get permission from you and the courts to raise her as if she were my own, but you are the one I am married to. You are the one I made a vow to before God and man. I may not be able to say I love you right now, but I hope to one day and I am hoping that we can start that journey today. You and I, with God in the center, for Celine, yes, and for any children, we might someday have, but also for the two of us and for however God plans to use us as a couple in the future." He took a deep breath to give him the courage to keep going, "I know your family hurt you with the marriage contract and I know I have hurt you too. I wish I could say it will never happen again but I cannot do that. I can commit that starting today, I will try to do things better. I guess the real question is, is that ever going to be enough for you?"

Biting that bottom lip again she stared at him for a long moment, tears shimmering in her brown eyes. "I always dreamed about falling in love and being swept off my feet. In my mind, love was supposed to come before the wedding, not after. I want to be loved Steffan, and to love someone in return, everyone does. But I also want someone who will always be there for me and who will stand beside me when things get hard. I think that's what a marriage is really about, so yes, it's enough. Although I can't promise to be any good at it I *can* promise to stand by your side no matter how hard life gets."

Emotion swelled his heart, maybe not love exactly but definitely a step in the right direction and he leaned over until their faces almost met. "Then I guess we have ourselves a deal." He smiled at her, "Maybe we need a new contract."

Karrine smiled back, silent laughter making her eyes dance, "I think one marriage contract is enough for this lifetime."

"Understandable," he agreed, "Maybe we could just work on the marriage part."

"Now that I think I can handle. Especially since this time, it gets to be our choice."

Grinning Steffan closed the last few inches between them to kiss his wife.

Standing in the doorway, unnoticed by the couple Tessa glanced over to see Celine grinning with tears shining in her eyes. Slipping an arm around the girl's shoulders she nudged her back down the hallway where they had come from so they would not disturb Karrine and Steffan.

"Maybe we'll come back later, huh?"

"Do you think they can really make it work?" Celine asked, hope battling with fear in her expressive brown eyes. Tessa felt her heart constrict for the teenager who had already been through too much in her short life. With a smile, she hugged her cousin close.

"With God, all things are possible." When Celine didn't respond Tessa let it go. All she could do now was pray. God would work out the details, but she was sure Karrine and Steffan were finally on the road to happiness and Celine would have two people dedicated to loving her and supporting her through her life. It might not be an easy journey but at least they were on the right path. "Hey, how about we find some ice cream before I take you home?"

And with that they headed out to the car, leaving the Daltons to get a little further down the road on the journey of their future without unnecessary interruption.

Epilogue

<u>**Nine Months Later**</u>

"Are you ready Karrine?"

Standing in her uncle's rock-climbing gym in Colorado she looked up at the wall of brightly colored hand and footholds and felt trepidation creep its way in. Her hands began to tremble and she shook her head. "I don't know if I can do this."

A hand gripped hers and Steffan interlaced their fingers. "I will be right beside you the entire time, we will do it together."

Despite the fear that was closing in she smiled at her husband, "You don't even know how to climb."

"But you do," he pointed out. "You can teach me."

Sadness and terror combined to wipe her smile away, "The doctors aren't sure if I'll be able to. You heard what they said. They don't know if my shoulder and hip can tolerate it."

"And a year ago we never expected to have a happy marriage." Steffan retorted, "Nothing is impossible with God, including getting you back to climbing. Are you ready?"

"No," she gripped his hand a little tighter and faced the wall again, "But let's do this."

*

One Year Later

Pulling herself up onto the ledge Karrine expelled an exhausted breath as she sat down and looked out over the island paradise she called home. In the two years since moving back to Yagos her life had changed in ways, she'd never imagined possible.

When she'd first found out about the marriage contract she had felt betrayed. Now she understood that her father had been trying to protect her all along and her mother, in her grief, had just been doing the best she could. They'd both made mistakes but Karrine had eventually learned to forgive them.

It had taken a lot of work but she and Steffan had made a life for themselves in Yagos, settling into their home and falling in love against all odds. Celine had settled into her new life and was staying busy with her high school equestrian team. She adored her brother-in-law and Steffan felt the same way about her. Life as guardians to a teenager wasn't always easy but they had figured out how to make it work even though they had chosen not to legally adopt her, at the teenager's request.

Karrine continued to keep an eye on her father's company but left the daily running to the longtime manager, Mr. Black, choosing instead to focus her time managing the rock-climbing gym Uncle Andy had opened right there in Yagos. Steffan's business had continued to thrive and it seemed he always had to hire new people just to keep up with the work.

God had blessed them more then she'd ever imagined and in the almost two years since her accident he had continued to teach her more and more about himself.

"Wow, it's beautiful here. I never get over this view."

Smiling at her uncle she couldn't help but tease him. "Well, you ought to enjoy it after it took you so long to make it up here."

"Hey! You saying I'm old?" Andy objected.

"Well I'm the one with the limp and I still beat you up, so . . ."

"Careful, I'm still your boss, remember?"

Laughing she turned her attention back to the view. "You know the first time I climbed here I thought about how pretty it was. It never really crossed my mind how every detail highlights God's glory. This is all His handiwork, not just a pretty sight."

"You've come a long way from that twenty-one-year-old girl who first came to Yagos," Uncle Andy agreed, leaning back on his hands. "I still wish you didn't live so far away but it's obvious that God brought you to the perfect place where you could find Him and grow into the beautiful woman you've become. Not to mention a wonderful wife and sister."

Grinning she resisted the urge to touch her stomach and add another title to that list but she had promised Steffan she wouldn't share the news just yet. Tomorrow they would renew their vows in a wedding ceremony that was designed to her dreams and not the one they had originally thrown together in a couple of weeks to meet the contract deadline. This year they would mark their two-year anniversary by renewing their vows with love marking their every word and on her part, with a commitment to God, that hadn't been there the first time around. Then, at the reception, they would make their big announcement. Until then it was only her, Steffan, and of course, Celine, who was in on the news.

"It's been an amazing journey Uncle Andy."

"And it will just keep getting better sweetheart," he promised. "Your life with Steffan and Celine, it's better than any mountain you could ever summit."

"You know at one time I wouldn't have believed that anything could be better than that," she admitted, "But now? I have to say, I couldn't agree more."

The End

Author's Note

Thank you so much for joining Karrine and Steffan on this crazy journey in beautiful Yagos! This book has been a long time in coming and I just want to take a moment to thank a few of the people who made it possible.

First, my parents who have always believed in me and pushed me. My Dad, who is always around to bounce ideas off of; this book would never have been finished without his input. And my Mom, who has been the driving force behind getting this published. She's acted as my editor, agent and publicist while continuing to juggle her own life and responsibilities. No one would ever have the chance to read this without all of her hard work.

A huge thank you to all of my wonderful friends and family whose encouragement and support made this possible. A special thank you to my critique group that has been working with me for the last couple of years. I would never have gotten to this point without them.

The amazing cover art was designed by Rosario Tamayo-Garcia. She can be reached at tamayogarcia.art@gmail.com

And finally thank you to all of you who have taken the time to read this book. I hope you enjoyed it. I'd love to hear what you thought. Please consider sending me an email to: klkirk@qwestoffice.net or follow me on Facebook at: Kattarin L. Kirk so you can hear the latest updates about what might be coming next. I can't wait to share more stories with you!

ABOUT THE AUTHOR

Kattarin Kirk is the youngest of five children. Her love of story telling came from her Mom who would make up stories to tell the kids in the van, and her Dad whose love of history often manifested in retellings of world events. She started writing her own stories as a young teenager. As she grew up so did her skill and love of writing. Although she enjoys writing many different genres, her most recent focus is inspirational romance and family dramas. Kattarin lives in the beautiful Pacific Northwest where she enjoys hiking, horseback riding and spending time with family and friends.

Made in the USA
Monee, IL
17 October 2020